Heron Mill

TENEBRIS

HERON MILL TENEBRIS

THE BLACKWELL BROTHERS

BOOK TWO

K.L. TAYLOR-LANE

ISBN eBook - 978-1-7392089-2-9
ISBN paperback - 978-1-7392089-3-6
Written by - K. L. Taylor-Lane
Cover design by – Leah Maree at Designs by LM.

❀ Created with Vellum

Mother said I'm strange, I am.

I am strange.
I am violent.
I am wanted.
I am *not* Mother.

Heron Mill is our home.
A fortress where there's solace in the shadows, obsession
in the darkness and horror in the basement.

I found love here.

But now there's a stranger in my house, another inside
my head, and something… *someone* is stalking me
through the shadows.

I am haunted.
I am hunted.
I am hurting.

I'm losing grip on everything I thought I knew, on
myself, on our safety, on *him*. There are dangers looming
that threaten to tear us apart, and I think, just maybe,
one of them could be me.

This one's just for me.

NOTE FROM THE AUTHOR

Please be aware this book contains **many** dark themes and subjects that may be uncomfortable/unsuitable for some readers. This book contains **very** heavy themes throughout so please heed the warning and go into this with your eyes wide open.
For more detailed information, please see pinned posts on the author's socials.

The characters in this story all deal with trauma and problems differently, the resolutions and methods they use are not always traditional and therefore may not be for everyone.

This book must only be read **after** Heron Mill. However, you do **not** need to read this book at all to enjoy Heron Mill or the books following. You can skip this one entirely if you so wish.

This book is written in British English. Therefore, some spellings, words, grammar and punctuation may be used differently to what you are used to. If you find anything you think is a genuine error, please do not report, instead, please contact the author or one of her team to correct it. Thank you!

This book and its contents are entirely a work of fiction. Any resemblance or similarities to names, characters, organisations, places, events, incidents, or real people is entirely coincidental or used fictitiously.

*Heron Mill Tenebris is a dark, MF, stepbrother, gothic, horror love story. This is **NOT** a romance, not in the traditional sense, anyway. Please read with caution, the characters in this book do not and will not conform to society's standards or normalities. This book does have a *happy ever after.**

CHAPTER 1

GRACE

Stars twinkle, glittering across a blanket of dark, the night's sky an endless ocean of black. Full moon, white and bright, beaming its radiant light down onto the thick bed of snow beneath. Illuminated, it glows, n... ...t any artificial light, it's as bright as a summ... ...nly more beautiful.

The ligh...

The darkness,

We belong in the dark.

Safest in the shadows.

Hunter and I.

I follow the moon. Toes numb, stocking covered feet frozen as they hammer across the frozen earth, the hard crunch of snow. Blades of grass poking through, whipping at my ankles like razorblades, wetting my legs, soaking into my tights. I race across the open meadow, darting into the trees. The wind throws my hair out behind me, thrashing through the night like golden streamers. My cheeks prickle, the cold needling my skin, assaulting me, stealing the warmth from my flesh, chilling me right down to the bone. But a single thought warms me.

He won't be far behind.

That's not how we play these games.

He can't stand to be away from me for too long.

I don't want him to be.

Breath puffing out in harsh clouds before my face, whistling through my teeth. I continue to run, my heartbeat erratic in my ears, lungs burning as they pump air too fast, too harsh. Goosebumps prick, razing across my skin, even beneath my thin tights and knitted dress.

Weaving through the bare branched trees, the clear sky making the late January night ever colder, the density of the forest somewhat helping shield me from the full force of the bitter wind. But then I'm pushing out of their protection, breaking through into the clearing beyond. The lake stretched out before me, glistening beneath the bright shine of moonlight, I slow my pace. Its surface still, not rippling like it does in the warmer months, no quiet sounds of it lapping at the pebbled shore.

The sandy gravel crunches with snow beneath my feet as I step closer. Little stones digging into the undersides of my feet, sharp against my arches. I tilt my head slightly, breathing slowing, chest still rising and falling rapidly, excitement now, adrenaline. Something new flushing through my veins, zapping through my icy insides like bolts of lightning.

I think of the rain then, the nights it batters against our bedroom window, in the farthest bedroom at the top of the house. Our large observatory style window, overlooking the forest, the water pond that used to feed the mill. The thunder and lightning that cracks and flashes whilst Hunter and I listen and watch from our bed.

The tips of my toes touch the edge of the ice, my thin tights sticking to the thick covering of the lake. I press a little harder, testing its strength, staring down at the frozen surface, the water beneath trapped, little bubbles locked below. The moon glints off its surface, a light dusting of snow rolling across it, the harsh wind like knives slicing my exposed skin.

Both feet move onto the ice, my stockings clinging to it, I shuffle across, peering through the cloudy surface, walking out further and further, eyes locked on what's below.

"Gracie."

A smile curls my wind chapped lips, my cheeks painful as they lift with the motion. Hearing my name on his lips, carried to me on the wind, my eyes close, chest warming. Slowly, I turn to face him, my Hunter, and I realise just how far out from shore I am. We don't even swim out this far, I can't, Hunter always with me, in case I get into trouble, I can swim now, but I'm not a strong swimmer.

"Gracie, come back," a harsh bark, an order that

sends waves of goosebumps rippling across my frozen skin.

Teeth chattering, I look up at him, across the stretch of frozen water between us, unable to make out his features, but I can see his black hair, thick and straight, hanging over one eye.

"*Now.*" A low growl, one loud enough not to be distorted by the wind.

A giggle bubbles up in my chest, a small, light sound, fluttering its way up my throat like an eclipse of moths. I shake my head, hair curtaining my face, taking another step backwards.

Further away.

This is our game.

"*Gracie.*"

My teeth tear into my bottom lip as I clasp my hands behind my back, take another step away. I cock my head, thigh length hair dropping forward over my shoulder, hiding one half of me. My chin dipped, I peer up through my thick lashes, take a further step back.

"No." Something like fear chipping away at his tone. "Get back here. *Right now.*"

A laugh then, pulled deep from my chest, I bite my lip harder, trying to lock it behind my teeth, but he hears it, even from so far away. My heart kicks at my sternum, fingers knotting together, knuckles cracking as I tug at them, my shoulders tense as I watch him step out onto the ice.

He's slow.

Cautious.

A meticulous predator.

Trained, unhurried, deliberate.

His head tilts, one side to the other. Long, thick neck straining as he cracks the tiny bones there, stretching out, he rolls his shoulders, curling and uncurling his fists. He starts forward, his tall, lean frame snuggly fitted in all black, thick joggers, cuffed at the ankles, a long sleeved, fitted t-shirt, tight across his broad chest, sculpted to the cut muscles of his abs. He's larger than when we first met, filling out more with age, thirty-one to my twenty-three. He's bigger, stronger.

Despite the cold, my blood begins to boil, skin tingling with awareness. I release my hands, body trembling, teeth chattering, I clench my jaw, already feeling the heat rolling off of his body in waves. Hot, sharp, overwhelming, crashing into my glacial skin. I stare at him, watching him glide closer, his heavy booted footsteps not heavy at all on the ice, light as a doe, silent, smooth, elegant.

He stops twenty or so feet away, this undeniable pull, making me want to drop to my knees, crawl my way to him. Worship at his feet like an altar, pray to the only god I acknowledge.

Let him have me.

His deep voice whispering to my psyche, *give in.*
Give in. Give in. Give in.

Hunter cocks his head, slowly roving his eyes up my body, climbing from my toes to my eyes.

"Where are your shoes, Gracie?" his breath fogs the

air before him, his hair flopped forward across one eye. "What did we talk about?"

I swallow, thinking back to our conversation the other night, the one we had with our eldest son. The first snow we've had since I arrived here. Almost five and a half years and we've only ever had a fine dusting that turned into grey sludge by the next morning. Nothing like this, thick, fluffy, up to eight inches deep, and the stuff just keeps on falling.

"Hypothermia."

"Mhm."

I shiver, his hum a dangerous thing, like barbed tentacles readying to strangle. The deep richness of his voice, vibrating through me, stroking the smouldering embers in my core. My muscles lock up, tight in antici-pation, coiling to spring, I release my lip, relax my hands by my sides.

Wait.

Hunter stalks forward, silent, smooth, deadly. Those dark eyes penetrating their way beneath my flesh, hooking in deep, heating my blood, boiling my insides, my soul light in a way only he can manage to summon.

"*Hunter,*" I breathe, his name pulled from my lips as though I'm possessed, by him, by what he does to me.

He stops a few inches before me, his body heat licking my skin like flames, igniting the flutter of moths in my lower belly, arousal roaring to life at the look he gives me.

Trembling in place, his hands never touching me, my

skin screaming for his attention. His dark eyes pierce mine, pupils blown, strong nose shadowing one side of his face, the moon bathing the other, bright and white on his naturally tanned skin. Square jaw sharp and angular, the jagged white scar through his right brow gleaming in the dark. I suck in a sharp breath as he moves around me, circling my quivering body, like a shark in water. Stopping behind me, he dips his face, nose in my hair.

"Are you the hunter, baby girl?" his deep voice rasps, ricocheting down the column of my throat. His lips brush the shell of my ear with every overly pronounced word, "or are you the prey?"

His tongue darts out, flattened, swiping up the length of my neck, wet and hot, his teeth latching onto my ear lobe, sucking and tugging. A hand clamps high up on my waist, his index finger flicking at my nipple as he squeezes. Rib bones bowing beneath his crushing grip, my knees wobble, legs threatening to give way at the sudden onslaught of touch. Breath rushing out of me, his other hand clamps around my throat, tilting my head up and back, the crown of it against his broad chest.

Hunter bites down my throat. Savage little nips that pluck and twist my delicate skin between his teeth. His breaths hot and heavy, breezing over my skin, I relax back into him, one of my hands coming up, finding the back of his head, fingers knotting in his thick strands. Hunter growls, low and raspy, the sound ripping up through his chest as I tear at his roots, little dark strands wrenching free, I feel them loose between my fisted knuckles, curling around my fingers.

He noses at the neck of my dress, his teeth sinking into my shoulder as he exposes it. My legs waver, my free hand clawing over his forearm, fingers tight against his around my throat. A whimper squeezes its way free, his hand at my waist climbing higher, thick fingers running over my ribcage. Thumb and forefinger finding my swollen breast, heavy with milk, he twists my sensitive nipple, razor sharp zaps of heat pulse through me, my clit throbbing with need.

Breath stilted by his hold on my throat. I lean back against him fully, let him hold me up, his tongue lapping over the tooth marks in my flesh. He sucks bruises across my skin, up my throat, into my hairline, flexing his fingers every now and then, so I can draw in a breath, release a breath, draw in a breath.

Hunter grazes his teeth along my jaw, his grip on my neck loosening, he twists me to face him, chin angled over my shoulder, his lips finding mine like a collision. My teeth smash into his top lip, his tongue licking into my mouth like a demon come to steal my soul. He palms my breast, over my dress, the thick knit separating us and I just want it *off*.

Whining, my tongue sliding against his, he sucks it into his mouth, slower, gentler, possessively, owning and claiming every inch of my mouth. His hard cock digs into my spine, his hips knocking gently against me, my fingers slide desperately over his forearm. My other hand tugging hard in his hair. He dips lower, breaking our kiss, the light dusting of stubble on his jaw, rough against my cheek, he pulls back, lips brushing just beneath my eye. Gaze locked ahead, the forest dark, its entrance lit bright by the full moon above us. The bitter night, clear sky, icy wind, his breath hot against my skin.

"Run, Gracie, and don't stop. I don't know how much of a head start I'll be able to gift you."

Eyes fluttering closed, I shiver, fingers loosening, slipping free from his thick hair, his hands leave my body and the second they do, I bolt. My eyes snap open, feet slipping and sliding over the ice, my tights sticking, and making it harder to throw myself forward.

And I can already hear him.

Feel him.

He can't wait, desperate to win, to chase, to *hunt*.

Just as I reach the bank, I feel the rush of air as his arm whips forward, I duck, swerving to the left. I slip forward, dropping into a forward roll, my knees slamming into the harsh gravel, stones and grit gouging at me beneath the snow, biting into my skin, snagging my tights. I push up onto my feet, racing into the trees, Hunter's feet hammering against the frozen earth behind me, and I know I must only be *just* out of his reach.

I drop my right shoulder, as if that's the direction I'm deciding on, darting into the dense trees, but fly left instead, swerving around a thick bush of holly, hopping over a rotting tree trunk. Hunter falls back, my smaller frame effortlessly weaving through the tangled path of undergrowth. Ice has penetrated the dirt, making it hard packed and unforgiving on my feet.

The cold seeping into my muscles, toes numb, heels sore, calves starting to cramp. Breath fogging the dark space before me, I whip around a thick trunked birch tree, slam my back against it, bark scraping and snagging my knitted dress. I hold my breath, straining my ears to listen over the erratic pounding of blood in them. Fingertips digging into the bark, nails bending back, grip tight, the tree the only thing keeping me upright.

Time stands still when a twig snaps behind me, the other side of my safety tree, the shield, the wall, *obstacle*, between my Hunter and me. But it's his warning, that he doesn't want this dangerous game to end yet, because Hunter knows this forest in the same way he knows me. Mapped out inside his head like pictures on a wall, no directions required to navigate, just him. He would never snap a twig beneath his foot by accident, which means he wants me to keep going, to run.

I push off of the tree, my cold feet making it hard to move as quickly as I'd like, but I don't slow down much. That is, until a rogue cloud smothers the moon, casting us in total darkness. I blink rapidly, trying to acclimatise my sight, see whatever may be in my immediate direction of travel. The *whoosh* of foliage rustling around my ankles, when I'm suddenly torn backwards, the wind knocked from my lungs as my back collides with Hunter's firm chest.

"Got you, *little sister*," he hisses in my ear, lips

brushing my skin, a shiver ripping its way up my spine at the nickname he now rarely uses.

His big hands land tightly on my upper arms, spinning me around in his hold, his foot effortlessly slipping behind my own, hooking around my ankle, he knocks me to the ground, his big body falling quickly with me. An oomph escapes my throat, my back hitting the hard ground, snow puffing up around us, a moan of pleasure slipping through my teeth at Hunter's hand already pawing at my inner thigh.

He rears up onto his knees, thrusting my thighs apart, forcing himself between my legs. Leaves and twigs trapped beneath my back get caught in the knitted wool of my dress, poking and prickling at my skin, snow soaking into the fabric and wetting my skin. Hunter dips down, his teeth assaulting my jaw, his hands roughly shoving up the hem of my dress, flipping it up onto my stomach.

He fists the crotch of my thin tights, the ripping sound as he grips and tears into them, filling the eerily quiet space around us, my breathing is ragged, his mouth sucking across my face. Plush lips kissing over my cheek, into my hairline, one of his hands thrusts my knickers to one side, his thick finger going straight for my centre, finding me wet and wanting, he plunges a digit inside. I groan, loud and low, arching my back at his intrusion, welcoming him deeper with the curved angle of my spine.

"*Hunter,*" the breathy moan of his name falling from

my lips, nothing louder than a whisper from a ghost, but it's just enough to turn him savage.

Hunter growls against my cheek, the vibration ricocheting through the delicate bones of my face. Goosebumps erupt over my flesh, he fists my thigh in one hand, tearing his finger from inside of me and working the elasticated waist of his joggers down instead. He gives me no time to prepare, slamming his thick cock inside of me just like that. I arch up from the frozen ground like he's exorcising the demons out of me, replacing them with his own. My hands fly up to his face, one tangling in his hair, the other desperately clawing into the side of his throat as the wide head of his cock crashes into my cervix.

The instinct to squeeze my eyes shut is overwhelming with the sting between my thighs, despite being drenched for him, but I keep my eyes open, on his. Hunter is a force of nature. Harsh and strong and devastatingly brutal, but I love everything about him. The possessiveness in his dark eyes as he stares down at me, his hands groping my flesh like he wants to claw it off, keep it, display it like a trophy. The contrasting way he dips his chin, his hips smashing violently into my own, but his lips find mine gently, caressing so softly, so lovingly, his tongue stroking into my mouth with so much love, it brings tears to my already glassy eyes.

"Gracie," he growls, tearing his lips from mine, breathing my name into my mouth. "Fuck," he pants, his nose sliding down the length of my own, lips sloppy against my skin.

I grip harder, hold him tighter, pull him closer by my hold in his hair. His long, thick cock slowing, growing impossibly harder as he looks into my eyes.

"Jesus, *fuck*, you feel so fucking good, baby girl," the words tumble free, unable to be kept inside. "You're so fucking wet for me, *fucking hell, Gracie.*"

The way he says my name, abandoning all self-control, has me clenching around him, my lower belly tightening. My lips part, a small gasp leaving my tongue, I arch my neck, driving my head back into the earth as he re-angles his hips, finding a new spot to thrust against inside me. Sparks shoot through my body, blood heating, toes curling, I twine my legs around him, tight around his back, desperate to have him closer, deeper. I want to rip open his chest cavity, crawl my way inside of him, forever tethered, stitch myself deep inside his soul.

Hunter grunts, one of his arms curling beneath my shoulders, drawing me up and into him. Hard packed muscles tensing and flexing against my softer flesh. My swollen breasts ache for his attention, breast milk seeping into the knitted fabric between us. He grips me tighter, thrusting into me hard and slow, balancing on his knees, holding me close, running his nose down my throat, tip of his wet tongue flicking over my pulse, sharp teeth nipping my skin.

Dropping back onto his arse, clutching me to his chest as he flips us into sitting, he thrusts up into me, my hands circling around his throat, fingers squeezing to cut off his breath, thumb pressing over his pulse. He groans, kissing me like a man possessed, hard and punishing, his hips lifting from the ground, undulating in a circular motion, dick grinding violently inside of me.

Groaning, I drop my head to his shoulder, sucking a bruise into the side of his neck, his hold on me so tight I can hardly breathe, the same way he can't breathe where I squeeze his neck, but I don't want to let go, let him breathe, I don't want him to ever let me go either. Let him squeeze the life out of me, keep my soul with his forever.

To walk the halls of Heron Mill for all eternity would be all I could ever hope for with Hunter by my side.

But it's not time for that yet. I loosen my hands.

"Gracie," he breathes into my ear, inhaling a huge gulp of air, his cock still slamming up into me, slow and hard. "You're leaking, baby girl," he rasps, hot breath feathering down my neck. "Let me clean you up."

And just like that, he's flipping me back into the ground, my spine aching at the impact. Hovering over me, cock still nestled deep inside my cunt, pulsing as he stares down at me, the moon above clear again, casting its bright rays down onto us.

Hunter's hands come up to the neck of my dress, twisting into the fabric, my chest rises and falls rapidly, watching the wildfire burning in his irises, and then he's splitting the fabric down the middle. It's not easy, the fabric woven, knitted, the wool thick, but he does it with such passion, such power, making it look like it takes no effort at all. The motion forces my body to lift from the ground, my breasts free, wet nipples pebbling further in the freezing air, but I don't have time to think about it for more than a second because Hunter's mouth and hands are smothering my chest.

His mouth descends, lips and teeth mauling across my breasts, cock still plunging in and out of me, our skin slapping. His hands come to the sides of my breasts, pushing them harshly together, he sucks across them, lapping over my sensitive, peaked nipples, milk for our new son beading before he laps it away.

Grunts and growls escape his chest, tearing their way up his throat, deep and primal, the animal he keeps caged inside ravaging me, licking, biting, and devouring my flesh.

Time stills as I stare up at the moon, his hands smothering my breasts, face buried between them, his hot palms massaging and squeezing as his cock punishes my pussy. I picture us from above, what we must look like to the stars, wild, savage, sick little creatures of the night, hunting and fucking and fighting in the safety of shadows, observed by a twinkling blanket of luminaries.

One of Hunter's hands lands softly on my face, redirecting my gaze onto him, his dark ebony eyes swirling with warm caramel, glinting like fragments of gold in black diamonds. Flop of black hair hiding one of them from view. My head cranes up, lips melding with his, pulled together like magnets. His other hand moves between us, the rough pad of his thumb grinding harsh circles into my throbbing clit. And that's all it takes to set me off.

Heat flares between my legs, warmth rushing out of

me, making me cry out as I come. The garbled sounds I make instantly consumed by Hunter, his tongue still fucking into my open mouth, eagerly swallowing my cries and whimpers. His hips snapping ever harder against my own. On one last punishing thrust, he holds himself deep, spilling inside of me, teeth sinking into my bottom lip before he tears away. Thick ribbons of cum decorate my insides, his cock hard and pulsing in time with his erratic heart rate as he empties himself inside of me.

Grunting into the side of my neck, hot breath ghosting over my cool, clammy skin, he places a kiss beneath my ear and lifts himself up. His weight disappearing from over me, the sudden loss of his body heat leaving me instantly cold and needy for his attention. A whine works its way up my throat, the desperation in the sound has his head snapping in my direction. Dark brow furrowed with concern, he runs his gaze over me, scanning for injuries, a logical reason for the needy sound. Finding none, he locks eyes with me, his rich eyes glancing between my mismatched orbs.

I stare up at him, eyes wide and glassy, my legs lay open, breasts exposed, chest rising and falling unevenly as I try to catch my breath. Exposed and vulnerable and confused about how I'm feeling.

All I know is I need him.

To creep through the shadows with me.

To play in the darkness.

To devour me.

Without a word, he dips forward, brushing his lips

across mine, up my cheek, pressing comfortingly to my forehead. His hands band over my shoulders, and slowly, taking his time, he draws me up to sitting, dragging me into his firm chest. Holding me close to him, I bury my nose in the hollow of his throat, my hands going around him, slipping beneath the fabric of his long sleeve t-shirt, fingertips grazing up and down his spine.

"What's wrong, baby girl?" Hunter's words make me shudder, the icy air whipping around our entwined bodies, making me want to go back inside, but I don't want him to let me go, I just need him to hold me a little longer. "You know you can talk to me." His strong fingers knead down my back, his other hand cupping the back of my head, holding me close. "If something's bothering you, you can talk to me, Gracie."

Shaking my head, I squeeze my eyes closed, mumbling into his skin.

"I love you." A confession, a truth, raw. "I just have this feeling inside of me," my lips brush his skin, his breathing deep and even, soothing my soul, like his hands soothe my body. "Like I *need* you to know."

So that you'll always stay with me.

He grunts softly, his hand stilling on my back, palm flattening and fingers splaying, he clutches me closer, my body squeezed tight against his.

"I *do* know," he tells me simply, reassuring me, but something on my insides is still twisting with unease, because I haven't told him about seeing her. "Just like *you* know, how much *I* love you, Gracie. More than anything, there are no words, no feelings, no poem or storybook. Nothing will ever be enough to explain how I feel about you."

And with that, he scoops me up into his arms, cradling me close to his chest, my legs wrapping around his tapered waist. I rest my head in the crook of his neck, breathing slow and deep, muscles starting to uncoil as I breathe him in, moss, daisies, the brook.

Clinging on tight, I settle into his embrace, and he carries me home through the snow.

CHAPTER 2
GRACE

Looking up, the morning sky blue, winter wind still bitter and shrill, heavy grey snow clouds hang low. I'm tired. The fourth night without sleep and I feel like I'm caught in a permanent daze. Pulling the collar of his coat tighter, tugging on the zip to make sure he's as covered as I can be, little gloved fingers squeeze mine with excitement.

Atlas's wide, mismatched eyes, one a deep dark brown, *Hunter*, the other a perfect split of us both, the bottom half a dark brown, the top of it an icy blue, like mine, stare up at me. Eager to take his first steps into the cold white fluff covering the grounds.

"It's cold," I tell him, a big grin on his chubby face, cheeks pink, tip of his little button nose red. "You need to pull your hat down over your ears, Atlas."

Releasing my hand, he grips the pink bobble hat in his little fists, sharply pulling and manoeuvring it so it covers his mess of dark hair and tops of his ears. When he's satisfied it's on *just* right, he looks back up at me where we stand on the back doorstep, a single black strand of hair across his forehead. Glancing over his shoulder, his puffy blue coat deflating under the pressure of his chin.

"Where's Uncle Archer?"

"Coming," I hum, his little warm fingers finding mine again.

He jiggles in place, looking right out into the woods, the trees bare of their leaves, dressed instead with delicate snow. His excitement pulses through me, up my arm, warmth travelling along my blood until it reaches my heart, warming me with love. I glance down at him, my chest aching enough to burst as he flicks his wide eyes up to me again. A beaming smile, one which I could never muster for myself, covers his face as he looks at me. It makes me feel different, different to how Hunter looks at me, my brothers, my dad. Atlas *needs* me.

It feels like a lot of pressure.

And I think of Mother again. My throat crushes in on itself, lungs tightening as I think about her. Those evil hazel eyes that I try to tell myself I don't see every time I look in the mirror. She's supposed to be gone now. Her evil expelled into the ether, something that will never touch me again, or my sons, Atlas, River and Roscoe. But she's still here.

I'm not like her, but I'm not sure what I am as a mother is exactly right either.

My sons are always smiling, happy, warm, loved, *wanted*.

So, I think I'm doing as okay as I can.

Tyson and Duke race towards us from the meadow, zooming around in circles as they reach us, kicking up snow like an ashy rainfall as it sprays over us in a wave. Atlas squeals, tugging me down the steps with him as he hurries towards the Dobermans. Leaving me on the bottom step, he leaps forward, his fingers releasing mine as he launches himself into the foot of snow. The dogs pounce on him immediately, licking his little face and circling him excitedly, stubby tails wagging. Tyson barks, Duke drops down in the snow, his bottom up in the air, tail wagging and then he pounces on top of Atlas. Atlas's little giggles of happiness hit my ears and I feel myself start to relax.

The door opens at my back, heat flooding out from the house before quickly closing off again. A tall, broad frame steps into the space beside me, hands going into the pockets of his black puffer coat. I turn my head, look up, Archer's playful smirk already plastered on his lips, he licks them, the plump pink flesh glistens just like the snow.

"Hunter's going to be irritated."

"I know," he snorts.

"*Really* irritated."

"I *know*."

"Archer," I sigh, his dark eyes glinting with mischief.

"Oh, sis," he chuckles, slinging a well-padded arm over my shoulders, drawing me into his side. "You worried about me?" he pouts, his bottom lip poking out, he bops me on the nose with a gloved finger.

I blink, wrinkling it, the cold having turned the tip of it numb, I return my attention back to my son.

"I don't think you should be fucking the nanny," I tell him seriously, but he snorts in response.

"Someone's gotta make her feel more welcome," he chuckles, but there's meaning to his words, I frown, unable to hide my feelings on that matter.

Something is off about her.

But then, something about *me* is off, too…

Let it go.

"Why do you like her?" the words pop out, unlike my usual quietness, Archer always makes me feel free to speak my mind.

"*Like* her?" A dark chuckle rumbles its way up his chest, his answer is not an answer at all, but another question, one I'm pretty sure is not for me to answer.

The whisper of waterproof fabric hits my ears when he falls quiet, his arms shifting, the material of his coat swishing as it slides over itself making my skin feel itchy as he shifts in place.

"Grace," he says it seriously, my name like that. "I don't *like* her."

I look up at him, a crease between my brows, "what?"

"You don't have to like someone to fuck them," his deep voice shakes his chest, the humour in his tone has me cocking my head. "You can find someone attractive enough to just stick your dick in them. I mean, really…

you don't even have to like looking at them all that much... It still feels good, ya know?"

I blink, hard. Once, twice, slowly. Wondering how sex feels good if you don't love the other person, let alone not even *like* them. It makes my brain ache the more I think about it. So I return my attention to Atlas instead.

"I don't like that." Is what I decide to say, trying to understand how that works. Eyes still straight ahead, I quietly add, "and I don't like *her*, either."

It's my truth, and Blackwells don't tell lies.

"Aww, come on, sis, don't be like that. She's really not so bad," he leans away from me, peering down at my face where I keep my eyes locked on my son, but his gaze heats my skin like lasers. "Why don't you like her?" it's not accusing, but I feel like his question is starting to peel away my skin.

I think of the bumpy scar on my thigh, how I wanted to pick my way inside of myself, and then push the thoughts to the back of my brain.

I lick my lips, swallowing down the words that want to bubble over, something dark I'm suppressing, this itchy feeling in the back of my throat where my words stick.

"Blackwells don't tell lies," he says quietly, it's to coax me into speaking, my neck twinging as I snap my gaze sharply up onto his. Green shards spearing his dark brown eyes, he looks straight at me, his lip curling in a half smirk, "tell me a truth, lil' sis."

My stomach knots. I can't speak *this* truth, this dark

thing I can't seem to avoid thinking about, the way it makes my blood hot, and my fingers twitch. So, to avoid a lie, I choose something else, a different truth.

"A truth?" I hum, my gaze going back to where Atlas hangs off of Tyson, little arms curled around Tyson's neck, Duke nudging at his wet bottom to help him stay on. "Hunter won't like you fucking the nanny."

"Har-*har*," he draws out, rolling his eyes, but I catch his smirk with a shake of his head from the corner of my eye.

He drags me in nearer, one of my arms lifting to curl around his back, rest around his waist as we watch my eldest son play. Thinking of my youngest two, inside, with *her*. My teeth grit involuntarily, and a wave of heat flushes my skin when I think of River clinging onto her leg at breakfast this morning instead of mine.

River is two, he clings to anyone available and I was feeding Roscoe, giving our baby my attention as he latched onto my breast. But it still hurt me, my insides felt like they were doused in acid, melting and dissolving in a fizzy painful mess. I drop my gaze then, eyes heavy with tears, I blink them away, the backs of them burning.

The boys seem to like her, and that's really all that should matter. I need to give her a chance. That's what Hunter said, Thorne hired her, he checked her, Thorne doesn't make mistakes. The problem must be me. I'm so up and down right now, I don't know how to feel about anything.

"Uncle Archer!" Atlas squeals, the sound loud and high pitched.

A peal of laughter rushing out of him as the dogs chase him around and around in a circle, kicking up snow and showering his already wet body.

"I can watch him," Archer murmurs, a lot more softly, his face on Atlas, eyes focused down on me, a frown on his lips, "if you want to go to your babies."

Swallowing, I sniff, quickly glance between Atlas and the floor, then slip out of Archer's hold, his arm dropping. Feet twisting on the snowy step, I head back inside through the kitchen door, thinking about why someone would fuck someone they don't even like…

CHAPTER 3
HUNTER

There are three bodies stacked up inside my fridge and a crease between my brows that just won't shift. I pinch the bridge of my nose, heave a sigh, dropping my chin to my chest. Closing my eyes, I take a few deep breaths before I straighten. Releasing my hold over my face, I shake out my fists, flex my fingers and roll my neck. Tension twists the muscles, twinges of pain pulsing down my spine, my lower back aching, all of the constant leaning over the cold slab the past few weeks seems to finally be taking its toll on me.

Slamming the newly fitted walk-in refrigerator shut, I grab surgical gloves, pulling them on, one hand at a time. Wriggling my fingers through the tight-fitting latex, I roll my trolley over, toeing the brake on two of the wheels. I want to get this over with as quickly as possible today.

Gracie is acting oddly, there's a stranger upstairs in

my house in the shape of a nanny, *Rachel*, who my Gracie really doesn't seem to like. I really need to make time to speak to the woman my father deemed an appropriate hire, after one of Thorne's very extensive background checks. I didn't have anything to do with it, letting them handle the whole process, so I could avoid speaking to her at all. And I desperately want to spend my son's first snow with him. But the bodies are piling up and it would be more than irresponsible to purposely fall behind.

I never fall behind.

It's why I work the mill.

Apron strings tied at my back, I select a bone saw and start at the feet.

Feet, calves, knees and thighs get carved into pieces, tossed into the metal cart. Wolf will collect it, take it back to the funeral home. Wolf's funeral home, handed down through generations of Blackwells, sits on acres of land. Large enough that we can scatter parts for years and years without anyone ever finding anything.

That's one of the main reasons the Swallows work with the Blackwells, it's historical, our families' relationship, plus, we have a great reputation, we never get caught. There's never any evidence, all tracks covered so well, that even if someone outright filmed me or one of my brothers setting a body on fire in the middle of Town Square, it still wouldn't be enough evidence to prosecute us.

It's on the disembowelment of the second body that I have to stop. Crouching beside the table, pressing my pounding forehead against the cold metal. Blood coats my hands, my grip slipping, but I hold tight, weight balancing forward on my toes. The stress headache I've been fighting off for the last week pounds hard in my temples, and I grit my teeth so hard my molars squeak. Breathing hard through my nose, I think of Gracie.

Those beautiful, mismatched eyes, plump, parted lips, cheeks and chest flushed pink, the way she hangs on my every word, always has to be touching me.

Needs me.

My three beautiful boys, their round, chubby faces, little button noses, tips slightly upturned, just like their mother's. How good it feels to hold them close, breathe them in, have them look at me like I'm their whole world.

I'm a dad.

And just like that I start to feel better.

The lines in my forehead smooth over, tension inside my skull bleeding away, I breathe in deep through my nose, let my eyelids flutter open. I go back to working on the body, throwing the pieces I sever into the metal cart. Focusing more on getting the job done than the art of it these days, but I have more to live for now. Plus, I prefer working alongside my girl than doing it by myself, it just makes it more… interesting. The way she reacts to things, admires them, carves them... Corpses are her chosen canvas, a beautifully brutal artist with a bloodied cleaver in her delicate hands.

My mind whirring, I think of last night, of Gracie, of chasing her beautiful body through the grounds. Her big, innocent, doe eyes, wide and glassy and so full of fucking love when she looked up at me, pinned to the icy, snow-covered ground, gold mane splayed out beneath her. The love in her gaze so strong, that even thinking of it makes the organ in my chest skip a beat.

But then I think of her after, in the aftermath of our game. The way she whimpered like a wounded animal, and my heart clenches for an entirely different reason.

Something is wrong with my Gracie.

Open your eyes, Hunter.

The saw clatters to the table, the thought as solid as a kick to the teeth, my brain rushing through a million different thoughts, sifting through memories. I sweep a bloodied hand through my hair, clearing my vision of dark strands, hands clamping down on the table, fingers gripping the edge.

I think of waking up in bed alone, the sheets beside me rumpled and cool. I sit up, rubbing my fists into my eyes, peering through the darkness, I find her watching over the cribs, back straight, fingers curled over the wooden sides. The way she's almost trance like, until I get up, steer her back, lie her down with me. She doesn't say why she's up, she seems confused, half asleep. She's tired but won't admit it. And then she rolls over, her tongue in my ear, hand fisting my cock and I forget all about why we're even awake, and she's suddenly on top of me, my throbbing length sheathed deep inside of her.

Distraction.

Even still, thinking of her, riding me, her hands pressing down hard on my chest, nails clawing deep into my skin. The way her full tits bounce above my face as she eases herself up and down on my dick.

My cock thickens, one of my bloodied hands going to the front of my jeans without conscious thought, over the apron, fist adjusting the sudden painful hardness pressing against the zipper, I breathe out hard through my nose. My eyes shut, I rest forward on my other hand, grip solid on the table. Nostrils flaring, I attempt to get my quickened breaths under control, thinking about the corpse on the table, the pieces I cut off.

But thoughts of Gracie's flawless skin flood my mind, drowning everything else, and before I can think it through, I'm shoving my way beneath my apron, popping the button on my jeans, dragging down the zipper and squeezing my cock. A loud groan leaves my lips with relief, my gloved fist roughly moving up and down my length, the heat of my cock warming the palm of my hand, fingers curling tighter. Breathing hard through my nose, I work my fist faster.

Gracie standing on the frozen lake, her pale skin glowing under the light of the full moon. Everything around her dims in my vision, it's just her and her reckless fucking self. The way she moved across that ice without any sense of danger, no concern of plunging into the depths below, lungs filling with water, whilst her muscles freeze up, hypothermia setting in too fast, heart slowing as her pale skin turns blue.

She has no fear.

Because she thinks you'll always save her.

My heart clenches at the thought, what if one day I

can't. Something stopping me from shielding her in the shadows, the darkness our safe space. Creatures of the night, led by the moon, the stars the only witness to our depravity.

Cum hits my knuckles, my pace only quickening as I pump my fist faster, eyes squeezed shut, head thrown back, a guttural moan tears through my teeth, pulsing through my chest at the same speed as my release. My chest heaves as I finish, cum slowly rolling over my fingers, the back of my hand, I drop my head forward, other hand still firmly secured to the table.

I breathe out hard, grabbing a clean towel, I wipe myself off, tucking myself away, re-collect my saw.

Something is wrong with Gracie.

Quickly switching out my saw for a short machete, I hack up the remaining pieces and shove them into the metal cart. I wipe down my surfaces, throw my rinsed tools into the steriliser and shove my apron and clothing in the bin for washing. I rinse off in the shower, the deep jade green marble calming as I rest my forehead against it. Running a towel over my body and hair, I dry off, throw on fresh joggers and sling the wet towel over my shoulder.

Heading through my old bedroom, locking up the two doors behind me, I take the stairs, locking that final door behind me too as I reach the top, pocketing the iron ring of keys.

The house is cool, the floorboards dressed with thin runner carpet, cold beneath my damp feet. The sky outside is dull, darkening the inside of the house with its aged wood and rich coloured features. Lamps are switched on at either end of the long hall, darkness of the empty sconces between their orange glows. I make my way to the stairs to change when I hear him, his two-year-old wobble starting, the only thing he wants when he gets in this state is me. I hesitate, my hand paused on the newel post when the screeching starts.

River.

I turn myself around, dropping the wet towel over the end of the polished banister, and head back towards the living room we never used to use. The double doors pulled open, pale green wallpaper, dark wood furniture with forest green sofas. It's full of toys for the boys now, a large pink painted doll's house I built with Wolf in the far corner, dinosaurs and cars spread out over the floor, Atlas's cuddly fawn toy on the back of the armchair.

And in the middle of it all is my boy. His little fists curled, head of dark blonde hair thrown back, face scrunched up, mouth open wide, tonsils rattling, his screeching so loud I'd be surprised if they didn't hear him in the seventh level of hell.

I step into the room, the new nanny on the far couch, a sleeping Roscoe propped against her shoulder. Her dark blue eyes find mine, a flare of panic in her gaze as I walk towards my middle son.

"River," I say his name quietly, drop down onto one knee so we're level.

His big brown eyes open wide, tears running down his pink cheeks, he sniffles, biting back his cry when he sees me. I open my arms, he looks at them, hesitating for only a second before he stumbles into my chest. I scoop him up, rubbing his back with my hand, other arm securely beneath his bottom.

"Tell Daddy what's wrong," I say gently against his ear, his little cries deep, his body shaking as he slows his breaths.

"Want you," he mumbles, dribbling down my neck, his breath hot and stuttered against my bare skin.

"You got me, Trouble, I'm right here."

Jiggling him up and down in the centre of the room, I continue to rub his back until he starts to nod off. I glance at Rachel, still unsure how I feel about having *help*. Dad *insisted* it was a good idea, to help my Gracie. Rosie can't keep up with three small boys, she's frazzled enough being our full-time housekeeper. I'm still not sure on this one though, but the boys like her, so I guess I'll give her a little longer before I get rid of her. But Gracie…

She offers me a nervous smile, dark hair cropped at her shoulders, she cradles my youngest in her arms and I work hard not to grit my teeth.

"I'm sorry, I thought I could get him under control, he's been restless all morning," she says quietly, but her voice still seems too loud.

"It's okay," I say gruffly, and she winces. Internally sighing, I lick my lips, thinking about how to be polite before opening my mouth. "Really, no one other than me or Dad can soothe him when he gets like that, he would have just screamed until he passed out."

The alarm in her eyes seems genuine, caring… but I'm just, *uneasy.*

"Wow, okay," she chuckles, "hopefully he'll get more used to me soon."

I stare at her for what is probably long enough to be deemed inappropriate, my head cocked, I think about Gracie, think about how she is right now, *fragile.* But she has good instincts, and I'm just… I can't stay silent.

"Rachel…" it's a deep rumble, quiet, because we all lower our voices in this house for our girl.

Loud noise overstimulating her sometimes.

I think about what to say, the things Gracie has been whispering in my ear, I know she's not sleeping well, she doesn't *know* anything, she has a feeling. Rachel makes her uncomfortable. I start to feel hot, anger simmering, but it's not really warranted, I'm winding myself up and I need to be careful, but this is *my* house.

Be nice, Dad keeps telling me. Does he not know I'm not nice?

"You need to tell me anything?" is what I ask, intimidation, it's the only thing I really know how to harness.

Rachel's eyes blink, fluttery, too fast, and I already have her flustered.

"No," she says in response, it doesn't feel defensive, but she's so *loud*, "what do you mean?"

"I mean," I say, stepping closer, very aware of my six-month-old son cradled over her shoulder, her neck craning back slowly at my approach. "You're making my missus uncomfortable, and that shit makes *me* uncomfortable. So, if it doesn't stop, you'll be out of here quicker than you can fucking blink. You need to prove yourself. Getting the job was not the challenge, *keeping* the job is." I raise a brow, dipping forward just slightly, "you understand?"

She nods her head, licking her lips, I watch as her throat bobs in a swallow and then I flash my eyes up to hers once more, making sure there's at least a little fear swirling there, amidst the understanding.

"Yes," she says, almost in a whisper and it's surprising how easy it is to tolerate her voice at this volume. "I understand. I really want to do well here," she tacks on shakily as I start to turn away from her.

I'm only half turned, so I flick my gaze back onto her, "if that's the case, I have some advice. Stop opening your legs for my fucking brother."

And then I give her my back. It's not my place to offer her encouragement, she's a nanny, she's supposed to just *be* good at the job, right? Turning on my heel to leave, I stop, finding Gracie in the centre of the doorway.

Heart skipping a beat in the same way it always does when I look at her, I give her a half smile, but she doesn't smile back. Her large, mismatched eyes rove over my exposed chest, eyes flicking to where the nanny sits behind me on the couch and then back to me. Without a word she holds out her arms, still wrapped up inside her thick white puffer coat. I blink at her, her eyes locked on mine, arms still outstretched, I close the distance between us and pass her our sleepy toddler.

She turns her back on me in silence, and I just stand

there watching her make her way down the hall, my eyes locked on the beautiful sight of her. Her long golden hair swishes against the backs of her thighs as she walks, her pace slow, hips swaying just slightly, everything about her movements so, *so* tempting. Even now, she still has no fucking idea what she does to me. She stops, turning her head over her shoulder, the opposite one to where River's head hangs carefully over it. Those eyes laser focused on me, ice blue and warm hazel.

"Bring me my baby, Hunter."

And then she starts up the stairs, and I, I go get our baby, taking him upstairs to his Mama.

"Hunter," Dad calls, his deep voice echoing down the hall from the front door, slamming shut behind him.

"Kitchen," I say back, not yelling, he can hear me, we've all adjusted our hearing in this house.

I lather soap on my forearms, a gentle vanilla scent wafting to my nose, foam and bubbles sliding down my skin. Using my elbow, I knock the tap on, pass each arm underneath the cold spray of water, feeling Dad enter the kitchen at my back. His usual seat at the head of the table, chair pulled out, the wooden legs scraping over the worn stone floor. I drag the chequered tea towel over my arms, drying my hands, I wander closer, drop into the chair to his left, cock my head.

Wavy, black hair slicked back, warm tanned skin bright despite the cold weather. Dark navy suit jacket fitted across his broad shoulders, tailored to fit his large build, pressed white shirt beneath, ever the professional.

Thorne is the same way, always dressed the part, unreadable. Dad's dark eyes glint with gold as he draws them up from the phone in his large hands to mine.

He sniffs, drops the phone, screen darkened, to the table, folds his fingers together, scarred knuckles bright and white, pale line of skin around his left ring finger. A small smile tilting my lips catches me off guard, thinking about the reason for the absence of a wedding band. Makes me want to abandon this table, find Gracie and fuck her for the next four hours.

Dad clears his throat, my eyes flicking back up to his, a crease between his dark brows.

"Hunter," he swallows, Adam's apple bobbing, "there's bee-"

Little feet pounding down the hall instantly steals our attention.

"Pops!" Atlas yells, running and jumping into Dad's waiting arms, little legs clambering him up into Dad's lap. "You're home," he giggles loudly as Dad digs his fingers into his sides, making him squirm and howl.

"Atlas, my boy, causing trouble?" he teases, stopping his tickling, Atlas almost looks offended, and I have to bite down on the smirk trying to free itself.

"Never! I'm a good boy," he tells Dad sternly, fists going to his hips. "Mummy said so just this morning."

"She did?" Dad raises a brow, corner of his mouth tilting up.

"Yes."

"Well then, who am I to argue with that, huh?"

"You can't argue with Mummy," he shrugs casually,

glancing at me before whispering, too loudly to really be a whisper, to Dad behind his small hand. "You all love her too much."

Dad's gaze flickers to mine, a smile in his eyes, my own dropping to the table, a real smile twitching on my lips, when the *tap, tap, tap* of heeled shoes interrupts. All three of us turning towards the hall, Rachel quickly appearing in the archway.

"Atlas," she says in a gentle scold, "you mustn't run off, what if I lost you?" that anxious bite is in her tone again and I feel my eyes tighten at the outer corners.

"How could you lose me? I live here." Atlas blinks hard, his words slow and drawn out, all of it reminiscent of Gracie, and a beaming grin plasters itself over my lips.

Dad clears his throat again, Rachel's lips popped open in surprise, Atlas just staring back at her in that unnerving way he and Gracie both do, unblinking, expression blank. Even at four and a half he's got it down to a T.

"Off you go, Atlas, do as Rachel says, please," Dad tells him, lifting him to his feet, and placing him down on the floor.

Atlas bends, tugging the legs of his black dungarees down over spotty orange socks. Bypassing the nanny altogether, he races around her legs and shoots off down the hallway.

Rachel stands there for a moment, gaze flicking between the two of us. I raise my brows with a tip of my head, and she gets the idea, swallowing quickly, she spins away from us and exits the room.

"Hunter."

"What?"

"Be nice."

I grin wide, feral, the look in his eyes something like exasperation, but he doesn't say anything else on the matter. It's not really having a nanny that I don't like, it's just, I guess, having someone in the house feels a little *odd*. She serves a purpose, I get that, I'm just, *adjusting*. And since my little chat with Rachel two days ago, well, I think she's trying harder because Archer brought home a different girl last night after complaining all day about his blue balls.

When I really think about it, I don't think I ever saw us needing a nanny... But then, I also didn't envision us having three babies in just over five years, so I suppose that was a deciding factor.

At that, I get this vision of Gracie, belly swollen, pale, flawless skin stretched, pale pink lines striping over her hips. I swallow, willing my cock to cooperate, not harden and seep cum at the thought of putting another baby inside of her. A girl, next time, I hope.

"I need to talk to you about something."

I blink, Dad's voice helping me find myself back into the room, that lingering headache, a dull ache in my temples.

God, I'm tired.

I tilt my head, watching his chest rise and fall with easy breaths, his pulse ticking steadily in the side of his throat, dark stubble, a light dusting on his cheeks, slight dimpled chin hidden beneath the density of it.

"It's about Grace."

Heart skipping a beat, slowly, I lift my gaze to his eyes, a slow blink and I straighten myself, shoulders already squaring, because I *knew* something was wrong with her. Dad always knows what to do, Gracie talks to him, more than me, but less than Thorne. She always goes to Thorne, he brings out her confidence, he's patient, she feels safe when he listens. It makes me wonder why she told Dad and not my eldest brother.

Not me.

"How did yo-"

"I've been contacted by a Michael Bishop," Dad cuts me off, attention and hands alike, back on his phone, my eyes snap up to his face, brow furrowing.

"Bishop?" I question, my brain ticking over on Gracie's last name, but he just continues.

"Forty-six, comes from Hammersmith, born in Surrey, wealthy parents, both deceased, works for a *Blaze McCoy*. Appears to be a lackey for The Ashes gang, low level grunt work, doesn't seem to be too trustworthy. Done a few stints inside, six months here, ten months there, battery, assault, theft, battery, possession, battery, driving while under a two-year ban, batter-"

I throw a hand up, flapping it in the space between us, he stops reeling off the information he's reading from his phone, eyes flicking up from beneath his dark lashes.

"Why are we talking about this?"

He presses a button on the side of the phone, locking it and pressing it down onto the table, the information disappearing with the darkness of the dimmed screen. Re-clasping his hands together, he sighs.

"Michael Bishop claims to be Grace's biological father. *Apparently*, heard through the grapevine about a girl with odd coloured eyes joining the Blackwells. Supposedly looked into his ex-wife, discovered her new last name, and well, he put two and two together. Not sure how, from what I've dug up about him, he doesn't seem like the brightest bulb in the box. But he's a gambler, and you know how the mob like to talk over a card game, son."

Goosebumps rip their way across my skin, hackles rising, nostrils flaring.

"He wants something," I bite out, the assumption thick in the air between us.

Jaw grinding, molars squeaking, I lick over the inside of my teeth. It sends a shock of pressure to my already pounding head and my fingers curl into fists, desperately wanting to pummel something.

"Most likely," Dad hums, then he takes a deep breath. "*However*," he says slowly, caution and warning in equal measures in his tone. "I have neither a confirmation nor solid suspicion that that is the case."

I raise a single brow, a snarl on my lips.

"So?" I growl out, the sound tearing at my vocal cords, already predicting what he's going to say next.

Something I love *and* loathe him for in equal measures, because he never treats Gracie like she's *lesser,* but if this were down to me… well, I already know I wouldn't be bringing it to her attention, like I know he's about to suggest.

"I think we should bring this to Grace and see what she would like to do about it. If she doesn't want me to get in contact with him, then I'll have it taken care of, silence the questions, lead him off base."

I drop back heavily into my chair, lungs deflating, the wood creaking with my weight, fingers squeezing the bridge of my nose.

"And if she does?"

"Then I shall make the necessary arrangements."

The next irritated word out of my mouth is bitter on my tongue, I spit it out sharply, my entire body secreting poison.

"*Fine.*"

I find her in the stables.

Thick white puffer coat zipped up tight on her small body, sculpted to her new curves, clinging tightly to her cinched waist. Hair pulled back behind her ears, teeny, tiny braids threaded through the gold lengths that fall down her back. Ones she's done herself, recently learning even the most complicated of plaits, surpassing both Rosie and Wolf with her skills. She sweeps her left hand down Lady's large black body, an oval brush in her palm, the strap of it snug over her pale knuckles. Her right hand splayed against Lady's side, the shire horse huffing happily as she pats her in an even rhythm.

Feet crossed, I fold my arms across my chest, lean against the open stable door. It's five o'clock, dark out now in the thick of winter. The seasons feeling as though they're changing, winter feeling much warmer in November, slowly cooling until it hits freezing in late January, early February. My breath puffs in front of my face, hers less so, with the warmth of Lady's body so close by. Stable closed off from the wind, arctic in temperature, I watch her brush Lady down. She knows I'm here, but she also knows how I like to watch her, just as I know she likes my eyes on her.

When she's finished, she drops the brush into the bucket, carrying it over to the corner of the stable, shelving it neatly in its usual space. Booted feet shuffling through the thick bed of hay, she collects the red rug, unfolding it as she heads back to the horse, mismatched orbs finding mine, a twinkle in them.

"Help me?"

I push off of the doorway, taking one side of the thick fabric, letting Lady push her nose into my palm as I pass around her to her other side. Between us, we manoeuvre Lady into her coat, Gracie dipping and sliding the fabric belt through its buckle, patting her on the side of her neck as she straightens and presses a kiss to her nose.

Gracie looks over at me expectedly, already reading the expression on my face, she knows we need to talk about something, through all of our silences, we still need no words. Being able to read each other like reflections of ourselves.

I walk around Lady, clasping Gracie's delicate hand in one of mine, pressing a kiss to the top of her head, I lead her out of the stables, bolting the bottom half of Lady's door and checking the others as we pass.

The moon is already bright in the sky, Gracie's skin soft against my calloused palm, her fingers tightening around my own. She smiles softly up at me as we follow the steppingstone path through the frosty grass, patches of snow glittering between the blades. A crescent dimple sits in her left cheek, dark, pinprick sized freckle beneath her hazel eye disappearing in newly formed smile lines. Smiles from my girl are few and far between, but receiving one is the greatest fucking gift.

I stop walking abruptly, turning my body into her, she mimics my movement on autopilot, her chest brushing my sternum. No concern or wonder about what I'm doing.

She trusts you.

A pang of pain suddenly hits my heart like a bullet, thinking about that first couple of months she lived here, how I fucked it all up, trying to protect her by breaking her heart.

Save her from going too far.

Protect her from her darkness.

From mine.

Little did I know, it's where she belongs.

In the darkness.

With me.

"I love you, Gracie," I tell her, the truthful words slipping free unbidden, my insides twisting with them at the same time I manage a full, if not stuttered, breath.

"I love you, Hunter," she replies, her soft voice gentle and coaxing, deceptive in a way she could tear my throat out with her teeth if she so wished.

She knows it.

I know it.

I'd welcome it if it's what she wanted.

"You want to talk about something," she hums, so quietly, a pinch of curiosity in her velvety smooth voice, it makes my veins sing with happiness.

I think about her skin then, the *not* so smooth scar on her thigh, the canine teeth marks she gave herself, chewing into her own fucking flesh.

To feel.

To remind herself she was still alive.

That I was real.

That what we had was real.

All of the pain she felt was because of me, but she wanted it, needed it to feel.

"The boys are here," I tell her softly, earning a slow frown, a single firm blink.

"Dad," she says then, confirming, as is usual when we're all summoned together, that he'll be leading the conversation.

Her eyes flicker over my face, her hand not clasped within mine reaching up between our close bodies, thumb ghosting over the curve of my chin, along my jaw, fingertips tickling the short stubble on my cheek.

The heat of her hand lands on my face, splayed fingers resting over the curve of my ear, my temple, thumb grazing the corner of my lip. My head falls forward, nostrils flaring as I pull in a lungful of her, honeysuckle, fresh ferns, a hint of hay, horse, but beneath it all, just her, like the forest that she loves so much.

"You protect me," she whispers, my eyes closing, a rumbling purr coiling in my chest. "And our boys," the words are spoken against my lips, her body leaning more fully into mine, weight pushing forward where she presses up on tiptoes. "My heart," she murmurs, plump lips feathering over my mouth. My free hand finds her back, gently leading her in closer, her spine curving. "*Soul.*"

The growl I attempt to suppress rumbles free, escaping through my barred teeth, like smoke through prison bars it drifts free. She shivers, falling into me as my hand fists the back of her puffy coat, twisting in the fabric and dragging her flush against me. Her breaths are harsh, dense puffs of warmth against my throat. My lips find hers like a moth to flame, her tongue instantly slipping into my mouth, long teasing licks of her tongue over mine. Unhurried, unrushed, silent, yet full of all the words we whisper to each other beneath the cover of darkness.

She pecks my lips, sucking my bottom lip into her mouth, slowly dropping back down on her heels. I rock into her as she sways, my cock hard against her hip. I dip my head, nuzzle her temple, kiss her cheek, a hot, wet kiss, my lips lazily puckering across her skin. Hand pressed against my chest, the other still locked with mine, she separates us, putting space between our bodies, my breathing ragged.

"*Fuck*," I mutter, running my free hand through my hair, "*fuck*."

I look at her, her eyes solidly locked on mine, wide and warm, a teasing smile on her swollen lips.

"I know," she whispers, turning towards the house, and leading the way.

CHAPTER 5
WOLF

Grace's face hardly twitches as she takes in the loose information we've gathered about the man claiming to be her biological father or when Dad explains the process of a DNA test. Hunter, on the other hand, looks though he's going to tear Dad's head from his shoulders and shove it into his exposed neck cavity. Or explode. Maybe both. Archer rocks on the back legs of his chair, the old wood creaking as he tips back and forward, back and forward…

"Fuck! Hunter!" he bellows, all four legs of his chair suddenly crashing back down to the stone floor with a clatter, both hands hitting the tabletop to save himself as Hunter violently shoves him between the shoulder blades.

Hunter huffs without a word, brow dropped low, dark, dangerous eyes lifted and locked on our father, who continues to speak with Grace, despite the interruption.

"Sit still, Archer," Arrow says quietly, nudging his older brother softly with his elbow, never one wanting a confrontation.

Archer sighs, *loudly*, eyes darting all over the room, one of his hands drumming on the table. I watch his fingers hammer quickly against the blue and white chequered tablecloth. My ears focusing solely on the sound, Dad's voice muffled in the background, until Raine clears his throat beside me, my eyes snapping up. I blink hard, re-focusing on the conversation at hand. Eyes flicking onto our oldest brother.

Thorne shifts slightly opposite me, in his usual seat beside our father, hands clasped together atop the table. Suit impeccable, scarred knuckles shining brightly beneath the overhead kitchen light. Black shirt beneath a black suit jacket, top two buttons open, collar pressed. My hair falls across one half of my face, I reach up, tucking it behind my ear, about to pull the thin elastic off of my wrist when I catch sight of it, it's hard to see on his tanned olive skin, but it's there, my eyes locking straight in on it.

A red, raised claw mark, just behind his ear, half hidden in his thick, wavy black hair, trailing down beneath his shirt collar. That's when I notice his hair's a little dishevelled, there's no wax in it, his eyes are bloodshot, and he has the beginnings of bags beneath his eyes. My head wants to tilt, eyes narrowing of their own accord to study him. My impeccably put together older brother looks… *ruffled.*

"But you're my dad," Grace's soft lilt hits me, my head turning in her direction where she sits at the very end of the table.

Her tiny frame, dressed in white, pale skin, wide, mismatched eyes, thick wave of gold hair, so innocently beautiful. Everything about her is built in a way to mislead you. Trip you up. Draw in a predator, just so she can attack first.

I've seen the evidence of her potential.

The way she hacks up bodies in that basement with my brother makes even me shudder, and I've seen some fucked up shit, but the things she does to those corpses… well, they'll be glad they're already dead, let's put it that way.

She blinks hard, just the once, no other expression on her soft face, Hunter shifts beside her, large, broad body exuding discomfort. She never once glances at him. She used to defer to him immediately, seek him out in an over-crowded space, difficult conversation, cling to his hand like they were physically stitched together. She still does that when we leave the mill, but not here, with us, at home.

"I'll still be your dad," Dad confirms, "nothing will ever change that, Grace."

That's her first tell, teeth tugging on her bottom lip, a soft crease between her blonde brows. Her gaze drops then, too much inside her head for her to hold eye contact anymore, it makes her uncomfortable, looking at anyone for too long. She's much better, but twelve years of barbaric institutionalisation would take their toll on anybody.

Hunter shifts again, his scowl, if it's even possible, carves even deeper into his features, lips twisting up into a snarl. He doesn't like this. I'm not sure any of us really do. But Dad's trying to do the right thing, offer her the chance to get to know a parent that may not be as terrible as the last… He might also be worse, but that's what she's got us for. To protect her, keep her safe.

I think of Eleanor, or what was left of her mother's body when I collected it, zipping away the gruesome evidence inside a black body bag. The stab wounds, parted flesh, tissue and fat oozing and seeping out of the blunt gouges. A letter opener. So innocent, the violence. Grace took her own mother's life in one of the most brutal attacks I've ever cleaned up, passionate. Stab wounds in the face, neck, chest, shoulders, her entire upper torso was destroyed, a couple wounds in her back where she was stabbed so hard the weapon went right through.

Grace looks to Hunter then, just a single swing of her gaze, he doesn't see it, still focusing on directing his anger at Dad.

"Will I have to leave if he wants me back?" she asks nervously, eyes raising beneath her lashes, gaze locked on Dad, an *almost* hidden crack in her voice.

My lips pop open, Hunter growls, and Dad instantly shakes his head, but it's Arrow who speaks first.

"Grace, you think we'd ever let anyone take you

away from us?" his softly spoken words seem to wash over the room like a wave of calm, everyone seemingly letting go of just a pinch of unease.

"It's just to meet him, nothing more, you'll have us there, we'll meet somewhere public, somewhere on our turf. You won't be going anywhere, and it's only happening if the DNA results prove he actually *is* your father," Dad reassures her, his words unhurried but firm, the way he always speaks to her.

We all seem to speak to Grace in a different way than we do everyone else, an unconscious adopted measure of calm and patience I never thought any of us would ever find in ourselves. But then, she makes us all soft for her. She has a way, something like a dark gift of magic, one she bestows upon us and our internal beasts, monsters and demons. Which is ironic really, considering I think, that just maybe, Grace's inner monster may be the most aggressive of us all.

"Okay," she says softly, her small hand sliding over one of Hunter's clenched fists atop the table. "Okay, I'll do it."

Hunter's teeth squeak where he grits them so hard, lips paling as he forces them closed. He was always the most silent of us all, he still is, unless it's something to do with our little sister. The man is as feral and as violently obsessed as they come. His chair knocks back as he stands, clattering to the stone floor. Grace's lips pop open in surprise at his outburst, she peers up at him, his face growing impossibly red.

"I'm not happy about this, I don't trust it, none of

it!" is what he barks, fingers curled tightly, knuckles blanched white at his sides.

Grace turns back to Dad, mouth opening briefly before snapping closed, stress lines wrinkling her forehead.

"How about we just agree to a DNA test, then after we get the results, if he is, we can discuss again and go from there?" Thorne directs the question at Grace, but the placating is for Hunter.

Grace nods, Hunter grunts, snatching up Grace's hand from the table, he presses a hard kiss to her knuckles, dropping her hand down into her lap, before he storms out of the kitchen in a red cloud of fury.

Once the discussion is over, and everyone's started parting ways, agreeing on a DNA test and nothing more until the results come back. I clear the table of the various cups, mugs and glasses that we used, placing them one by one onto the countertop beside the sink. I gather my black hair up in one hand, using the other to tie it up in a bun on the back of my head, a piece falls forward and I huff, tucking the rogue strand behind my ear. When I turn around, Thorne is there, silent as ever, hands in his pockets, body stood casually in the open archway of the kitchen, but there's nothing casual about the way he stares me down.

"Brother," his tone cool, a thread of something else present.

I eye him, dark circled eyes, expensive outfit, shined shoes.

"What's going on, Thorne?"

The table between us, I lean back against the sink. His nose twitches in irritation at my question, I reach up to my neck, trace a finger behind my ear in a line down to my collar, gesturing to what, is very clearly, a claw mark on his skin.

He barely twitches, but he does, one of his shoulders jumps *just* slightly, you wouldn't notice it unless you knew him as well as I do. We're only a year apart in age, we've spent my thirty-two years on this planet causing trouble side by side, I know *everything* about my brother. So I know he's keeping something from me.

He steps further into the room, hands sliding free of his pockets, he runs a hand down the front of his shirt, before coming to stand beside me, his back to the kitchen entrance. Laying both hands flat on the counter beside me, he drops his head forward between his shoulders, chin practically flush with his chest. I've never seen my brother like this before, it spreads an uncomfortable trickle of nervousness through my bloodstream.

"Thorne?"

"I need your help with something. No one else can know," he peers at me from the corner of his dark eyes, waiting for my reaction.

"Okay…"

"I need you to come with me somewhere and help me with a body," his words are quiet, and they're calm, but he still looks… *ruffled*.

"Why is this a secret, Thorne?" I question quietly, a slight frown on my face, we don't keep secrets in this family, no secrets, no lies.

"Because of *who* it is."

My mouth opens and then closes a few times before I manage to get my question out.

I feel a spark of anxiety flare to life in my chest, he never kills without payment, his body count is just his job, Thorne is controlled.

Never reckless.

"Who is it, Thorne?"

He watches me, expression clear of any and all emotion when he says, "Shane O'Sullivan."

And I gape at him.

I actually *gape* at him.

Of all the Irish mobsters he could have picked off, he went for one of the Kelly family's favourites.

A large hand scrubs over my face of its own accord, my eyes closed, features squeezed tight. I open my mouth, about to ask the million-quid question when he speaks first.

"You can't ask any questions."

"The *fuck?* Thorne, I-"

"Really, Wolf, you need to trust me on this one, no one will find out it was me, no one will ever know."

I sigh so hard I could cough up a lung, but apparently, he's not finished yet.

"This isn't a disposal."

"I'm sorry, what other help is needed with a *body,* that *isn't a disposal.* What in the fuck does that even mean?"

"It means we're going to collect the body and we're going to make a statement with it."

CHAPTER 6

GRACE

The stone is cold against my bare feet as I stare out of the window. More snow is falling, large, fluffy flakes of white, settling on the patchy leftover snow that fell just a few days before. It's dark out still, comfortable, ___ ___ pressed against the fogged glass of the ___ bedroom window. The heat of my hand forming little droplets of moisture on the inside of the cold glass. I watch each one as they bead and then roll down, creating a path down the windowpane.

Eyes locked on my hand, fingers, thin and spindly the knuckles in the middle of each finger looking a little too round for each digit, I run my other thumb over each one, blue veins bright beneath my skin. Each of them carrying blood through my body and cells, white cells, just the right amount of each. It all pumps effortlessly beneath layers of skin, the heart in my chest making it all keep going around and around and around.

It feels strange that your heart can still work so well when it hurts as much as mine.

I shift my weight from one leg to the other, the soft, well-worn cotton of Hunter's t-shirt, combined with the long tresses of my hair, tickle my bare thighs. I tuck wisps of gold behind my ear, one-handedly smoothing it down over the crown of my head. My attention returns to the forest beyond, my favourite place, the full boughs of trees, dense shrubbery, the brook running through its centre. Especially at night, it's even more beautiful, once my eyes have adjusted, my feet are bare, the damp earth seeping between my toes.

I'm free.

No one can judge me when I'm in there. One with nature, the animals around me aren't frightened of me, they embrace me. The insects, the moths, the toads, everything croaking and screeching, singing their night-time chorus. My fingers itch to go down there now, hand clawing down the window, leaving elongated finger marks in the condensation on the glass. I could head outside into the snow, let the wind whip through my hair, the icy snowfall thrash my cheeks, my toes numbed by the cold as I race through the undergrowth.

My head snaps up sharply, a whimper coming from River's crib, ripping me violently from my thoughts. Silently, I pad across the floor, a collection of rugs now scattered over the wood, but I try not to use them, I walk in the spaces between, liking the feel of the cool wood beneath my bare feet.

Goosebumps prickle my legs as I curl my hands over

the wooden bar of his cot. His little hands and feet curled and twitching. A soft smile tugs one corner of my lips, I wonder if he's running through the trees too. I reach down, my cool fingers smoothing over his fluffy head of golden hair, a little darker than my own, he has my pale skin, but he has his father's eyes.

I wonder if I have my father's eyes... Is my blue eye the same shade as his, glacial and cold? Do I have his skin tone, his build, his mannerisms? Or is that something that's learned? Perhaps I have his face shape, his laugh, maybe his teeth, or his lips.

River turns his head, my fingertips still gently moving over the top of his head. He's so warm against my cooler skin, his cheeks a little pink, I feel his forehead with the back of my hand, just in case. He kicks gently inside his sleep bag because he doesn't sleep as still as Atlas did at his age, so he doesn't have a blanket yet. I worry about him wriggling around, a blanket twisting around his head, knotting at his throat, suffocating him. A sob chokes me, even as I stare at his slightly flush cheeks, how they're round and full, not sallow and blue. His lips a bright pink, not a washed out violet, little chest rising and falling with good, strong breaths.

I squeeze my eyes shut, a tear tracking down my cheek. I try to breathe in, my lungs squeezing so tight I can't get any air in. My eyes snap open, one of my hands clawing at the skin over my heart, nails burying deep in my flesh. I hurry over to Roscoe next, his cot right beside his older brother's. His tiny body is as still as the dead, his head turned to one side, his pulse ticking hard in his throat, a strong pounding visible beneath his light skin.

Without giving it a second thought, I head to the door, my breath still stuck inside of me, unable to escape until I know.

I have to know.

Hunter sleeping soundly in our bed, the boys safe with him in the room.

I leave the door open behind me, entering the long hall, pushing through the first door on the right. A soft orange glow emits from the far corner, a nightlight, because Atlas doesn't feel as secure in the shadows as I do yet. But he was a child born into the light, never forced to seek safety in the shadows, hide in dark corners from monsters.

I stand over his bed, wooden frame, a woodland scene carved into the headboard by his Uncle Wolf. I pull his duvet cover back, red pyjamas on his body, I press my fingers to his throat, his chest is working, slow and even but I need to feel it. When his pulse kicks against my fingers, I finally take a breath, it's gasping, desperate, my eyes watering, throat burning. I bend over Atlas, gather his warm body up into my arms, his legs curling around me even in sleep.

I turn to leave the room, swallowing hard at a strange shadow cast over the wall in front of me, the door open, hall beyond in pitch darkness. I squeeze my eyes shut tight, Atlas's warm breath ghosting across my throat. I open my eyes, attention on the tops of my feet, turn myself back into the room, I pad over to the corner, keeping my eyes locked on the little light plugged into the wall and not the horror silhouettes cast over the pale grey walls. Lifting a foot, I use my toe to flick off the switch, plunging us into the dark. Tightness in my chest restricts my breathing, but it's better now, in complete darkness.

Slowly, I make my way out of the room, knowing the layout of this house even better in the dark than in the light, I use my free hand to pull Atlas's bedroom door closed behind me. Keeping my eyes low, I turn left to head back into my bedroom, and stop, my hands tightening on Atlas so hard he stirs in my arms.

The woman blocking my bedroom door is petite, my eyes are wide, unblinking as she takes a step towards me, closing the small four-foot gap between us. I tremble, unable to move, fear slithers through my veins, locking my muscles and joints into place. I squeeze Atlas so hard to my chest, he whimpers in his sleep, but I can't loosen my hold, I can't make myself ease him from my tightened protective arms.

The woman's face is cut up, an eyelid severed, flappy piece of skin almost covering one eye, but she still blinks, as though she can't see it, feel it, lashes like spikes stabbing into her eyeball. Blood is congealed, jellylike, dripping from her parted lips, stab wounds cover her face and neck, gashes that once oozed her insides onto her outsides are clogged with gelatinous substances. Blood and tissue and fat.

"Grace!" Mother snaps, thick globules of blood drop from her mangled face to the carpet. "What do you think you're doing wandering about the house! You should be locked up! You don't belong here. This is *my* house, *my* family, *none* of them belong to you. Take your filthy little leech and get out of my house! Get out, get out, get *out*!" she shrieks at me, lunging forward, arms outstretched, blood-soaked hands grasping for my son.

I spin on my heel, my hair twirling out around us, shielding us as I rush down the hall, my bare feet padding hard, the floorboards creaking beneath my feet. Without looking back, I take the staircase, hurrying downstairs, my breaths coming thick and fast. I rush through the dark halls, racing straight for the kitchen.

"Mummy?" Atlas whispers groggily in my ear.

"Mummy's just getting us somewhere safe, baby," I whisper back, my voice cracking with unease.

Without another word, he loops his arms around my neck, trusting me, it eases the ache in my chest slightly, but panic is rich in my blood.

I clutch Atlas to me with one hand, the other fumbling with the locks on the kitchen door. When I finally get it open, I almost slip on the icy steps, body bowing backwards, I push myself forward and throw us outside, rushing into the trees, snow hitting my face as I bundle Atlas tightly in my hands and run into the forest.

When my legs can't carry me anymore, I lean back against a tree, straining my ears to listen for her, even though I know she can't follow me out of the house. It's been over five years and she's never been able to follow me outside.

Breathing hard, I sweep Atlas's dark hair back from

his face, his eyes are closed, lips parted, his breath still warm against the bare skin of my chest. I cradle him to me, rocking us both slowly, my feet sinking into the thick snow, hard mud beneath. The dense canopy of fir trees overhead protects us from the worst of the wind and snow, the moonlight buried behind low, heavy clouds.

I let my eyes close, my heart rate slowing, my breathing evening out. A cold sweat pricks my forehead, soft wisps of hair sticking to my temples. I keep Atlas's legs around my waist, his dead weight making my muscles burn but I won't ever let go.

I don't know how long we sway at our tree for, the buzzing in my head slowly subsides, the pounding in my ears stilling. I hear the call of an owl, high up in the trees. I breathe in deep, the scent of the forest calming my nerves, the freezing air makes me cough, a cloud of white puffing in front of my face. Atlas shivers in my arms and a new wave of panic floods me for an entirely different reason.

I stroke his hair back, dip my head down, my cheek to his, he's warmer than I am, but he shouldn't be out here in these temperatures. Kicking my feet back to life, the cold seeping beneath my skin, digging painfully into my bones, I move as quickly as I can.

When we reach the stables, the soft glow from the light above the door guiding the way. I unbolt the latch, turning to look back at the house over my shoulder. The huge stone building looming, its shadow swallowing me, I turn back, entering the stables, grab a spare horse rug from the shelf at the far end and pull it around Atlas. He stirs in his sleep, his breaths still warm against my icy skin, I pace a short while.

Lady stirring in her stall, not appreciating the disturbance to her sleep. Stopping in front of her, I pat her nose, rubbing my free hand up and down her face. She huffs into my palm, lips nibbling over my empty hand, wet and warm. I brush my hand over her, her head dipping over her gate for me to scratch the spot behind her pointed ears. I let myself in with her, her stall surprisingly warm, heated from her big body. I sit down in the far corner, the thick hay and straw mixture beneath my bottom taking the chill away.

My teeth chatter as I pull the horse rug further around us, Atlas still lying on my front, I slump back against the wall. Try to work out from the sky outside how many hours are left until the first signs of day will start, but then I remember the heavy snow clouds, hanging low in the sky, so the likelihood of the sun penetrating them is slim. Atlas sighs against me, my hands gently soothing over his back, little hot puffs of breath tickle the hairs tangled around my throat and shoulders, but it eases the tightness in my chest a little, knowing he's not cold.

Lady scuffing her hoof over the floor jerks me awake, Atlas's wide mismatched eyes already open, he reaches up, brushing his little fingers against my cheek. My back is cold, but my front is warm, I blink at him, and a small smile pulls at his mouth, a half smirk learned from his father.

"Are you okay, mummy?" he asks in a gentle whisper,

a tear sliding down my cheek, he watches it roll down my face before his thumb wipes it away, smearing it across my jaw.

He snuggles in closer to my chest, his hands and feet all balled up, as if he's trying to get as close as possible without clawing his way inside of me.

"Mummy's okay," I tell him quietly, heat burning at the back of my eyes.

Blackwells don't tell lies.

A phrase that's ingrained into my very soul.

But mothers must sometimes lie to their sons.

That's what Dad told me when Atlas had asked me what job Mummy and Daddy do in the basement and I was unsure what to say.

Atlas squirms in my arms slightly, pushing at my chest, I loosen my grip on him, little red lines from my shirt imprinted on one side of his face. I watch as he stands to his socked feet, the stripey fabric hidden in the bed of hay. Brushing down his pyjamas, he straightens, pushing back his shoulders, he reaches forward, offering me his hand.

I push to my knees first, my cold back stiff, a shiver wracking my body as I stand and take his hand in mine. Both of us patting Lady's side as we exit her stable, sliding the bolt into place as we leave. Atlas and I walk through the thick snow, side by side, I imagine the sky lightening far off in the distance, but the sun's rays are still hidden behind thick grey clouds, cloaking us in darkness. The sky so low it feels as though if I stretched up on tiptoes, I'd be able to touch it.

I lift Atlas over the three icy steps, placing him on the top one, reaching forward and pushing the now closed kitchen door open, he races inside. My cold, wet skin sticks painfully to the ice as I take the slippery steps up, my teeth chatter, skin prickling as warmth from the house rushes out of the open door. As I enter, closing the door behind me, my eyes fall on Arrow, sat in the dark on the opposite side of the table, a steaming mug in his hands. He offers me a sad smile and I let my tears fall.

CHAPTER 7
HUNTER

The sun is smothered by snow clouds beyond the stained-glass window overlooking the staircase, hiding away from the horror of the day, a bit like I wish I could.

I've never not known what to do before.

I don't think.

I have to have a certain amount of control, timings, tools, days, people, all of those things need to be just *right*, anything that disrupts that makes my brain ache and I tend to get *irritated*.

But I don't lose my temper often, that band is impenetrable, tough elastic inside of me, that wouldn't snap for anyone. And then I met my Gracie. And then she had my babies. And that changed everything. The thought of one of them being in danger or hurt, sick, sad, injured, *anything*, well, it spikes an anger that seems to tear out of me like a fork-tongued demon, spitting acid, chewing venom, gnashing it's dripping maw.

But anger can't fix whatever is wrong with the woman that is my whole heart.

A piece of me feels like it's missing.

Broken.

Something is very wrong.

I *knew.*

Why didn't I do anything about it?

I take my time walking down the long hall to our bedroom on the top floor of the house, where she was placed back in bed beside me by my younger brother at just after five-am. My chest aches, forcing me to stop, hand slapping against the wall, my legs feeling too weak to continue. My head dipped, eyes squeezed tight, I take in a deep breath, nostrils flaring. How didn't I know she was gone? Why didn't I wake up? Why couldn't I feel her panic? Sense it?

I've been sleeping so heavily lately, exhaustion, it's hard to even open my eyes some days, and the headaches are intense, like a scratching at the inside of my temples. I feel like I walk around in a trance for half the day before I can finally wake up.

I shove my free hand through my hair, squeezing my nape, tension coiled tight beneath my skin. I force my shoulders to relax, huff out a few breaths and get my shit together.

For her.

The bedroom is empty, enough light from outside flooding through the window. The door clicking closed at my back, I enter. Bare feet halting, I see the bed clothes rumpled, but the bed empty, my eyes dart over the room to her favourite sitting spaces. The chair beside the window, angled towards the view, the small gap between the side table and the glass, where she often squeezes herself to get closer to the forest. All empty.

A memory flickers through my mind at that. Her second or third day here. The room in darkness, both of us seated on the floor beside the window, rain pattering the glass. She wouldn't look at me. It was... frustrating. A red handprint upon her pale cheek. I asked her who hurt her. I'd never heard her speak before. I desperately wanted to hear her voice. And when I finally did, my eyes practically rolled into the back of my skull. The first spoken word from those plump, sinful lips was my name.

My fucking name.

I'm pretty sure it was that moment that I knew. Obsession tugged on my heart, my mind, my soul. Tangling together with hers.

I thought I wanted to hurt her.

I thought I wanted to destroy her.

But the tables were turned.

She destroyed me.

In the best fucking way possible.

"Gracie?" I call softly, cooing, like we do with baby Roscoe, although, I don't know why, that boy's only six-months old and he's already a fucking bruiser.

I think of that night again, when I told her I'd hurt her, *wanted* to, and she replied with *'everybody hurts me'*.

Even now my pulse spikes. Rage making my nose twitch, eyes narrow.

As I head to the en suite, the door ajar, I step in

water. It stops me in my tracks, the carpets laid out on the wood, soaked right through, I hear the water then, still running, despite the water flooding the floor. My gaze snaps up, the bathroom door hiding what lies beyond and my heart thumps so hard in my chest, I think it might burst. I rush forward, hand slapping against the wood, the door hitting the top of the water sending droplets spraying up in an arc.

Gracie sits in the overflowing tub. Her knobbly knees pulled up tight to her chest, thin arms wound around them. Hands tight around her elbows, face turned toward the opposite wall, cheek resting atop her drawn up knees. Golden hair floating through the water as the flow from the taps carries it half over the lip of the tub.

I step through the water, one hand gripping the rim of the bath, I reach over and turn off each tap, her back to me. The water a very low temperature, it's barely lukewarm, on the verge of cold, what was left of the house's hot water is likely the same water soaking through our bedroom floor.

Taking my time, heart thundering in my chest, I pad through the water, around to the other side of the bath, the way she's facing. The slapping of my skin against it loud and echoey in the small space. When I stop in front of her, her beautiful eyes closed, tears streaming down her face, she looks like an angel, peaceful, delicate… *tortured*. And it cuts me up inside like a physical blade.

"Baby girl."

"Hunter," she whispers, that soft lilt, her gentle tone, everything about her so beautifully fragile.

I drop to my knees beside the tub, cold water soaking through my joggers, fingers of both hands curling over its edge. And I realise, as the water soaks into my clothes, tears streaking down her beautiful face, that the bathroom's not just flooded with water, but with grief too, pain, it's so much you could drown in it.

I would drown with you, beautiful girl.

I reach up slowly, my large hand smoothing wet hair back from her innocent face. My thumb sweeps beneath her left eye, the other unreachable where it's flush with her knee, I gather her tears on my skin, trying to steal her pain, her torment, take it unto myself, destroy it for her. The unseen. The thoughts that plague her mind. The things that scare her. Whatever they may be, I want them.

I'd do anything for her.

"You found me," she whispers, voice cracked and sounding so, so tired.

I swallow down the lump in my throat.

"I will always find you in the dark, Gracie," I murmur, my hand cupping her face, her cheeks flush despite the cold water she's sitting in.

"I'm sorry about the water," her voice trembles with those words, my lips pop open to scold her for apologising, but she cuts me off. "I could see her in the reflection and then I couldn't do it."

I frown, my eyebrows knitting together.

"Do what?"

"Stop the taps."

I nod to myself, my features smoothing out just a fragment, such a simple explanation.

My fingers stroke her face, over the back of her head, her eyes still closed, tears still dripping from her chin, the salty droplets running down her knee. I think I already know what she's going to tell me next, I don't want her to be frightened when I ask her.

She's emotional, three pregnancies in just over five years, it's a huge thing, I know that, I let us spiral out of control. I like getting her pregnant, I *love* her being pregnant, she loves being pregnant just as much. She's fucking perfect for me. But I know better. I'm supposed to be fucking looking after her. She's so young and we get carried away and I just, I lose my fucking mind around her. It's not an excuse, it's just the truth.

I'm sure the surge of pregnancy hormones hasn't helped, all of those thoughts and feelings piling atop one another with nowhere to go.

Because Gracie doesn't talk.

We don't even need words between us because we read each other so fucking well.

But it makes me lax, I get lazy, I should push more for her words if only to help her free herself from things that plague her.

There are so many things going on right now, it's hard to find a balance.

And then there's the other things, the little things she does, like not knowing how to tell Atlas no, and no one wanting to speak with her about it, because she's Gracie and we love her. She'll give our eldest son whatever he wants because she loves him. And it's just that fucking simple to her. It doesn't matter that I'd say no to a second bowl of the sugary breakfast cereal, or that I'd demand he brush his teeth even if he throws a tantrum. She'll always indulge him, and he doesn't take advantage of that, because he knows no different. Because he's fucking four and a half and it's always been this way. But it's not *supposed* to be this way.

But I can't tell her to stop. I don't even fucking want to. I just want her to parent however the fuck she wants, because despite all these things, she's perfect. The perfect mother, the perfect partner, the perfect fit for me. For us. Our family is fucking beautiful, and that's all down to her.

I have the same problem she does. Because I can't seem to say no either. I can't say no to *her*. I can't deny her anything. Especially when I probably should. I just… *can't*.

And she's been… *sad*. She won't tell me why, maybe she doesn't even really know. And I've been comforting her as much as I can, but with the work coming thick and fast in the basement and trying to split my time with Dad and my brothers, our three boys. I'm exhausted. And I know I need to be with her more.

I need to do better.

I can't believe I didn't wake last night when she got up, took our son out in the snow…

I know she's drained, breastfeeding, restless sleeps, I have to practically force food into her mouth some days.

I don't know how to help, what to do, how to fix this. Us.

This is why we've got that fucking woman in our house, the *nanny*.

She's supposed to be helping.

"That's okay, Gracie," I stroke my hand down her back, beneath the tepid water, over the little bumps of her spine beneath her gold mane, her skin so fucking soft against my rough fingers.

We sit a while, her eyes closed, tears slowing to a stop, my hand soothing her, stroking her hair, her skin, her face.

"Open your eyes for me, beautiful girl," it's a gentle command, but a command all the same.

Those long, wet lashes slowly flicker open, mismatched eyes squinting with the onslaught of light. I frown, instantly pushing up to my feet. I pad through the water, flick the light off, plunging us into darkness, a small amount of sunlight streams in through the open bathroom door from our huge bedroom window beyond, but it's still dark. Her eyes relax, her pink tongue poking out, smoothing over her bottom lip, then the top. I reach into the overfull bath, lace my fingers with hers.

"Why did you do that?" she whispers, her eyes on mine.

I lick my lips, shift my weight on my knees, urge her to turn a little, so she's facing me fully, giving me her full attention. Her chin on her knees, golden tresses cloaking her small, curled body.

"We're safe in the darkness, aren't we, baby?"

She stares at me for a long moment, and then her eyes close, a sob choking its way up her throat, she nods her head at me, the smallest of movements, and she cries. Her entire body trembling, sobs wracking through her, the sound of it fucking breaks me and I find myself holding back a choked sound of my own. I lean forward on my knees, pressing up, I grasp her face in my hands, cupping her cheeks, thumbs stroking through her tears, tracks of them streaming like rainfall down her face.

"I frightened Atlas," she gasps, her voice this fractured, tortured thing that strikes me like a sword through the chest.

"You didn't."

"I did, I-"

"You didn't." My words are louder, sterner, they broker no argument because they're true.

She blinks those beautiful eyes open, one a warm hazel, the other a glacial blue, all wide and watery and hopeful.

"I didn't?" she blinks hard, swallowing.

I massage my fingers into her hair, pull her closer, her hands flying to the side of the bath when I tug her sharply.

"He's been telling everyone how you had a sleepover with Lady, and it was, in his words, *'the greatest thing ever'.*" I raise a single brow, silently reminding her that Blackwells don't tell lies.

Gracie gives me a slow, gentle nod, one I feel more than see, her head in my hands. I lick my lips, readying myself, trying to think through what I'm going to say, how I'm going to react to the answer she's going to give me.

"Gracie," she tries to lower her head instantly, but I tut lightly, "nu-uh, show me those pretty eyes, baby girl." She does, always obeying, something I will *never* take advantage of. "Who did you see in the reflection?" Her eyes squeeze closed, breath held captive in her lungs, before she exhales the shakiest breath. "Was it the same person that spooked you last night? That's what happened, right? You saw someone?"

My words are so fucking slow, carried out, I don't want to frighten her into keeping secrets from me. But I've seen her looking off in the distance, the way she stiffens at things that aren't fucking there. Closing her eyes, holding her breath.

I looked up postnatal psychosis, scared the shit out of myself with what I found and promptly deleted my search history. But she already has problems, trauma, PTSD, she's already got so much going on inside her head, I thought I didn't need to do anything, thinking I'm enough, to make it better. And she's not normal, I'm not fucking normal, we're different, she can't see a therapist. This is the life you live, the sacrifices you make, when you work for the criminal underworld.

"You can tell me, Gracie." A small shaky breath escapes her lips as I lean in, my mouth hovering over hers. "I'll protect you."

Her eyes flicker between mine and I wonder what she sees, other than sincerity, what do I show her? Does she see my soul? Does she see how it only lights up for her?

She licks her lips, my gaze dropping to her mouth, her plump pink lips glistening even in the low light.

Tenebris, our safe place.

"Mother." She exhales the word like a curse, like it's a poison infecting her brain, something foul and acrid tainting her blood.

My eyes draw up, locking onto hers, such deep longing in them that it actually cracks my heart in two, I swallow, lick my lips, keep my hold gentle on her face.

"When do you see her?" I whisper the question, the water still lapping over the edge of the porcelain every now and then, a steady drip onto the flooded floor beneath my knees.

"All the time," she whispers back. "And she's… she's all… *wrong,* and she tells me to get out, and that this is her house an- and-" she chokes back a sob. "She said Atlas was a leech."

"Oh, baby girl," the back of my eyes burn, and I breathe in deeply through my nose.

So many thoughts rush through my head, her mother is not haunting our house. She's haunting Gracie's head. But the things she *says,* are they a projection of how my girl really feels? A manifestation of fears and discomfort, worries, stresses.

"You don't think he is though, do you, Gracie?" It's a half question, because that's my fear, does she regret our children?

Does she regret me?

All the dark and twisted things I've exposed her to by being mine…

We did this all too soon. I *know* that. She was pregnant within six weeks of fucking moving in. That's on me. Virgin or no virgin, I know what a fucking condom is. I can be responsible. I'm just not. Something inside of me just snaps when I look at her. Self-control sails out of the window like a paper aeroplane caught in a breeze and I just turn feral.

My desire and love for her are a dangerous combination.

We are toxic.

We are wrong.

But the way we love each other is anything but.

"I love Atlas," she says, a simple, but heartfelt truth.

"Gracie, do you…" I lick my lips, thinking about how to phrase my question. "Do you see anything else?"

She shakes her head as much as she can in my hands, her head dipping slightly, she looks up at me through dark, wet lashes, sucking her bottom lip between her teeth.

"Are you telling me a lie?"

She drops her gaze too quickly, I tilt her chin up, move a little closer, my lips caress a kiss to her wet cheek, mouthing at her skin.

"What else do you see, Gracie?"

I don't look at her, keeping her cheek flush with mine. Sometimes eye contact is still too much for her and that's okay. She doesn't have to make herself uncomfortable for me.

We stay quiet, her breaths a little laboured, I curl an arm around her back, beneath the water, one hand still cupping her opposite cheek.

"Our babies dead in their beds."

My eyes close and I try hard to control my body's reaction, but she stiffens in my hold, feeling the slight tenseness in me. And she's trying to pull away, and I just… I can't have that. I throw myself up, water splashing beneath my feet, I vault myself into the over-filled tub, gather her into my arms and drag her onto my lap. Water sloshes over the sides, joining the rest of it on the floor. I shiver instantly, the water unbearably cold and she's been sitting in it for fuck knows how long.

The water soaks through what's left of my dry clothes, her naked, trembling body in my arms, she rests her cheek against the hollow of my throat, the side of my face going to rest on the top of her head.

"You know I would never let anything happen to our boys," I rumble quietly.

"I know, I just, sometimes it's what I see," she whispers.

"Is it only at nighttime?"

"Yes."

"Then I want you to wake me up, okay? Every time, any time you see something, I want you to get me, scream for me, shake me, just get me to you, okay? So we can both see that they're safe." It's the only thing I can think to suggest, I can't make her unsee things just because I tell her it's not real.

"Okay," she swallows, nodding her head against me, "I can do that."

"I love you so fucking much, Gracie." The words are so true, so raw, so vulnerable. "You mean *everything* to me. I am nothing without you, my beautiful, beautiful girl. I've been so busy and that's not fair on you, but I'm going to be here for you, be more present, do you think that might help a little?"

Her breaths come in short pants, her warm breath on the underside of my face where she turns her face up slightly, I shift off the top of her head, let her peer up at me with those wide mismatched orbs. I dip down, her neck arching up to meet me. Our lips almost touching, but not quite.

"I miss you, Hunter."

"I'm right here, baby, and this is exactly where I want to be, where I'm always going to be. It's you and I together. Always and forever."

CHAPTER 8

GRACE

I t's been a few days since I last saw Mother. I've slept a little better too, since Raine swabbed my cheek and sent it off for DNA testing. I've never really thought about my biological father. I never spent time wondering wh... ...... who he was, what I did to make him hate... ...much when I was just a baby.

I've nev... ...ked at any of my s...ns and felt anything but love. I think it might be something even stronger than that, the way I feel about them. I don't know if there's a word for it, but I'll make sure to ask Thorne next time I see him. He'd be the one to know if there were, he's very good at crosswords.

Muffled words reach my ear and I stiffen, eyes unblinking on the view, my shoulders tense and I try to work out what it is I'm hearing. It doesn't sound like Mother, and I find myself breathing just a little easier, but then I turn my head slightly, listening, the hushed voice out in the hallway.

"I told you- no- no! You need to wait…"

I frown, blinking and the voice stops, dying off.

It isn't real, let it go.

Scraping off carrot peel from my wooden chopping board into the food waste bin, the sound of the large carving knife oddly soothing as it slides against the smooth wood. I flick the plastic lid of the bin closed, place the board back onto the worktop, the knife atop it. The copper sink filled with warm, soapy water, I rinse my hands, glancing up, the kitchen window above the sink looking out onto the forest. It's darkness inside the trees, a shadowed tunnel between the thick trunks, despite the world around it bright and white, thick and glistening with snow. It's still falling from the sky. The dense clouds hanging so low it's a wonder how the men of this house don't have to duck beneath them.

"Muuuuuuuuuuuummmy!" River squeals from the hall, his happy voice high, his feet pounding down the wood towards the kitchen.

The feeling to smile is right there, and I force my eyes closed as his footsteps approach, desperately clawing at the feeling of joy, but I don't manage to grasp it in time as his little body collides with my legs.

The force of it unbalances me, knocking my hips forward into the sink. Fingers curling over the edge of it, I straighten up, reach across the counter to grab the tea towel. Wiping my hands off, River wedges himself between my shins and the cupboard beneath the sink's doors. His hands clinging to my legs, hot, sweaty fingers plucking at the thin fabric of my tights. He buries his face in between my knees, peering through my legs towards the kitchen archway. One of my hands goes to the top of his head, my own turning over my shoulder just in time to see Atlas come careening into the room.

"Found you!" he shouts with glee, jumping into the air as River screeches with a high-pitched giggle, the dogs lying beneath the kitchen table shift, grunting at the noise.

I smile then, the curve of my lips coming naturally.

"Mummy, you have to move, I have to catch him! I'm the hunter!"

My lips press together, curling between my teeth, I drop my gaze, a small laugh on my tongue at that.

"Noooo! Mama!" River screams with a raucous chuckle, pressing his wet mouth to my knee, his hands squeezing me tighter.

Like he needs me.

It makes my heart warm, my hand palming the top of River's head, he looks up at me, where I look down, a big toothy grin on his face, *for me.*

"Boys!"

The shrill sound, *too loud*, makes my body tense, I turn around to face the kitchen entrance, keeping River behind me, I step back into him just a little, trapping him in against the cupboard door. He grips me tighter, pinging the elastic material of my black tights.

She moves into the kitchen archway and stills, her eyes dropping from mine, going between the boys, dismissing me completely, it makes my insides tighten even more. She starts speaking to Atlas, his eyes still on his brother like a predator, River sucks a sloppy kiss onto the back of my leg, wet and dribbling, he's teething, I think his back molars are coming in, so he's constantly sucking and chewing on things.

I stare at her.

The nanny.

Rachel.

"Mama," Atlas says, ignoring her presence, "can I please have one of those little cheeses?" he asks me with his hands clasped before him, his eyes darting between me and his brother hiding behind my legs.

"Yes," I say quietly, watching as he moves to the fridge, reaches up on tiptoes, he tugs on the door, reaching inside one of the drawers blindly, he pulls out the small stick of cheese.

"Thank yo-"

Rachel snatches the cheese out of his little fist, cutting him off, dropping down into a crouch before him, *too close*, my eyes narrow, but Atlas holds his ground.

"It's almost dinner time," she scolds, standing back up, she opens the fridge, drops the cheese back inside, *in the wrong drawer*, and then turns back, smiling at me, it doesn't feel like a nice smile.

She's older than me. Taller. She has a thin waist and a round arse, her breasts are large and always pushed up high beneath her tight tops, jeans clinging to her shapely legs. Her hair is dark and shiny, and her blue eyes are dark like sapphires, *matching.* She's very pretty.

I glance down at my black pinafore dress, tight on the top, flared on the bottom, it stops just above my knees, and I have a long sleeve white shirt on beneath it. Buttoned up to the top, a frilly collar around my throat, chunky knit white cardigan over top. You can't see any of me beneath it.

I turn away from her, an angry flush working its way up my chest. Her voice like a nail scraping down the inside of my skull. I tune her out as she speaks to Atlas, trying to *tolerate*, that's what Thorne tried to advise, telling me she was safe, that I will get used to her with time.

River still hanging onto my leg, I shuffle back to my chopping board, retaking the knife in my right hand, I reach over, picking up a peeled potato, lay it on the wood, and slice it in half, then cut each half into quarters. I scoop them up, drop them into the empty pan. Repeating the process until I feel River tighten his hold on my legs, fingers curled tight in my stockings, then they're suddenly not.

A wail spills from his throat, loud and deafening, alerting the dogs to his distress, their bodies bashing into the wooden chairs, one clattering to the stone floor as they rush out from under the table. I spin around, eyes darting to where Rachel has River in her arms just a foot or so away from me. I glance at Atlas, his little mouth popped open slightly, the dogs stood before him, separating him and the nanny.

"We're going into the other room, River, not a dungeon," she chuckles, the sound making me grit my teeth.

I step forward, closing the space between us, my son

wailing in her arms, sobbing, where less than a minute ago he was happy and laughing. When she finally deigns to look at me, her eyes widen, the colour draining from her face, she takes a step back, my feet closing the distance instantly. Toe to toe.

I feel hot, my heart thundering inside my chest, a prickling cold slowly slides down my spine like an icy trickle of water, my fingers tighten on the knife. That's when I realise what she's backing away from. I cock my head at her, her feet still taking her backwards, *my* son in her arms. I take in a slow, easy breath, my lungs filling, my skin tingling, I lick my lips. The knife at my side, her back hits the wall beside the entryway to the kitchen.

She swallows, I'm too close for her to slip away from me. My head tilted, I watch her pupils grow, the black bleeding into the blue, a swirling sea of fear. A thrill rushes through me, something sick, violent. I think about slamming my blade into her neck, it'd probably go right through, the point of it hitting into the wall. I could pin her here, take my boys outside to play in the snow.

Hunter will be home soon, it's Friday, the boys all have jobs with Dad on Fridays, but they always come home early enough for family dinner. I stay home with Rosie and my boys. Rosie's gone into town; we didn't have enough steak for the pies we were in the middle of making, she put Roscoe down for a sleep about an hour ago, which reminds me, I need to go wake him.

Rachel swallows again, her pulse thrumming aggressively in the side of her throat, it makes me want to smile, giving me the confidence to look her right in the eye.

"Hand me my son, please."

The front door opens, more than one set of footsteps thundering into the foyer, but I don't let it distract me, even as they start to approach.

With trembling hands, she turns my baby around so he's facing me, his big brown eyes wide and wet, cheeks red and splotchy, spiking my irritation further. I wrap my arm around his waist, his bottom resting in the crook of my elbow, he hooks his arms around my neck as I draw him into my chest. His sobbing slowing to sniffles instantly, but his heart beats hard against me, and I feel my insides prickle.

My gaze flickers between her eyes, I have to look up at her because she's so much taller than me, but, in this moment, it feels like I'm the taller one, *I* have the power. *Knife or no knife.*

A shadow stops in the archway, *Arrow*, then another, *Dad*.

I see them in my periphery, but I don't look, keeping my eyes trained on her.

"Do not snatch my son away from me," I say quietly. "Ever." I let my words sink in for a long few seconds and then I turn back to my potatoes.

CHAPTER 9

GRACE

His eyes aren't blue.

That's the first thing that stands out to me whilst staring down at a photograph of my confirmed biological father. Hunter wasn't particularly happy with the picture, but as Dad said, you can't change blood.

The man looks old, his skin is wrinkled, hair is scraggly and greying, and his eyes are, in fact, a muddy brown, rather than the ice blue I expected. They look like the many useless eyeballs I've popped out of faces down in our special work room below the house. He isn't smiling in this picture, it's no bigger than my hand, and it's only from his chest up, the corner is bent on one side, and I focus more on the white crease line than the man on the worn, glossy paper.

Arrow said I might feel something when I looked at it. Like maybe I'd get a feeling of familiarity, sense of belonging, something inside of me might feel warmth.

But when I look at this picture, the man in the picture, it makes me hold my breath, my insides churning with anger. Warmth floods through me, but not in the way Raine suggested it might.

I swing my dropped gaze to the left, where I sit across from Dad in the living quarters of his upstairs suite, the place his letter opener used to sit, occupied with a different one. This one is silver, the handle curved, leaves engraved into the shiny metal.

I can feel the weight of the old one, a solid gold sword, in my fist, how easily I used it for violence.

I thought I was dead.

With glassy eyes, I finally blink, my hearing coming back with a low buzz. I gently place my fingers over the man in the photograph's face, pushing it back across Dad's desk.

"Grace?"

The room is warm, the fire cracking and spitting, my fingers curl into fists, short, sharp nails digging little divots into my clammy palms. I feel sweat bead at my hairline on my forehead, the nape of my neck, little hairs along my arms stand up on end when I glance at where it happened.

The cream carpet has been replaced with a deep green, it reminds me of the forest, my safe place, but I can still see the spreading puddle of red where my mother laid. So many holes in her upper body, blood oozing and seeping free. I feel the sticky residue of it against my skin, the places it splattered as I buried my weapon inside her. Stabbing through skin, tissue and fat, veins and arteries, over and over and over again.

My fingers reach up absentmindedly, wiping at my cheek, I draw them back, clean of red. I stare at my fingertips, think of them bathed in crimson, swipe my other hand down my chest, my heart hammering, I can hear my blood pounding in my ears. Spikes springing to life in my chest and then I find myself out of my chair. Standing in that same spot. My eyes bore holes into the new carpet, I can still see the cream one, the blood, the body.

Mother.

A hand touches my shoulder and I jolt. I jump so hard my heart rattles inside my chest, thumping and pounding on my ribcage, trying desperately to escape.

"Grace," the large, warm hands on my shoulders turn me, I blink hard, my vision cloudy and strained.

Bringing the heel of my hand to my head, I press it firmly between my eyes, squeeze them shut tightly. Everything feels foggy.

"Grace," Dad places a finger beneath my chin, his other hand curls around my wrist, drawing my hand gently away from my face.

He tilts my head up, my bleary eyes blinking open, I look up into his dark ones, warm and familiar. My chin wobbles, his thick arms wind around me, dragging me protectively into his chest, I keep my eyes open, locked on the floor, ear against his chest, his heartbeat calming.

"Your mother was not a kind woman, Grace," his

deep voice rumbles through me, his arms not too tight around me.

"But you married her."

It's confusing. The contrast of character in the two of them. The way Dad is so warm and comforting, he loves us and he's kind, he's funny and smiley. He has crinkles around his eyes that prove it. I don't understand why he would marry Mother. She was cold and wicked, and her rules were strict, nails too sharp, grip too tight. I shudder just slightly at the memory.

I feel Dad's chest inflate beneath me, my arms linking around his waist, he blows out a breath, fanning the top of my head.

"I think I liked the idea of a new start, a marriage. I wanted a second chance to get it right, the boys were grown, and I'd been alone a long time. And when I met your mother, she seemed, well, I think I was a little taken aback by her beauty at first, and I overlooked everything else. A young woman like that giving me her attention, well, it made an old man feel special, so I rushed things. Chose to only see what I wanted to, over-looked everything else." He shrugs, his hands gently smoothing over the top of my back. "I was a fool, Grace."

I swallow hard, arms tightening around him, thinking of a marriage like that.

A rushed marriage, all because a pretty woman gave an older man her attention…

It's odd and I don't understand. I won't pretend to. It just… it's too puzzling.

It makes me think of what Archer said about sex. Sex with someone you don't even have to like...

These men are so confusing.

"But," he pauses, his tone growing a little happier, "there were some good things too," he tells me quietly.

"What were the good things?" I question, my head still resting against his chest, my heart rate calming, even as I struggle to think of a single good thing Mother could have brought to their relationship.

"Well, actually, there was just one, darling girl," he unwraps his arms from around me, my own dropping back to my sides, he steps back a little, looking down at me.

I peer up at him, his head full of wavy black hair, dark eyes that look like voids but carry a warmth that always makes me feel happier on the inside. He grips my upper arms gently, turning me away from that place on the carpet. He bends his head down, our eyes only on each other's.

"What was it?" I ask again, a crease forming between my eyebrows.

"A daughter."

I catch my bottom lip between my teeth, my eyes filling again, I bite down hard on my lip, breaking the already fragile skin, but I'm too teary lately, and this isn't a sad thing. I don't understand my own reaction to his words. We've always had a loving relationship, he's one of the best things to ever happen to me. This family. He created it all. And I fit here.

I finally fit somewhere.

"You are so brave, Grace. Beautiful, smart, and you, you are the *best* mother your boys could ever dream of. I am so incredibly lucky to call you my daughter. And nothing, not your mother, not your father, no one and nothing will ever take that away from me. You have blessed our lives, Grace, you just need to remember that whenever you're feeling unsure or uncertain. I am the luckiest man alive to have a daughter like you. And when you meet your father, whatever the outcome, I'm always going to be your dad."

He smiles down at me, his thumbs wiping away the stray tears that fall. My breath still held in my lungs, everything inside of me feeling so full I could burst, my gaze drops, his dark eyes suddenly feeling too intense. He chuckles, swiping his big hands over my head, brushing all of my loose hairs back from my tear-streaked face.

"So, dear daughter, do you think you'd like to meet Michael?" he asks me with a head tilt, I catch it just as I lift my gaze.

I'm not really sure of my answer, how to feel about the biological father that has suddenly decided to seek me out. Hunter won't say anything, but I know him better than I know myself some days, even when I don't understand the world in the same way that everyone else seems to. I know that Hunter is not happy about the prospect of this man coming into our lives. He wants to protect me, from anything that could hurt me, *us*. And this man could do that.

It's a big decision to make, meeting the man who

fathered me and then left me. With Mother. It makes a bubble of rage boil up inside of me, which makes me think that I should decline. Say no. Ignore this entire thing and move on. Never think of it again. Because like Stryder said, he'll always be my dad. And, yet, despite my reservations, I have an automatic answer, that my tongue knew before my head or my heart, it shocks me much more than it shocks Dad. Like he already knew what I would say. Much, much before I did.

"Yes."

CHAPTER 10

HUNTER

To express my distaste for the situation I find myself in would be pointless.

Gracie wants to meet her biological father, which means that *I* will be meeting her biological father. My chest feels tight with unease, and an anger I can't quite seem to tamp down seems to simmer in my chest, pushing and prodding at my sternum, clawing teasingly to escape.

My head pounds, and I feel tired, fucking drained, inside of my skull feeling too tight for my fucking brain. I've been knocking back migraine pills like they're the only thing keeping me alive some days and no matter how long I sleep for, I still feel like warmed up shit.

I crush my girl's hand in mine, fingers laced, resting on the centre seat in the back of the car that my eldest brother Thorne drives. Wolf in the passenger seat, the rest of the family in a separate car ahead of us, probably already inside the meeting place, waiting. With *him*. Her knuckles creak beneath my grip, but she doesn't bat an eye. If anything, she squeezes back just as hard, which in turn, makes *me* hard.

God, I'm so gone for this girl.

We're meeting in a closed restaurant. A friend of Dad's loaned us the space that sits exactly halfway between our home and Gracie's father's address, if it even *is* his address. The important thing here though is, that he doesn't know where we live. He couldn't find our house if he tried. Safety is the most important thing, and we never take strangers back to Heron Mill, well, not anymore.

There was a time we had parties, gatherings, and dinners at the mill, so there *are* others outside of our immediate circle that know where it is, but not since our boys were born, and certainly not anybody we don't explicitly trust. Our circle remains extremely small.

It's one thing to put my girl in a situation that she might not be able to navigate well, but doing it in an unfamiliar location as well, has my jaw clenched so tight, my teeth ache. Everything in me roars to protect her and to do that, I need to obliterate anything that might hurt her. Physically, emotionally, psychologically, whatever it may be, and meeting her biological father that's crawled out of the woodwork like some sort of festering parasite is something I desperately want to keep her from. But I know I can't, because, regardless of my feelings on the matter, Gracie comes first, and, for whatever reason, she *wants* to meet him.

Quite frankly, I don't know why I haven't just given

into my baser instincts, stolen her away, chained her down to the cold slab in our work room below the house. Because that's what it is now. *Ours.* The place we dismember bodies, slice and dice corpses and then fuck each other like feral animals on the cold stone floor afterwards.

Ours.

I imagine her body lying there, those clashing-coloured orbs shining as they stare up at me. Blank and lifeless. Until my dick slams inside her aching cunt, her hot, slick walls swallowing me whole, the way she clamps down around me as I thrust into her, forcing life back into her. That's how it starts, then we work, and she creates a macabre masterpiece out of the flesh I present to her and then we fuck again.

It's deranged.

Sick.

We are sick.

Her and I.

A filthy, rotten, twisted thing.

Something dark binds us and I don't ever want it to let us go.

Let it continue to creep its way inside us.

Infect us.

Poison us.

Choke us.

Ruin us.

The car comes to a stop and Gracie's hand turns to stone inside mine, fingers rigid. My head snaps in her direction. Her eyes are wide, too wide, fear floods through her, it's palpable, I can taste it in the air between us, thick and heavy and acrid.

"Everyone get out of the car," I bark it out aggressively, but neither one of my older brothers argues, exiting the vehicle and slamming the doors shut behind them.

With my free hand, I unsnap my seatbelt, then hers, threading her arm out of the restraint, her eyes locked down on her knees, unblinking. The car quiet, the engine fan the only thing I can hear, a low whir in the background, my heart thuds in my ears, but it's not deafening. I'm her anchor, right now I need to think about her and her alone, I need to be the all-consuming darkness she finds comfort in.

"Gracie," I murmur, "breathe for me, baby girl."

Finger hooking beneath her chin, I tip her face up to meet my own, sliding across the bench seat so my leg has to lift, knee bending to lie flat on the leather, I turn into her, my shin against the outside of her thigh. Her knees pressed together, free hand like a claw over her kneecap, knuckles blanched white, her nails claw in deep. Releasing her face, I reach over, place my hand over hers, pull it back and clasp both of her hands in one of mine, our hands resting atop her thigh. She still doesn't look at me, so I force her face up again, my grip on her jaw just a little too tight, but she blinks, and I know I've got her back.

"Talk to me."

She rolls those eyes up, flicking between my own, one gifted by the Devil, filled with fire and passion, the other by a god, cold and icy and seeing. She watches me watching her and I feel her exhale, a soft breath against the skin of my throat, then she breathes in, matching my own breaths. She slows her heart rate, the rapid beat of it like a drumming in my ears. I cup her face, my thumbs sweeping over the apple of her cheeks, her eyes fluttering shut, lashes tickling the rough skin of my hands.

"I'm afraid," she whispers, her lips brushing over mine, I drop my forehead to hers, her face blurring where my eyes cross to stay on her.

"Tell me what you're afraid of," I let my own eyes drift shut, her pulse thumping steadily against my little finger stroking her soft skin, "I'll keep you safe, scare away the things that frighten you."

"Because you're the bigger monster," she mumbles against me, a soft huff of a laugh.

My lips curl on one side, a smile that's just for her.

"That's right, baby girl. I'm the bigger monster." I brush my lips over hers, let them linger, pulling back before she can kiss me fully, her breath hitching, hands coming up to my chest. "But, Gracie," one of my hands sliding down her throat, squeezing gently, she swallows, I feel it beneath my palm, fingers tightening my hold, I tilt her head back. "You're a monster too."

Lips teasing hers, she groans so softly it sends a shockwave of goosebumps prickling their way across my flesh like one of the ten plagues spreading across the land. Heat unfurls inside my belly, spearing out like blood in water, searing through my veins, my tongue flicks across her bottom lip. I feel her try to push forward, into me, against the grip on her neck, connect us. Smirking, I huff a breath of laughter, feel her huff a breath of frustration, which only widens my grin. My fingers flex, making her think she can kiss me, but I snap my hold back into place so hard I cut off her breath.

"Show me, little monster," I tease, a smile settled firmly on my lips, my cock as solid as steel beneath my jeans. "Show me how unafraid of the bigger monster you are."

Her hands shove at my chest, hard, startling me just enough to force me away from her. Her palm connects with my cheek so fast and hard that it has my head snapping to the side, my neck cracks and my cheek burns, and I swear I can feel every imprint of her fingerprints on my fiery skin. I laugh then, deep and melodic, a sinister echo inside the empty car.

She's breathing hard, chest heaving, her scent invading my nostrils like the sweetest toxin, sweet honeysuckle, fresh ferns, a deeper woodsy spike of something darker, and *me*. I smell myself on her perfect fucking skin and my brain just about implodes.

"That's right, beautiful," I nip her lips, the bottom then the top, "you're the monster."

I groan, my tongue plunging its way into her mouth, forcing its way through her lips with a brutal force, licking deep. Her tongue tangles with mine, her teeth nipping at it to retreat, but I stay, even when she bites down savagely, blood and all. She tears her teeth into my bottom lip so hard, I feel the evidence of our kiss slither down my chin, heavy droplets dripping onto my jeans, iron tainting our kiss in full force. She attacks my mouth like she's trying to chew her way inside of me, fingers clawing at the skin of my neck, gouging my flesh.

My grip on her face tightens like I'm going to crack open her skull, force her head open so I can fill it with nothing but thoughts of myself. A growl rips its way up my throat, feral and desperate as she breaks away from my lips, the flat of her tongue running urgently up my bloodied chin. Coming back to my mouth, she sucks on my lip, swallowing my crimson essence down, her breaths erratic, eyes wild.

She fists my shirt, ripping at the button of my jeans with her other hand. Her teeth tugging on my earlobe, her hand shoving down into my jeans, the zip tearing open, my head dropping back, her slim fingers close around my erection and my hips buck into her.

I slide my hands roughly into her hair, fisting the gold lengths, knocking her head back into the window with a thunk, my mouth descending on her as I climb to my knees. Her soft hand squeezes my cock, the other pushing up under my shirt, nails scratching down my back like blades.

I want to rip her to pieces, tear her apart piece by tiny piece, shatter her into a million fragments and then put her back together again.

My tongue licks into her mouth, her legs spreading wide beneath me, a foot thudding to the floor, the other foot flat on the leather, knee bent, outside of her thigh flush against the back of the seat. With one hand planted on the window above her head, my other grasping roughly at her waist, I bite her lips, lick her jaw. Her hand tugging and twisting hard at my throbbing cock. It *hurts*. And I love it.

Tearing myself up, weight leaving her, our chests heaving. Staring down at her, laid out beneath me, her white dress rucked up around her hips, puffy white coat parted open, revealing the delicate treasure that was wrapped inside. I lick the blood from my lip, seeing it smeared messily over the bottom half of her face, mesmerised as it drips from my parted lips, splattering down onto her pale face.

She stretches up, her neck craning, back arching, her full breasts press against my chest, her hand on my back clawing me down to her. I take her mouth with mine, our kiss savage and violent, full of the darkness that constantly simmers between us. She guides me to her entrance, her grip impossibly tight, I bite into her tongue, sucking it into my mouth, I thrust my cock inside her.

We groan together, my fingers skating down the fogged glass of the window, other hand palming and squeezing around her ribcage. Glancing down between us, I pull out, thrust back in roughly, watch my thick, hard length glisten with her like diamonds, compelling me to keep my gaze locked on the place we join together.

It's too much and not enough, and we don't have much time, but I'm not going to waste time worrying about that. I live for these moments; every one I get to spend with her is yet another gift I feel like I've stolen. I'm not a good man, I don't pretend to be, I don't want to be, but I'm a good man to her, in a way that only we understand. I'm what she needs. And if in this moment what she needs from me is this, then I'm going to give it to her.

"*Hunter*," my name is barely a breathy whisper from her swollen lips, an unconscious plea to the devil she knows.

My hips snap against hers, harder and harder, her pale skin flushing, pink blooming against her icy skin, outfit of all white, like she's some sort of angel. My cock slams into her, her walls so fucking tight around me that I bite my own tongue to stop myself from coming too soon. My fingers find her clit, my hand releasing her thigh, her back arches up into me like I'm performing a demonic exorcism, but all I'm really doing is infecting her with one. The whine that claws its way up and out of her throat is a beautiful, desperate sound.

For me.

"You needed to feel something, baby girl?" I grunt into her ear, my teeth grazing the shell of it. "Something real?" my thumb presses between our colliding pelvises, circling and grinding into her swollen clit, fingers splaying over her lower belly. "You feelin' this, Gracie? You feel me? All of this," I bite her earlobe, tug it sharply into my mouth, breathe down her neck through my nose, "all of it's for you. *Me.*" I pant against her cheek, my nose pressing beneath her eye, the one with the tiny dark freckle beneath it, the one gifted by the

Devil. "*I'm* for you, Gracie, all of me is for you, *I'm yours.*"

And then she comes, shattering beneath me, hands clawing at my skin, fingers pinching and twisting at my shoulder, nails in my back. The vice-like grip around my fucking dick is so intense I can hardly breathe, I don't slow my pace, there's no gentle working her through her orgasm, there's only desperate, carnal brutality.

Hips smashing into hers, cock thickening, I push up on my hands, hovering over her, she stares up at me, mouth open. Chin dipping, I let saliva drip from my mouth, into hers, she pushes out her tongue, mouth open wide, showing me. My blood smeared across the lower half of her face, beaded at the corner of her lips, my saliva glistening on her tongue. It's the prettiest goddamn thing I've ever fucking seen.

There's a feral glint in her eye that makes my heart stutter, and then I find out why.

Her hand flies up, cracking me across the jaw, snapping my head to the side, but I twist back to look at her just as fast. She swallows my spit on her tongue, throat working in a harsh gulp, and then she fucking slaps me again. Fire razes across my cheek, my eye temporarily blurring over for a blink or two. I come then, dick buried deep inside her, my cum filling her and filling her, and it doesn't feel like it's ever going to fucking stop. The thought of which only makes my cock pulse harder. Heartbeat thudding in my ears, breathing erratic, side of my face hot and numb. I flex my jaw, an ache already present.

Breathlessly, I drop my face to hers, kiss her fiercely, tongues loving now instead of fighting, stroking and hungry. Her warm palm passes over my face, fingers dancing delicately over my glowing cheek, not quite touching. Eyes connected, souls tangled, hearts in sync, I kiss her slow, deep, and feel the tension start to drop out of my shoulders.

"Fuck, I love you, Gracie."

She smiles up at me, soft and blood streaked, and I feel my insides twist with want, need, this endless, desperate desire to claim her again, mark her, show everyone that she's fucking mine, put another of my babies inside of her. But I can't, at least not right now, because we're meeting her fucking father.

CHAPTER II
HUNTER

Red and white tiles cover the large expanse of the restaurant floor, the tables wooden beneath crease-free, white tablecloths. The chairs are wood too, without cushions, small and uncomfortable, creaking every time I, one of my brothers or my dad, shift in place.

The pale man across the table has brown eyes, coloured a bit like dirt, or maybe drying mud. The stubble on his face is too short to be a beard, but too long to really be stubble, the short, coarse hairs are patchy, growing oddly along one side of his jaw. A scar, fresh, slashes through the hair, dark pink, raised and jagged. His hair is an ashy brown, streaked with a just as ashy, grey, its length tucked behind his ears, a piece of his left one missing, a little triangular shaped piece in the top curve of the shell. Like someone grabbed a pair of those tiny nail scissors and just snipped the piece right out.

I cock my head, take him in, watch his mouth flap with useless words I'm not paying attention to, thin lips cracked, a silver tooth tucked behind his canine. His t-shirt is an off white, holes around the neck of it on one side, a beaten-up hoodie, the zip only halfway done up, a navy Barbour jacket over top. I crack my neck, roll my head on my shoulders, rock my shoulders back, another click sounding from my tired bones.

The man, Gracie's biological father, *Michael*, looks at her like he's trying to figure her out, which only serves to bring a little smile to my face because he won't. She hasn't said much, sitting beside me, Dad on her other side, her hands in each of ours beneath the table. She stares at him as he speaks, eyes unblinking, I'm on her right, her blue eye keeps flicking onto me. Despite having hold of her hand, she's making sure I'm still present. I squeeze her fingers in mine, letting her know I'm right here and she finally blinks.

"… and Eleanor, she told me you were at boarding school, that you were happy there, I didn't want to inter-fere if you were happy, so I le-"

"An asylum," Gracie interrupts, the first words she's said since we got here, other than the very quiet *hello* she murmured when we first arrived.

I'm glad she's finally speaking, interrupting at that, but the short snap the words are said with makes my spine stiffen. I glance up, watching Michael's face turn a little paler, his mouth working without sound, a crease forming between his brows.

"I'm sorry?" is what he eventually blubbers out, but

nobody says anything, Gracie just shifts slightly in her seat.

I look to Gracie, everyone around the table is looking at Gracie, but she's only looking at Michael, and I wonder what she sees. How he feels in her mind, in her heart, in her gut. Is it something bad?

I think of just throwing myself across this table, the too small chair I'm perched precariously on shattering against the red and white tiled floor behind me as I fling myself out of it. My hands going around his neck, squeezing, his Adam's apple popping beneath my grip, eyes bulging.

"Why did you leave me with her?"

I blink at that, it's… unexpected. Thorne carefully lays his hands on the tops of his thighs, across the table from me to the right, the table round, but no one sits directly beside Michael. His fingers flexing against the expensive fabric of his slacks. Hands free to reach for his gun, should we need to take this man out, in case she says too much. I never told her not to mention what she did to her mother, but I just… I didn't really think it was something that needed to be said.

It's possible that before midday today, I'll be regretting that decision.

"Where did you go when you left?"

"I-"

"She was evil, *Michael.*"

Her last word is said with such cold disdain it makes my pulse hammer hard in my neck and I suddenly wonder what it is about this man or his words, perhaps both, that has triggered something dark in my perfect girl.

Thorne shifts again, no doubt the use of a past tense word registering as quickly in his head as it did mine. Gracie doesn't seem to be phased; the words don't feel clinical like they usually do. Her words aren't usually brought forth by emotion, they're usually very well thought out before they're spoken.

This all just feels off.

Something is wrong with Gracie.

Her nails dig into the back of my hand, her thin fingers crushing mine, her arm tensing.

"Do you know the things that she did to me *before* she sent me away? It was bad there, at my school, but nothing like living with Mother."

I swallow my own gasp of breath; Gracie has *never* spoken about life before her *school*. When she first came to us, she said she didn't really remember, just small bits and pieces. She's told me things, but they're fractured memories of a five-year-old that went on to experience so much more trauma than anyone ever should. They're warped memories, possibly not memories at all, sometimes she can't make head nor tails of anything she says when she talks to me about it. All of the evil clouded in her mind with confusion.

Michael's low chuckle has my gaze snapping to his, my spine going ramrod straight.

"Is she always on rapid fire like this?" he aims his question at me, like his *daughter* is suddenly not here anymore, like they're not the ones having a conversation, like I'm her fucking *keeper* and I goddamn almost fly across the table.

His question isn't to smother his awkwardness, it's mocking, mask slipped.

Gracie's grip tightens to the point of punishing, her arm trembling against mine, her tension flooding me. I want to absolve it from her, take it into myself, soothe her. Slowly, his dull brown eyes on mine, slimy smirk playing at the corner of his mouth, I lean forward. Chest almost flush to the tabletop as I get as close as I can without physically throwing myself across the circular tabletop at him.

"Don't talk about her like she isn't right. *Fucking. Here.*" I keep my words calm, slow, spaced out with meaning.

His pupils widen, but his expression is kept blank. Practised. Mask sliding back into place.

I want to leave. Take this all back, go back in time. Tell Dad no when he brought this to me, tell him absolutely not, make Gracie disappear from this man's thoughts. Never to be thought of again. As though she never existed. He never produced a child, and not a daughter at that. Not one he can sit here and insult.

But I don't decide for her.

My teeth gritted, Gracie's nails gouging divots into the back of my hand, I sit up straighter, cock my head.

"Why don't you answer her goddamn fucking questions, *Michael.*" The words slither out, not a question, dripping with venom I want to spit in his fucking face.

The smarmy fucking chuckle he rasps has my brain spinning with violence.

"This was probably a mistake," is what he finally says next, switching his attention now to Dad instead, because I'm not giving him whatever it was he wanted.

"A *mistake*?" I laugh then, "meeting your daughter? Being *gifted* with the opportunity to be in this woman's presence, *at all*," I swallow, roll my tongue over my bottom lip, the corner of which curls up in a vicious smirk. "Is a *mistake*?"

I'm a shark in bloodied water, trying not to lose my mind in a frenzied attack.

He stares back at me, suddenly a little warier, but he still has to open that goddamn fucking mouth of his.

"Yeah," he leans back in his chair, the wood creaking beneath his spindly form. "A *mistake*," his eyes flicker back to Gracie as he says that last word, picking up on the double meaning he thinks she won't…

"I'm going to rip your beady little eyeballs out of their sockets and choke you with them," I inform him calmly, wondering how quickly I could do just that.

His chin dipped, eyes flicked up onto mine, he cocks his head to one side and the similarity of that action to the one my Gracie makes, makes my blood boil.

I don't want there to be *any* similarities between them.

They're not the same.

They're nothing alike.

She's just Gracie.

She's mine.

I envision it right then, cracking his legs backwards, snapping his fucking kneecaps, making him slither his way across the floor, nothing but a smearing of crimson in his wake.

My girl's knuckles pop in my fist, making me forcibly relax my hold, smoothing my thumb over the back of her hand in apology, but she doesn't loosen her hold on me. If anything, she tightens it, then she's releasing it all together. Standing, placing both of her hands flat on the table, fingers splayed, her chin dipped, eyes flicking up onto her father's. They mirror each other, but the difference, the difference is that her demon snarls *much* louder than his in the silence.

"Why did you come?" it's calm and said in that special Gracie way that makes you believe she wouldn't hurt a fly. "What do you want?"

Michael clucks his tongue, sitting forward, arms folding atop the table, his focus stays on her, perhaps, finally sensing she's a deviant too. The thought alone makes me want to smile.

"I wanted to meet my daughter, get to know each other-"

"That is not your intention," Gracie says coolly, and I'm momentarily a little shocked, she takes words as they're spoken.

Exactly as they're spoken.

Gracie doesn't really 'get' hidden meanings.

His shoulders shrug and I'm waiting for him to just spit out what the fuck it is he really wants, because this, this is all fucking weird. And I don't like this shit. I knew it was a bad idea. Having my girl exposed like this, we like staying at the mill, locking ourselves inside the safety it brings us. More importantly, it's where *she* feels safe.

I want to keep her safe.

We're never leaving the fucking mill again.

"You can think what you like, I just wanted to reach out, maybe build a relationship, the years I lost w-"

"Years lost while I was locked up in a sanitorium."

He blinks, eyes narrowing slightly with irritation.

"No one ever tell you it's rude to interrupt when other people are speaking?" His dirty brown eyes flicker onto Dad, his question aimed at Gracie, but spoken at my father. "Your new *daddy* not teach you anything about how to communicate with *normal* people?"

Gracie blinks, my eye twitches, a growl rumbling deep in my chest, I snap my teeth, half lunging across the table.

"I'm going to make you eat your own fucking teeth if I have to look at you for one more goddamn second, you piece of fucking shit. Get the fuck out of here before you *can't*."

It's snarled, snapped, spittle flying across the table, Thorne stands at the same time I push to my feet.

Michael staring up at me, a smirk still on his face.

"Touch a nerve, did I?" he asks smugly, and I'm getting twitchier about what in the fuck it is his cocky arse thinks he's doing here.

In a room full of killers.

He's just some low-level lackey, working for the fucking Ashes, I want to scoff, they're a fucking gang, they have no power. No connections. Unlike us. Black-wells are entrenched so deep in The Firm even death won't set us free.

Dad and my brothers all move, everyone getting to their feet, Michael to his. Chairs squeaking, creaking, their wooden legs scraping across the floor as they're shoved back across the tiles.

This meeting's fucking over.

My nose twitches, top lip beginning to curl up over my teeth, words like fire burning my tongue to free themselves, but Gracie's gentle touch to my back has me stopping. I snap my gaze down onto her, I can hear Dad talking, but sound's always muffled when she has my full attention.

Her big, beautiful eyes flick between mine, filled with something dark I only ever see her uncoil when we're working on bodies in the basement. She licks her lips, drawing my attention to her mouth, my cheek begins to burn then, the one her hand connected with in the car, before this shit show happened. I think of letting her do it again, on the way home, whilst sinking my cock deep inside her, fuck the pain away.

Someone jostles me, drawing me back into the room, raised voices, I pull Gracie protectively into me, glance back across the table. Michael's hands stuffed in his jean pockets, standing behind his chair, a look of irri-tation on his face, something *else*, that I can't read, but know I don't particularly like. I turn her away from him, my hand cradling her head to my chest, her face turned in the opposite direction, my other arm banding around her back, body flush with mine.

Head turning away, cheek resting atop her golden head of hair, I speak lowly, words soft enough to reach only her ears.

"You want to see him again?"

She doesn't speak, but she shakes her head sharply, I smooth my hand down her back, squeeze her hip.

"I think that'll be all, *Michael*," I toss over my shoulder dismissively.

I turn Gracie towards the door, using my much larger body to shield her from the room, and walk her to the exit. Only once we're inside the car, her seatbelt buckled by my hand, her fingers clasped in mine, resting atop the centre of the bench seat in the back, do I close my eyes. Head slumped back against the seat, tension bleeding out of my neck and shoulders, I finally take in a full breath.

CHAPTER 12

GRACE

Temple pressing against the cold glass, light condensation dampens my cheek where I lay curled up against our large bedroom window. More snow is falling outside, big, thick, fluffy flakes, stark and bright white in the expanse of darkness that is the night.

It's February 14th and Rosie said the weatherman forecast us at least another week of the stuff. It's unusual for England, this much snow, but my boys, even Roscoe at his very young age, seem mesmerised by the stuff. I can't deny it brings a small smile to my face too, if only because it makes the forest beyond look even more beautiful than usual.

I'm reading, albeit slowly. I'm at the part in *'The Shining'* that always gets my pulse racing, the topiary animals chasing Jack through the snow, and I'm still unsure whether it's because I'm scared or excited. I prefer it when Hunter reads to me. He gets all the words right every time. But, because he's read this book to me so many times, enough times, in fact, for the binding of the old book to be cracking, pages starting to part from their spine. A little like the things I do in the basement. Severing things from where they're held in tight. I can kind of make up the words I still don't know.

The floor creaks somewhere behind me, making me stiffen, fingers still delicately curled over the edges of my book, a fragile page squeezed between my thumb and forefinger that I don't turn. Breath held; I strain my ears. Listen to the silence. I can hear the blood rushing through my veins, loud in my ears. I swing my gaze to my right, eyes scanning across the two boys, Roscoe closest to me, River nearest to the door, the door I can't quite see the entirety of at this angle. Neither boy's moving inside their crib. I calculate the time it would take me to reach them. How quickly I could get myself up, uncurl from this position, throw myself in front of them.

Hunter is in the basement working through the backlog he doesn't want me to worry about. Dad is in his suite, a full floor below me on the opposite side of the house. It's the first night in ages that most of the boys aren't here, only Archer, a floor below me, two doors down, three more from the stairs to reach me. He put Atlas to bed, they watched a film together, so I could put my two youngest down. River gets excitable at bedtimes; it always takes a little while to get him in bed, and if Atlas is nearby, he won't stop for anything to get his big brother's attention.

Rachel offered to do it… *wanted* to.

I wanted to snap her vertebrae.

She's been overly eager to *help* me the last few days, and I think of her that day on the sofa in the boys' playroom. Hunter bare chested, way too close to her, the way he turned to face me, not knowing I was there, and behind him, her face red, she was all *flustered*.

Archer told her to go home tonight, but only after staring at me for a little too long, a little too closely. It made me uncomfortably hot, like he was seeing too much.

The thoughts I have when I'm around her… something's not right there.

The floor creaks again, further away this time, the darkened corner directly behind me, the one I cannot see *at all*. I think of having eyeballs in the back of my head, how Dad always says he has them, but we just can't see, how he always knows what all of us are up to because of them.

And in this moment, I wish I had some too, because an icy chill whips across my shoulder blades, fanning my hair, before I can react, a hand clamping firmly over my mouth and nose, breath rushing out of my stilled lungs. I kick my legs, feet smacking hard into the window as I'm pulled up and out of my cubby hole, book thunking to the floor.

Twisting and turning my body, I push off of my captive's shin with the flat of my bare foot, arching my entire body up and away from them, their thick arm banded around my middle stopping me.

I think of the purple folding knife in my bedside table, the only thing inside the drawer on my side, how I feel a little better with it being there when I eventually fall asleep. But then, I'm not even really sure if I'd know what to do with it on a live person if it came down to it anyway.

Hot breath pants down the side of my throat, ruffling the long, long lengths of my hair that's looped itself between their bare chest and my shoulder, the rest of it trapped between our bodies. The ends of it swishing between us, over the bare backs of my thighs, and it makes goosebumps spring to life, erupting in a cold sweat across my cool skin.

I can't breathe, desperate for air and I just want to be *free*.

I bring my arms up, curl my fingers over their exposed forearm, my neck pulled back at such an obscene angle, I think they might snap *my* vertebrae. Sinking my short nails into their skin, I squeeze hard, use the heel of my foot to kick at their kneecap. Their leg dips, they don't go down, but their hand over my mouth loosens enough for me to claw in a half-breath.

That's when I smell him.

Moss, daisies, the brook, earthy and clean, masculine.

My body instantly goes lax, and even though my vision starts to cloud around the edges, lungs deprived of oxygen for so long I could pass out right now, I relax. Body becoming a dead weight in his arms, he grunts in my ear.

"Don't give up the fight now, baby girl, we're just getting started," it's a hiss, his teeth latch onto my earlobe, a short sharp sting as he bites down hard before throwing me onto the bed.

I bounce as I hit the mattress, drawing in a desperate gasp of breath on impact, then his body comes crashing down over mine, knocking the air right back out of me. His arms bracket my head, the length of his body flush with mine, thin joggers, bare chest. His firm muscles, heavy and hard, hot skin, pushing down on me, sinking me into the mattress.

"Hunter," I breathe out his name like a prayer, his fingers instantly clamping over my mouth, side of his hand smothering my nostrils.

He grinds his erection into me, long, thick and hard between us, making me go deathly still. Tiny, panted breaths hot against his skin, my nostrils flare as he slides his way down my body, my eyes following him, my head held still by his biting grip on my face.

He shoves up my –his- shirt, buttons fastened down the length of the white cotton, it hits the top of my thighs, white cotton knickers beneath. Using his nose, the rough scrape of his short stubble prickling over the soft skin of my stomach, he bunches the fabric up, belly and cotton covered pussy exposed. Staring down at him, my arms at my sides, both hands fisted in our dark green sheets, he glances up, dark eyes on mine.

A cruel smirk curls his lips and then his teeth descend. Biting and nipping and sinking into my flesh. I arch my back, try to push up into him, one of his hands still clamped over the lower half of my face, the other, palm flat, fingers splayed, heavy and firm over my sternum. His mouth scrapes deliciously down the centre of my belly, tongue and teeth assaulting and soothing my skin all in one breath, a breath I'm still unable to take.

Then his teeth clench over the low waistband of my underwear, tugging them down. I lift up, as much as my hips are able, the soft cotton sliding over my arse, stopping halfway down my thighs, shackling my legs together.

I can't move, breathe, think, none of it as the flat of his tongue swipes up my slit, the tip of it nudging my clit as he does it over and over. I'm trembling beneath him, my legs locked together, his face burying itself between my thighs. Hunter sucks my clit between his lips so hard I see stars, and when he bites it, overly hard, I come, just like that, a muffled cry beneath his tightened palm. Hands flying to his head, my lips part as he shifts his hand and then two fingers are sliding into my mouth, moving quickly over my tongue, curling into the back of my throat.

Throat constricting around him on reflex, saliva pools in my mouth, dribbling from the corners of my mouth, over his hand, my chin, yet his fingers remain, depressing my tongue. Orgasm like a white-hot poker slicing through my skull. I twist and turn and thrash beneath him, his weight holding me down, mouth still suctioned between my legs. The room silent around us, buzzing fills my ears, my head feeling so full, blood running too hot, I collapse against the sheets, my knuckles aching with their iron-grip in his hair.

Hunter doesn't give me any reprieve, his fingers tearing out of my mouth and plunging straight into my pussy. The surprised noise that leaves my throat is swallowed by his mouth as his tongue fucks between my parted lips. Hand working the slick heat between my legs, thumb rolling harshly over my clit, hand crushed between my thighs. I shatter a second time, my tongue licking against his, tangled and wanting and desperate. He bites my lips, fingers thick and brutal between my thighs. I'm gripping his face in my hands, fingertips curled painfully into his skin, he doesn't flinch.

This time when I finish coming, his tongue laps over my chin, swirling down my throat, sucking and bruising and marking. Rearing up onto his haunches, my legs beneath him, he pulls his fingers free of me, scissoring them in the space between us. The little light from the moon through the window revealing just enough for us to see his fingers glistening with me. Lazily, making sure he tastes every part of me, he sucks them into his mouth, dragging it out, dark eyes penetrating, stare hard on mine, he makes a show of swallowing.

I reach up for him, desire for his attention a hot, sharp thing beneath my bones, but he's already shifting off of the bed, something uncomfortable starting to unfurl inside the pit of my stomach, stinging heavily at his sudden rejection. Since I had Roscoe, it's been this way, I feel unusual, overwhelmed, and Hunter has been absent. It makes me wonder what's wrong with me now.

What I'm not doing right. Why he hardly spends any time with me anymore. Keeping me away from the basement.

It makes me feel a little, among other things, *strange*.

His back to me, muscles tight beneath suntanned skin, his olive complexion enhanced by last summer spent outdoors. I fly up to sitting, tugging my shirt down to cover myself, the thick scar on my thigh, eyes on the twisted knickers locked around the middle of them. Eyelids hot, cheeks searing, I start to draw my legs up to my chest, Hunter's hand whips out, closing around my ankle like a human shackle, yanking me back down onto my back.

"Gracie," his voice barely a whisper, I tug to free my ankle, his fingers only tightening more firmly, dark eyes focused on mine. "We're not done, beautiful girl."

My neck snaps up so hard it makes the bones crunch. He drags me towards him, rucking my shirt up, sheets wrinkling beneath me. He dips forward, pulls my knickers down my legs, gaze on mine all the while, he drops them to the floor. Arm sliding beneath my back, he tosses me up into the air, throwing me over his shoulder like I weigh absolutely nothing at all.

Arm banding across the backs of my thighs, bottom exposed to the elements, goosebumps rip their way across my flesh. His big hand palming my arse cheek with his free hand, massaging the bare, pale flesh whilst walking us across the room.

Craning my head up to check on the boys, my heart in my throat because we're heading towards the door, and I don't have the monitor and what if something happens whilst I'm not watching them. Panic seizes my heart, squeezing, fear strangling me, suffocating everything that's happening in the moment.

"Hunter," the plea is a cracked, distorted, almost silent thing, but it stills him, dead in his tracks.

"They're fine, baby girl," he says after a moment, head turned slightly over his shoulder, towards me, even though I can't see him, words whispered, lips a caress against the bare skin of my thigh.

It's reassuring, the way he speaks the words, soft and confident, but my eyes squeeze shut all the same, burning in their sockets. Like a fist around my heart, my chest aches, my body lurches to get to them, all things out of my control, a sob threatens to choke me, cut off in my throat when we continue to the door. The boys feeling like they're much too far away from me, they *need* me, and it makes me think, *I hate you, Hunter*.

And that's worse.

So much worse.

Because I don't mean that at all.

But I feel the separation like a piece of me is stitched to them, and the further away I am the more painful it is, as the skin stretches, stitches pull, ripping free.

Hunter's hand covering my nakedness in the dark, we step out into the hall, the bedroom door left wide open behind us, making my anxiety spike harder.

What if she comes for them?

They don't yet know the darkness like I do.

They aren't yet familiars with the shadows in the way in which *we* are.

I arch up, hands pressing into Hunter's lower back, my spine and neck screaming at the angle, so I can keep my eyes on them for as long as possible. I don't know why he doesn't know. Why he doesn't understand that I can't leave them by themselves. Why he doesn't *get it.*

Why doesn't he feel me?

Thoughts a tangled flurry inside my skull, tiredness and phantoms a curling smog inside my head. Panic sparks to life, thick and heavy, when a tall, wide figure emerges from the shadows, blocking my view of my boys. I squirm, Hunter's hands tightening, everything tumbling around inside of me like a raging storm. The figure shoves a big hand through his black hair, feathering it through his parted fingers. Familiar cocky grin pulling at his lips, shadowed and lit up all at the same time from the moonlight reflecting in our bedroom.

"Have fun," Archer chuckles in a dark whisper, walking his way backwards, heels of his feet entering our bedroom first, he tracks us with dark eyes all the way down the hall before closing the door.

CHAPTER 13
HUNTER

Her slight form hangs over my shoulder, the ends of her hair trailing along like a bride's veil behind us, dusting the floors and stairs in our wake. She hangs like a corpse over my shoulder, body limp, relaxed in every loose muscle in her body, and it gets my fucking attention.

The fucking trust she gives me, it makes my blood run hot. I can smell her, her skin, honeysuckle, ferns, the sweet, earthy scent of arousal between her thighs. I grit my teeth, swallowing the taste of her still on my tongue. This woman drives me fucking wild, and lately, she doesn't seem to see it, *get it*, the way I feel about her.

Why doesn't she get it?

It grows stronger inside me every day, it's so heavy, the feeling, this *love* that I think I'm going to drown in it. Sometimes I look in her eyes, and I think she feels it, and then it's gone, a shutter falling over the feeling like she's stopping herself from believing in it, in *me*.

Wood cold beneath my bare feet, I wind us down the stairs, the house in darkness, silence. Gracie's breaths even and slowed, the panic from only moments ago, dead and gone, because of Archer.

Because someone she trusts is watching the boys, and the dogs are sleeping with Atlas.

Effortlessly, I take us down the main hall on the ground floor, slipping the ring of iron keys free from my pocket, the quiet clattering of the heavy metal clicking together. Large wooden door before us, I place the key in the first door to the basement stairs, twist it, the door unlatches, a low creak of the hinges as I push it open, step us through and lock it behind me.

"Watch your head, baby girl, hold on tight to me."

Never hesitating to do as she's told, her arms draw up, winding around my waist, her fingers lacing together over my lower belly, her elbows drawn into my sides.

Muscles jumping, her soft fingers tickling over the V between my hips, joggers riding low. I make my way down the steep steps, going through the motions of entering through the second door once I reach the bottom. Her arms loosen around me as she feels the lower temperature of our old bedroom.

"Did I say you could let go?"

Her hands tighten at my words, and I smile, dropping my gaze to the cold stone beneath my feet. I walk through the room, heading towards the door at the far end, pausing beside the desk, the top drawer containing the things I need, matches, candles, and tucking them in my pocket. Unlocking the final door, bitter cold rushing out, both of our bodies shivering as I move us inside, closing the door behind us.

Darkness.

Shadows.

A place we both feel safe.

Before we found each other.

I was always skulking around in them.

She was always locked inside of them.

I chose them.

They chose her.

Slowly, I lean forward, carefully sliding Gracie over my shoulder, her bare feet placed tentatively on the ground. Arm banding around her small waist, I keep her in the crook of my elbow, my other hand coming up, brushing her long gold hair back from her face. In the dark, no windows inside this room, the door closed, my eyes adjust, as do hers, years of wandering around here in the dark helping us find ourselves.

I breathe slow and deep, hearing her breaths between us, a little faster than mine, but not by much, I cup the back of her head, drawing her into my chest. She's looking up at me as I do, her chin bumping my sternum, hands trapped between us, the palms of them flat on my stomach. Eyes still on mine, her upturned nose, high cheekbones, the shadows play with her soft features, carving her cheeks hollower, eyes wider.

Dipping my head, tip of my nose touching hers, she inhales, short and sharp, holding it in. My lips move over hers, barely touching, the tip of my tongue rolls out, tasting her, caressing over her plump bottom lip.

She doesn't move, letting me play with her, our senses heightened all the more because of the darkness. It encases us, protecting us in its bubble, a fragile thing, that could be shattered at any moment by the simplest of things, the spark of a match, flick of a lighter.

I kiss her cheek, her perfect, blemish-free skin soft as silk beneath my lips. My hand clamps onto the nape of her neck, the other still banded around the small of her back, she's arched over it slightly, hips pressing closer. My cock throbs between us, hot and hard and aching. I know she can feel it, but she doesn't move, doesn't try to get closer, rub herself against me. The level of control we've built between us, something dark and depraved. It's a sick thing. Making each other wait for what we both know the other wants.

My mouth over the highest point of her cheekbone, nose against her temple, I breathe her in, her scent driving me wild, my eyes roll into the back of my head. Knowing I have her here, in the darkness, at my mercy. *She trusts me.* It's a dizzying power source, something I could get intoxicated on.

Her silken hair hangs like streamers down her back, the arm around her waist, my fingers of that hand latching in the lengths of it, gentle, teasing tugs as I pluck at the loops around my fingertips.

She gasps then, her senses finally adjusting, her soul dropping back into her body, melting into the space that's just for her and I. Sometimes I want to drag her down here, and not even for anything nefarious, just for something selfish, *for me.* To tuck her between my knees, cuddle her into my chest, the pair of us hidden away in the darkest corner of the mill. Because sometimes, sometimes I just need a fucking break. And so does she.

So the fuck does she.

Help her Hunter.

Sloppily, my lips, my tongue, my teeth, all of it moves over her face, tasting her, sucking along her jaw, nipping at her earlobe, teeth scraping down the column of her throat. Our bodies flush together, her hands slide down my abs, the muscles rolling beneath her touch. Lips finding hers, I suck her bottom lip into my mouth, fold it between my teeth, groaning into her mouth as her nails gently claw over my skin.

Tongue licking into her mouth, through her parted lips, her breaths short and uncontrolled. Every touch of her hands sets me aflame, one of her hands moving around to my back, climbing up my spine, she pushes herself against me, my body bowing over hers. She sinks her nails into my shoulder as her arm moves up my back and curls over it. I hiss between my teeth, into her mouth, she bites my tongue, sucking on it hard. Any semblance of control I had shatters when she jumps, both feet leaving the floor like she just expects that I'll catch her.

I always fucking will.

Her thighs lock around my waist, her bare cunt grinding up and over the hard planes of muscle in my abdomen. My fingers delve into the flesh of her thighs, gripping and parting her cheeks, I spin us, slam her up against the door. Air rushes out of her lungs into mine and it fills me up. Our exchange of life force. She's moving more vigorously now, back to the door, weight in my arms, grinding herself against me, breathy moans falling free from her throat, my dick so fucking hard I can hardly think. The slick between her thighs coating my skin, I can smell her, her tongue fucking into my mouth, her cunt slipping all over me.

Every nerve in my body is sparking, my muscles trembling, blood running hot. I bite into her lip, the top one, forcing her tongue to retreat, I sink teeth into her flesh, making her cry out as I split her pouty little cupid's bow, it's so defined, so delicate, she's so *pretty*. It makes me want to ruin it. *Her.* I never knew what to do with gifts I was given, like pulling the wheels off of toy trucks when I was small, skinning my teddy bears, plucking out their eyes and tearing out their insides.

I wanted to see how it all worked. What made it look the way it did. The same way Gracie wants to know how everything works, why things *are.* I was worried. When we found out we were expecting that first time. Worried of what she'd be like, carrying a baby, learning about her body, the things she'd have to go through because I couldn't put on a fucking condom.

I should have known I'd have nothing to worry about. The way she handled her entire pregnancy with Atlas was a mixture of awe and curiosity, an ethereal calm that would put meditation experts to shame. When he kept her up all night kicking the shit out of her insides, and she'd laugh and watch and feel.

I think I fell deeper then.

Feelings, obsession, possession, all of it tumbled and tumbled and tumbled. Evolving into something even more dangerous than before.

That first night she woke me with her quiet chuckle. Sat upright in our bed in the basement, back resting against the headboard. Both dogs ears pricked, their eyes on her from the base of the bed. Her exposed stomach just a small gentle curve to her belly, her delicate hands splayed over the tiny bump, her white skin glowing in the light from the moon. I thought she'd be scared, because I hadn't really explained, but she was grabbing my hands and pulling them to her belly, her hands over mine, her eyes alight in the darkness.

"That's our baby, Hunter."

A tear slides down my nose, her lips stilled beneath mine, and I wonder when I stopped making love to her mouth, how long I've been lost inside my thoughts, how long she just waited for me. I move my lips again, the taste of iron tainting our kiss. She kisses me back with the same gentle urgency I switch us to, no questions asked. I kiss her for long, slow moments, needing her to know, to *feel*.

I want to destroy you, baby girl, but I want to fucking love you just as much.

"I love you, Gracie," I whisper it into her mouth, let her taste my words, I suck on her wound, lick over the parted flesh. "I love you."

My head against hers, our eyes on one another's, darkness swirling around us, the cold air of the room pricking at our flesh, goosebumps and a shiver, the chill in the room forcing me closer. I squeeze her cheeks in my hands, and then I'm lowering her slowly to the floor, her shirt covering her, hitting the tops of her thighs. I sweep her hair back, cup her face, press a fierce kiss to the top of her head.

"What are we doing down here, Hunter?" her voice is soft, a caress in the dark and I love that she always says my name like that, just this innocent, worshipping thing.

My fingers encircle her throat, stroking gently, my other hand moving to her waist, a light squeeze. I swallow at the same time she does, beneath my palm, her hands at her sides. I can feel her on me, the wetness from her arousal smeared and drying all over my abs.

"I have a body for you," I whisper it like a dangerous confession.

And it is, *sometimes*.

I've seen people play with bodies before, live ones, dead ones, but I've never witnessed the things that my girl does when she's got someone on the slab. She likes the pretty ones I've noticed. And I'm not sure if she's carving them up to make them *more* beautiful or because she wants to destroy them.

I can relate to that, beautiful girl.

I turn her, hands on her hips, walking her forward until her hips, my fingers curled around them, are flush against the cold metal table in the centre of the room. She sucks in a breath, thin cotton shirt between her and the metal, but a tremor runs through her all the same, the chill in the air, the anticipation, the things she knows I'll let her do in this room.

There's nothing not allowed here.

I know it.

She knows it.

This is the place our sickness unfurls in safety, our madness circling us like smoke, no fear, no judgement.

"Hunter?" my name is a breathy whisper from her lips, my erection digging into her spine jumping at the lilt in the word, the question.

My hands find hers, fingers lacing together without protest, I bring them up, onto the forearm of the body on the slab. Her breath stills in her chest, my back flush with hers, her heart is pounding, thrashing like a bandit trying to free themselves. Adrenaline courses through my veins, like an electrical current of shock, I step in closer, pressing her hard into the table.

I spread our hands, the right ones sliding down to the back of the corpse's hand, our left sliding up, over the elbow ditch, until we stop at the shoulder joint. Skin cold, smooth, a little dry beneath our joint hands, her palms in direct contact, mine over the backs of hers, touch heightened, everything sharper, clearer, more intense in the dark. She exhales a slow breath when I stop moving our hands. Shaky and drawn out, before she pulls in a similar inhale. A smile teases at my lips, anyone else would think this was nerves.

I know much better than *everyone*.

Except maybe Wolf, he removes the parts when we're done, transporting them to Cardinal House. He's seen what my girl can do. The artwork she creates.

"Yes, baby," I answer her finally, my words whispered against her ear, a shiver wracking through her, wisps of hair fanning across her face.

She swallows, it's almost loud in the silence of the room, nothing but her heartbeat and mine, our breaths, hers much faster than my own.

"Keep the lights off."

Something inside my chest spikes, a flicker of panic passes across my vision, the candles and matches suddenly feeling very heavy in my pocket. I nod against her all the same. Keeping her calm, happy, at ease. This isn't a place for judgement. This is a place of freedom.

Safety.

"I've got you, Gracie," and it's like my words mean far more in this moment, like she *knows* they're true.

She presses back against me, flexing her fingers between mine.

"Who did this one?" she asks in a fragile whisper.

She sometimes wants to know about the bodies we work on, who they were, what they did, who killed them. Sometimes I know, sometimes I don't.

"Thorne."

"Our brother would kill anyone for the right price," is what she tells me, and I can't help but laugh, nodding against the side of her face, because she's not wrong.

It's not the money our eldest brother's interested in, it's the people, the reasoning, the job, the organisation of a kill.

"Hmm," a thoughtful sound, quiet, "what do you think this one did?"

I actually *know* what this one did. There's a lot going

on right now if you're a mafia associate, all of the crime families are organising a meeting to discuss what the fuck is going on, there's discord in the factions. So there are bodies being dropped left, right and centre. Too many secrets being spilled, too many tongues wagging.

"She talked too much."

"Ah, a rat," she hums quietly, only recently learning a few more details about what The Firm actually is.

After the Swallows took up a semi-permanent residence in our home a few years ago, we had to start explaining a few things to her.

"Such a cold dismissal, *little sister*."

A tremor wracks through her, vibrating through my bones, a smirk crawls it's way to my face.

"What do you need?" I ask, kissing her temple.

She starts to move our hands, feeling the skin beneath her fingers, her palms caressing the body, thinking about it, what she wants to do.

"A skinning knife," she finally decides, long moments of silence before the breathy words.

I let my eyes fall closed, my head dropping back, face tilted towards the ceiling, head a little dizzy, because all of the blood in my fucking body just rushed to my dick.

Kissing the back of her skull, I release her fingers, even as she continues to trace her hands over the corpse. Eyes consumed by darkness, I imagine my pupils to be like saucers, desperately seeking out the tiniest flint of light, but I know this room, I know the location of everything, so I move around in the dark. Senses heightened, loss of sight making everything louder, sharper, the air feel thicker, my skin prickles.

My hands find the knives, years of my tools being in the same place, muscle memory has me reaching for the correct knife, there're a few, I collect a longer and a shorter blade. I place the knives down on the edge of the slab, Gracie's hands moving delicately along my arm, to my hand where my fingers close over the edge of the slab.

"You want help, beautiful?" I whisper into the darkness.

Heart pounding now, because I like when she instructs me, tells me what she wants me to do. Remove a foot, scalp a skull, gut them and let her play with their insides. I feel like I'm giving her something she craves, but I like to watch her too, maybe more than the assisting. The way her large eyes hardly blink when she's concentrating.

She turns her head over her shoulder, looking up at me, and I can't see her, but I can feel her eyes on me. One of her hands going to my chest, I'm not ready for it, my body jolting at the featherlight touch, goosebumps ripping their way across my skin.

"No, thank you."

I smile, a big, wide grin, that probably looks feral, but is swallowed by the darkness.

"Okay, baby girl, you do your thing."

I take a step back, intending to lean up against the wall, settle in for the long haul, but her cracked voice stops me.

"Don't leave me alone," it's a raw sound, desperate, like it's clawed at her vocal cords on its way up.

My mouth just sorta pops open for a second, and I know she's looking back at me again, and I'm not sure what to say. So instead, I step back into her, and it's like the tension drops out of her as my chest touches her back once more.

"I'm here," I breathe, swallowing down the lump of emotion in my throat, "I'm right here."

I hear her shift, the cotton shirt sweeping over itself as she extends her arms, outstretched in my direction. I reach out, fingers running down her forearms, I roll her sleeves, folding the cuffs up and up, into the crook of each elbow, and then she begins.

CHAPTER 14

HUNTER

Time seems to pass slowly and too fast all at once. Teeth clenched around the curved end of the thin metal twine, I dig in my pocket for the candles and matches.

"Your stitches won't be neat if you can't see," I tell her through my mangled tongue, my tongue catching the warmed metal held between them as it curls around the words I speak behind closed teeth.

"Hmm," she hums softly, a thought of agreement, but not permission for what I'm suggesting.

The wax feels almost sticky in my cold fingers, neither of them very many clothes, the temperature in this room ice cold, the way it always is to slow decay.

I wonder about her hesitation, what it is she's thinking, the things she won't fully talk to me about, secrets that she's holding inside herself.

Let me in.

"I don't want to see the shadows," a quiet confession, one that makes my gut twist.

Crease forming between my brows, I frown. I don't speak immediately, patient, waiting for her to give me more, *hoping* that she'll give me more. But her silence extends, it's practised, and I know she's still wielding a knife between her dainty fingers, the wet sound of it snicking against flesh.

"What's in the shadows, Gracie?" I ask, but I already know.

These hallucinations of her mother, but I need her to talk to me about it, properly.

With a clatter, her knife hits the table, as though my question startled her somehow.

"Gracie?"

"Be quiet, *Hunter*," she hisses my name with disdain so sharp it cuts.

Fingers coming to my mouth, I remove the suture held captive between my teeth. Stepping forward until I reach the table, I place it down on top. Hands clamping over the edge of the slab, candle and matches crushed between the table and my fists. Knuckles cracking with the harsh grip. Head dropping forward between my shoulders, eyes squeezing shut tight, I force out a deep breath.

"Baby girl," I lick my lips, swallow, look up, across the table to where I know she's stood, even though I can't see her. I can feel her, her eyes boring into me through the density of the darkness. "What will we find in the shadows *when* I light this candle?"

Her hand bangs down on the table, something clanking, metal on metal, a strangled sound caught in her throat, something she's trying to suppress. Like she's in pain.

"Tell me." I demand it from her, because we don't tell lies.

She doesn't keep secrets from me.

We don't do that.

Not Gracie and I.

"Now, Gracie."

I feel the air shift, my spine straightening, a nervous energy filling my chest, cold seeping into my bones, freezing me in place, grip on the table so tight, my fingers go numb. I feel her rage like it's a palpable heart-beat inside this room. Loud, harsh, thumping at a million beats a second, its speed increasing the longer the silence stretches on. She doesn't do this. She does not *ever* let her emotions creep out of her very careful control. But I *like* it. I *crave* it. *Her.*

Bring the fucking pain, baby girl.

"I'm waiting," I tell her, there's a vicious quietness to my words that she'll feel compelled to do something about.

Something violent.

"If you can't tell me what's in the shadows, baby, I'm lighting this candle," it's not a threat, it's a fact.

Very slowly, I release my hold on the slab. Pinch the small box of matches between my fingers, pushing the little cardboard drawer out of its sleeve. I rattle it, ensure she hears exactly what it is I'm doing. Match pinched between my thumb and forefinger, I lick my lips, raise my eyes beneath my dropped brow to hers. And despite the darkness, I know she knows I'm looking at her.

"*Hunter*," I freeze, the way she says my name, the plead in the word, the rawness to it. "*Don't.*"

"Tell me why."

A choking, gasping sound fills my ears, and it takes everything inside of me not to go to her. Not to love her, not to hold her, not to save her. But I coddle her too much sometimes and I know that's not healthy either. In some of the ways I protect her, I'm shielding her from life and it's not fair on her.

"*Now,*" it's a low growl, the cardboard matchbox bending under my grip.

She always does as she's told, she's better without rules now, something she always needed just to get her through the day, a routine. But we don't do that now, we allow freedom, for the mind, the body, there are a few things we say, to make her feel more secure, like she has structure, but they aren't really rules. I want her to want to live freely. But she's a good fucking girl and she does as she's told because she knows I would never tell her to do something that would put her in danger.

"*Gracie,*" I hiss her name, just as her wet hands come to my throat.

Momentarily caught off guard, I drop the matches, the little wooden sticks scattering across the stone as they hit my feet. Gracie's slick hands close tight around my neck, thumbs pressing hard on my windpipe and for a second I'm stunned, body turning to stone because she has *never* attacked me before. And then all at once, we're both moving.

My hands clasp around her waist, rib bones bowing beneath my palms as I lift her, her legs wrap around me, high up on my waist, back arching, elbows tucked. She's wet, the entire front of her shirt is soaked right through, and I can only imagine she's been wiping her bloody hands down it.

Tight at the crown of her head, I twine a fist into her hair, wrenching her head back so hard her neck cracks, but she doesn't let go of me. Thighs squeezing around my middle, sticky fingers digging into the corded muscles of my throat. I can't breathe, and it turns me on, because the only thing I can feel is the way her bare, slick cunt grinds against my muscles as she squeezes me between her thighs.

With my free hand, I grab her jaw, chin caught in the webbing of my thumb and forefinger, I grind her bones, applying pressure with my fingers over the side of her neck. Her nails gouge into the skin at my nape, hair caught between her fingers, she's panting, breath fanning over my face hard and fast. I'm hurting her, but she can still fucking breathe, *unlike me*. Her hands loosen enough for me to catch my breath as I jerk her head back further. Hand moving rapidly to clamp over the back of her neck, my other still squeezing painfully on her jaw.

"Enough." The word rips between my teeth,

commanding, it's rough, stern enough for her to falter. "Let go, Gracie, *right. Now.*"

Her hands fall from my throat, my grip on her face instantly loosens, fingers at her nape relaxing and she falls forward. Her head burrowing into the crook of my neck, hot tears dampening my bare skin, but she's silent, there are no sobs, no shaky breaths, no evidence of crying except for the salty streaks tracking down my chest.

I smooth my hand down her back, clawing air into my shrivelled lungs, my other arm propping beneath her arse where she clings to me like a small child.

"I want to help you," I murmur against her hair, cheek resting against her head.

She shudders in my arms, her hold on me impeccably tight, like she's scared I'll let her go.

I'll never fucking let you go.

"Let me help you," I repeat it softly, over and over, reassuring. "We're safe in the darkness, aren't we, baby?"

She nods against me, a very quiet, "yes," that reassures *me* in the moment. "We are..." hesitation rolls through her, like she's not sure she can tell me, and guilt eats like a wild beast at my insides. "It is always safe in the darkness," she swallows, but I can tell she's not finished, something more waiting to be freed. "But it's not always safe in the *shadows*," her words are but a breathy whisper, but I can hear her perfectly well over the drumming of her heart. "There are things that want to hurt us there, Hunter."

I let her take her time, smoothing my hand over the

back of her head, my fingers light as they pass over her scalp. My eyes close, nothing to see in the pitch room.

"I *can't*… I don't want to see *her*," she mumbles the words against my shoulder, her plump lips wet with her tears, I stroke over the back of her head, my hand splaying over her skull, keeping her tucked into me. "And she's always there."

I think of what Dad might say, the way he'd reassure her she's safe, something about facing your fears. Thorne and how he'd explain the ins and outs of death, how corpses are not animated beings that chase you around in the shadows. How Arrow would be kind with his words, offer her some kind of comfort and pet the back of her hand.

None of those things are going to work for my girl.

"Gracie," my voice rough, no more whispering. "Your mother is dead." She stiffens in my arms, but she needs to understand without any of the embellishments or softening. "You killed her."

It's the first time I've ever said it. Half frightened of what might happen if I put it this bluntly. And I suddenly feel entirely responsible that this shit, these hallucinations, this psychosis is my fault. For not talking this through properly, right away. I just, moved on. Thinking she did too. How long has this been happening?

Her breath comes in fast, brutal pants, hot against the cool skin of my neck, raising the hairs on my arms and neck, but I don't stop and she's not crying anymore.

"You stabbed her thirty-eight times," that, I whisper,

with awe, directly into her ear, my lips grazing the shell of it, her hair separating our flesh. "With a letter opener."

Breath ruffling her hair, she shivers, and I can feel her getting slicker, her bare cunt pressed up against my abs. I kiss the side of her head, my hand still gentle, but my dick growing ever fucking harder.

We both like this dangerous game we play.

I grit my teeth, nostrils flaring, I inhale a lungful of her, honeysuckle, ferns, sweet, woodsy. Let it soothe me. It's all I can do not to fuck her in this moment, thoughts of her asking me to escort her to hell, covered in blood after she murdered her mother, all rushing through my head like a film. A groan works its way up my throat, low and feral and she trembles in my arms.

"She can't haunt you, beautiful girl, because you made sure she could never haunt anyone ever a-*fucking*-gain."

Teeth driving into the side of her throat, she pushes against me, bare pussy wet and hot and desperate. She coats me in her arousal, her thighs clamping harder around me, bending forward, I slam her down onto the slab and she fucking *yelps*.

"You are the bigger monster in the shadows, baby girl. *You.*"

Gasping beneath me, my mouth unable to stop its journey across her jaw, biting hard, sucking harder, she whimpers, following the needy sound up with a moan as I buck my hips against her.

"Let's face her together," I speak the words into the side of her face, nipping across her cheekbone as I do.

Her nails sink into my shoulders, fingers curling into the muscle, she yanks me down onto her, her body draped over the mutilated corpse beneath her. I haven't seen it yet, but I'm sure it's a fucking masterpiece. My cock throbbing where it presses against her dripping pussy, her wetness soaking into my thin joggers. My tongue fucks into her mouth, long, desperate licks over her lips, the top split, *by me*, the copper tang fuelling our kiss.

"*Hunter*," it's a gasp, a short sound, the only thing that separates me and the clanking sound of the metal table where I dry fuck her against it. "*Stop.*"

I rear back, realising her legs are no longer wrapped around me, hanging limply over the edge of the slab. Blinking in the darkness, I shove a hand through my hair, wishing I could see her, wishing I knew what she was thinking.

"Baby girl?"

"I want to finish *her*," I blink, her body shifting away from the table, gentle rustle of fabric, her feet sweeping over the floor as she closes in on me, I can *feel* her.

Her hand comes to my chest, palm over my cool skin, heart hammering against her small fist.

"Okay," I say reluctantly, lungs working overtime to catch my breath, but I should have known she'd want to carry on, her mind only half-focused on me.

I don't want her unless I have her full attention.

"Hunter?" another whisper, more unsure than before. I wait in silence, breath held, for her to finish. "You can light the candles."

Knee to stone, I bend down, without hesitation, finding one of the candlesticks first, fingers fumbling over the spilled matches, regathering some and their box. I stand, and I can feel her moving closer just as her hand makes contact, fingers curling over my forearm.

"I'm right here, and we can do this together," I assure her, wondering how I'm supposed to fight off her demons when I can't see them.

She takes a shaky breath, pressing her body against mine, she trusts me to help her, to fix this. It makes something inside me preen, and despite being sick, deviant little heathens, we are something more.

"Gracie," I lick my lips, index finger curled around the candle, thumb and middle finger gripping the small match box.

"Yes, Hunter?" the soft lilt of her voice lights a fire in my soul, the way whatever I'm about to tell her will be taken into her as gospel.

"Baby girl, we are *sick*. You and I." Air whistles between her teeth as she sucks in a sharp breath. "But we are all the more beautiful for it. The world isn't only made for whole people." I turn my head to look down at her, despite not being able to see her, knowing her face is already tilted up, eyes on mine. "Some people are only pieces, fragmented and sharp and broken. But those people-"

"Like you and I," she interrupts me, and a small smile finds its way to my face.

"-those people find a soul similar to theirs, a darkness akin to their own, and when they come together, despite the ugliness the world has inflicted on them, they become whole. Perfectly, imperfectly whole. Thing is, Gracie," and I know I have her whole fucking attention right now and I'd be lying if I said that didn't make me feel like a god. "Even though those people are whole now, different to the others, but whole all the same. They sometimes have to deal with things that are scary, scarier things than the other whole people have to deal with. But they can do it because unlike the others, there's two of them. Do you understand what it is I'm telling you, beautiful girl?"

There're slow seconds of silence, her fingers gently circling over my arm, I keep looking down where I know she's looking back up at me.

"That I don't have to be scared. And because I've got you, I'm not alone," it's not a question, she knows it's the answer, sure and true.

"We're toxic, filthy and insane. You've infected me like the sweetest poison, Gracie. Our sickness, the *strange* things we do in the dark, it all makes us whole when we're together. You're not alone, baby girl, not anymore and never again."

It's a confession, and I think back to when she first arrived here, that morning after my birthday, when I thought I was fucking destroying all the innocent parts of her. Thought *I* was the poison, thick, black tar injected straight into her veins. Sucking the life out of her, instead of infecting her with it. I took her heart and shattered it like glass, I thought I was doing it *for* her.

Truth is, I was scared, the moment I laid my eyes on her, high above me in the window, I wanted to destroy her, and then the second I didn't… I did anyway, just not in the way I thought.

I suddenly feel choked up, my throat closing, tongue too big and dry for my mouth. Thinking of how fucking far we've come, my heart fucking aches for her and she's right fucking here. She never made me work for her forgiveness, never required or requested an explanation. I just swept back in, recaptured her heart without any effort at all. And now it all feels wrong. She's given me *everything*. And I haven't earnt it. None of it. I own her. But fuck, does she own me too, and I don't think she even knows it. The power she wields over me.

I am her fucking slave.

Make me fucking worship, baby girl.

"*Gracie*," the word comes out like a plea, a prayer, a curse, my skin prickles with unease.

"What's wrong?" voice so soft, so perfect, so *knowing. So. Fucking. Innocent.*

"I'm just…" I lick my lips, squeeze my eyes closed for just a second. "I just need you to know how much I love you."

It feels like a confession, like I don't say it enough, I'm too busy, too carried away, mind elsewhere. And it's reminiscent of the words she whimpered to me out by the frozen lake.

"I just have this feeling inside of me," I repeat her words back to her. "Like I *need* you to know."

"Hunter?" another whisper, her fingers flex where they curl over my forearm.

"Yes, Gracie?" I whisper back, scared to shatter this bubble with too many loud words.

"Light the candle."

My finger and thumb follow her order before my brain can even register. The match sparks as I strike it, flame flickering, I hold it against the candle wick, the orange glow dancing over the stone room. Blinking my eyes in the sudden light makes them burn in their sockets.

Eyes falling onto Gracie's slight form, she blinks up at me, wide eyed and head cocked. Blood up to her elbows, streaked through her hair, slathered down the front of her white shirt where she's wiped her hands down it, across her face. The soaked fabric sticking to her skin beneath, clinging to her peaked nipples.

She holds my gaze, her chest not moving, lungs not working. Her nostrils flare, eyes glazing over, she doesn't blink, her eyeballs don't dart around in their sockets, I don't sever our moment, knowing she's looking to me for support. Holding her gaze, captivated, enthralled, bewitched, enchanted, completely and utterly drunk on her, I exhale, a long deep breath.

"You want to finish her now, baby girl?" gesturing to the woman on the slab without breaking eye contact.

My eyes flicking between hers, ice blue a dark sapphire in the flickering orange glow of dim candlelight, warm hazel turned a red, fiery brown. She licks her lips, finally breathing, short, sharp, almost painful pants of air whistling through her teeth, chest heaving beneath blood drenched fabric. Candle held tight in my fist, hot wax rolls down the side of it, over my curled fingers, a gentle sting over the split skin of my knuckle.

"I want to stitch her up now," she finally whispers and *god*, the things I'd like to do to her when she says shit like that to me.

Her fingers slide from my arm, hand dropping to her side, and then she moves around the table. I turn my body towards the slab, closing the small distance to reach it. I'm unsure what it is I'm seeing at first, and it's still so, so dark... but this is just...

"Gracie..."

Strips of skin have been peeled off of the shins, laid out over the exposed flesh and bone, some parts carved deeper than others, uneven, a little gouged in places. Holding the candle close to the body, Gracie on the opposite side of the table, her fingers pinching the curved end of the suture. I take the light further up the body, all of it perfectly intact, spots and smears of blood in places, but not too much. Until I get to the throat.

"Baby girl, did you... cut out her tongue?" this is *different* to what she normally does in here.

I look up at her, the tongue resting in the open palm of her free hand as though on display for me, a trophy of sorts, her eyes already on mine when I look up to her face.

"Yes."

I stare at her for a moment, a little bit in awe, a little bit in confusion…

"Okay, what's next?" I ask, which I think is brave in itself because I have absolutely *no* idea where this is going.

"I need to stitch these pieces together," she tells me, indicating to the strips of skin she's laid out. I nod, still moving the candle over the body to get a good look. "And I need you to watch for Mother."

"*Gracie.*"

"Just in case, Hunter."

I sigh heavily, "she's not in the shadows, she's gone, she's rotting in hell, she is not coming back." I stare at her, my expression stern. "You know now that you're the bigger monster, you always will be, even when I'm not with you. You're enough, Gracie. Strong, beautiful, kind, smart. If you see Mother again, you kill her dead, Gracie, you hear me? You close your eyes, you count to five, that's enough, that's all you have to do. Show her how little you care; how little she matters. You are the darkness, baby girl."

She drops her gaze, twirling the curved needle between her finger and thumb, before glancing up at me from beneath those thick, fanned lashes, her mismatched gaze on mine. She nods, a look of determination crossing her features.

"Okay?" I ask her.

"Okay."

"Good. Now, start stitching, beautiful," I nod my

head, flicking my gaze to the grisly pieces of carved flesh as I do.

Her fingers work delicately, weaving, and pulling and pushing, tying off each and every meticulously placed stitch, until the pieces are joined, length of skin just over two-foot long. My head cocked, wax rolling over my knuckles as the wick burns fiercely, I hold the candle beside her hands. Glancing around the cold, dark room every now and then, making sure she knows that I'm keeping watch for her mother.

When she's finished, bloody hands gently holding the patchwork strip of skin. Severed tongue stitched onto one end, she glances up at me, her face awash with an innocence I don't think God himself could question. Her lips part, blood smeared across her cheekbone, jaw, in her hair where she's pushed it back. She licks her lips, rolling them together, I'm so distracted by the movement I almost don't hear her request at all.

"Roll her over?" I repeat as a question, blinking hard.

"Please," she hums, looking back down at the patchwork piece in her small hands.

Holding out the candle, without looking at me, she releases one end of the length of skin, taking the candle into her small, bloody fist. Light dancing across her pale skin.

"Step back," she does, bare feet shuffling her away from the table.

Hooking my arm beneath the top of the spine, the other threading under and between the thighs, I lift and flip, the body thudding face first down onto the metal slab.

Gracie runs her eyes across the body's back, smooth, untouched skin, she looks across at me, my hands gripping the side of the table, she passes me back the candle. The second one I've had to light since she started. I take it, watching as she runs a waxy finger down the corpse's spine, almost tentatively, stopping at the base of bones in the back. She taps her finger in the spot once, twice, and then re-takes the curved suture, replacing her finger with the length of skin, tongue-free end placed down.

In silence, I watch on, the way she bends herself over, dainty fingers pinching skin together, bottom lip pulled into her mouth. She threads the curved wire through both pieces, tying off each stitch and then starting another, all of it perfectly symmetrical. When she straightens, cocking her head, surveying the piece she's just completed, plump lips in a curved pout, she smiles. Eyes glittering, face shadowed with the flickering glow from the candle, she looks right at me, outer corners of her eyes tilted up with her joy.

"She's a rat," she explains so carefully, proud of herself with the results.

And I… I just stare at her.

Thoughts rush through my brain, blood rushes to my dick and my heart pounds harder and harder trying to get it there. In my silence, her smile drops, a little unsure of herself now that I'm seeing it. *Understanding it.* But she's got it all wrong. I already know what she's thinking and that's not it. *God,* that's not it.

"*Fuck*, you're so perfect."

Arm across the table, hand closing around her pretty little neck, I tug her forward, leaning across the slab to meet her halfway. Our eyes locked on each other's, lips a hair's breadth apart, my breath is her breath, short, sharp pants being sucked down by hers. It's *me* filling her lungs.

"See?" she whispers, like she thinks I don't get it.

A wicked smirk curls my lips, tongue rolling out over the bottom one, catching hers in the process. Sucking my bottom lip into my mouth, letting it pop free with a smack, I slant my mouth over hers, eyes dipping to that perfect cupid's bow, a viscous split in it, made by *my* teeth. I lick over it, the top lip, the flat of my tongue rolling over the top then the bottom, tasting, swallowing. Breathing her in, I let my lips ghost hers, my words only meant for her to hear, to be swallowed down into her soul.

"You are so perfect, baby girl, so, so perfect for me."

Shyness overwhelms her, my intensity, compliments, raw feelings a little too much, she drops her gaze. Candle still burning, stinging my hand as it drips, drying over my skin, a heat, not unwelcome, where the wax is stacking up. I tilt her head back, face up, my hold on her throat punishing.

"Look at me, beautiful girl, eyes on me," I purr, my insides so heavy, twisting in my gut when she does just that. The power of it otherworldly. "I love you, Gracie."

"I love you, Hunter," she whispers, lips sliding over mine with every overly pronounced word, her tongue rolling around the letters with a husk that only makes me smirk more.

"Good girl," I whisper in a growl, before plunging my tongue into her mouth.

Our kiss is violence, her hands pressing down on the corpse between us to keep her up. My hard cock digging painfully into the metal table, she's already on tiptoes where I grip her neck, my thumb over her hammering pulse. Her tongue slides over my own, desperate, licking strokes into my mouth, like she's trying to eat her way inside of me, and I'd let her if I could. Keep her locked beneath my bones, our souls physically intertwined, her heart inside mine, I would keep her selfishly.

One of her hands comes up to my face, nails curving into the skin of my cheek, not to hurt, just to hold, and my dick kicks in my joggers, precum weeping from the tip. I groan into her mouth, her throat echoing a similar sound back to me, a keening, growling, hungry sound that drives me fucking insane.

Releasing her throat, I toss the candle, the wick going out as I do, descending us into darkness. Her breathing erratic, I reach forward, hands going under her arms, I heave her up and across the table. A squeal escaping her on a breathy chuckle, I throw her over my shoulder, her legs flailing wildly as she catches herself on her hands, fingers grabbing at my hips to steady herself.

"Hunter!" she squeals, high pitched and loud, too loud for the tentative silence we've built here, but it's fucking beautiful.

"*Gracie!*" I mock back, laughing as she does, burying her face in the small of my back.

And that's how we end up in the basement shower. The spray ice cold, our clothes still on, my dick buried inside her sweet cunt, brutally fucking the darkness away until we're greeted by morning light.

CHAPTER 15

GRACE

"Shane O'Sullivan has been found," Dad announces over breakfast a few days later.

I'm only half listening because I have no idea what the boys do when they leave this house, so I'm sure *Shane O'Sullivan* has nothing to do with me. Roscoe is snoozing softly on my arm, his bottom resting on my lap, milk drunk after his morning feed. My other hand clasps a plastic purple spoon, outstretched in offering to my toddler, porridge with berries on the end of it.

River in his highchair, sits beside me at the kitchen table, his little fist reaching out, he scoops the breakfast off the end of the spoon and slaps it over his closed mouth. Dark brown eyes looking at me with confusion, when he realises his mouth is empty. I take the spoon, I swipe it off of his lips, his chin, re-offer it this time only once he opens his mouth.

Atlas is upstairs with Hunter, wanting to talk to his

dad about *boy things*. I'm not really sure what that means, but I'm not a boy so I guess it doesn't really matter.

Thorne and Wolf sit in their usual seats on either side of Dad, Arrow beside Wolf, Raine beside Thorne, an empty seat between Arrow and I. I pass River the spoon, giving up on trying to feed him the last little bit of his breakfast, he just wants to bang the spoon like he's playing the drums, he'll eat when he's hungry. Finger smoothing down the length of Roscoe's nose, his lips parted, arms thrown above his head, little foot twitching inside orange striped socks, he snores softly. My hand continuing to smooth over his little features, head of black hair, so fluffy and thick.

"Outside of the Kelly's largest safe house," Dad continues, knife and fork scraping over the china of his plate.

Arrow reaches across, placing a glass in front of me, filling it with cranberry juice. I tilt my head in thanks, a kind smile on my brother's face before he returns his attention back to Dad.

"Decapitated head displayed on a pike."

The clattering of cutlery halts, an eerie silence falling over the room. Wolf looks up, Thorne does too, but they glance at each other before they look at Dad. I tilt my head, watching them both, Arrow and Raine staring silently at Dad. It feels uncomfortable, the heaviness in the room and I look to the head of our family for *something*, because Hunter's not here and Arrow isn't giving me reassurance. But Dad isn't looking at me.

His black eyes are entirely focused on his eldest son,

and it feels as though everyone around the table is suddenly waiting, for what though, I'm not quite sure. And then, just as quickly, the tension in the room seems to bleed out, like someone sliced right through it, squeezed the wound, sucked the poison out. Arrow looks at me, smiling again, his plush lips pulled up higher on one side than the other, like it feels a little strained to be doing it.

"What do the Kelly's want us to do about it?" Thorne asks in that rough, gravelly voice of his, it's a sound that's confident, always drawing attention, always *heard*.

People always listen when Thorne speaks.

Tiny hairs stand up on end all over my body, my eyes drawn to him, his broad shoulders in a black suit jacket, slate grey shirt beneath. His hands fold together on the table, his plate pushed back, knife and fork placed together atop it, indicating he's finished. Wolf's face reveals nothing as I glance at him, his hands fisted tightly around his utensils.

"Nothing," Dad shrugs, dark eyes all too seeing. "Just keeping my boys up to date," he says nonchalantly like he was merely making conversation, but it feels as though that's not it at all.

A shudder rolls through me, Roscoe stirs where he's perched in my arm, I feel his little breaths, his chest rising and falling deeply, heartbeat in his back strong against my forearm. And I breathe just a tad easier once it all registers.

Footsteps start down in the hall, multiple pairs of

feet, but my hearing automatically zeros in on the tapping of heels moving closer, my hand instinctively tightening on my son.

And it's her I see first. *Rachel.* Shiny brown hair, bright blue eyes, a smile that makes my jaw click. I could never smile like that; I don't even think I have the muscles in my cheeks to do so. She's just so… *glittery.* Perfect and pretty and *normal.* Hunter steps in behind her, a curve to his mouth that is unfamiliar, and I just stop breathing. He looks… *happy.* And he's coming to breakfast with her…

I'm up and out of my chair before I really realise I'm moving, manoeuvring Roscoe over one shoulder, unclipping River from his highchair with my free hand. River wails as I take the spoon he's banging on his tray from his fingers, curling my arm around his back and heaving him up into my chest. He sobs louder, Arrow pulling the chair I was sitting in back and out of my way without question. All of my brothers watching me as I skirt around the table, eyes downcast and breath held because the sudden anger that's swirling around in the pit of my stomach is struggling to stay there.

River wails louder and it takes everything inside of me not to react, not to stop, not to pass him off to Dad, who can settle him with less than a look. I'll get the boys into the playroom, out of this kitchen, sit somewhere I can breathe.

"I can take him, *Grace,*" my steps falter, hearing her voice as I go to make it past her, the way she always says my name, when she deems it fit to address me at all, makes me grind my teeth.

She's always different with me when someone else is around. *Nicer,* more smiley, and I hate it, because it isn't real. I *know* it isn't real, I can feel it. But I'm tired, and I've been *seeing* things, and it makes me wonder how much of the happenings inside this house are real at all. Plus, Hunter said she's trying, I should ride it out a little longer, see if I just got a bad first impression. But all that happens when I think about that is anger blooms in my chest, and my teeth grind, thinking about him thinking about her…

And I'm not entirely sure now if it's her, or myself, that I find I have a bigger problem with. Sometimes I want to crack my own skull open, pull out the part of my brain that's upsetting me so much.

I glance up, Hunter standing strong in the centre of the archway behind her, thick arms folded across his chest. Dark eyes on me, tracking every little tic of my face. My eyes narrow slightly, causing his to widen. I turn my body towards her, eyes slowly rolling up her body, stopping when they connect with hers.

Her skin is perfect, make-up expertly applied only enhancing it, she reaches up, tucks a strand of shiny hair behind her ear, and then stretches out her arms. My hands curl tighter over both of my sons, and I think about putting *her* head on a pike.

"Gracie, hand over one of the boys, let Rachel help you," Hunter says, his deep voice stroking the embers in my belly, but all my brain latches onto is the way he says *her* name.

He doesn't even like her.

Archer says that doesn't even matter.

My eyes flash from hers to his, looking up through my lashes, watching one of his dark eyebrows climb his forehead, jagged white scar tugging up at the arch.

"I do not *need* help, Hunter," I'm well aware my words are a low hiss, that everyone is listening, watching, taking it all in. "I can look after your sons just fine."

River goes deathly quiet in my hold, like he can feel the tension, which makes me feel like the absolute worst mother. But then he's bringing his thumb between his lips, sucking on it, settling himself, dropping his head to the crook of my neck, snuggling into me, his eyes, too, going to his father.

Hunter just gives me a *look*. And I know what he's saying, *that isn't what I meant at all*. But I can't let it go, and I can't stop thinking about what Archer said.

'You don't have to like someone to fuck them. You can find someone attractive enough just to stick your dick in them. I mean, really… you don't even have to like looking at them all that much… It still feels good, ya know?'

And Hunter is beautiful. Rachel is so *pretty*. And I'm just… unusual.

Strange.

I'm not sure I've ever cared before. Hunter is obsessed with me. But I'm not pretty like her, and he's been stuck in this house with me for what probably feels like forever to him. And I wonder if he only stays here because I like being here. Does he feel like he has to stay with me because once upon a time I was his stepsister? Would he rather my father had been decent, so that he'd offer to take me away from here? Am I too much hard work, I don't understand things the way other people do. Rachel does. Because she's normal. And I'm just not.

I don't think he would hunt someone else. He never had before me… and until today he's never taken her side over mine.

And I wonder if I've been ignorant this whole time or if now I'm just seeing things that aren't really there… Thinking about her too much.

It makes my cheeks heat, and an uncomfortable itch starts over my skin, because I don't know what's real anymore, and what's not.

I bite my lip, the top one almost healed where Hunter tore into it, but I don't care, I suck it between my teeth, gnawing on it savagely as I think about someone else touching him.

Rachel touching him.

Anyone…

I would cut off their fingers.

And I've had three babies; *she* hasn't had any. *She* doesn't leak breast milk, *she* doesn't stay up all night staring at her sons, making sure nothing harms them. *She* wears tight jeans, with an arse that's round and high, hips that aren't too wide, skin that has never seen a stretch mark. I think of the white lines I have now, zig zags across my belly, boobs, hips. I grit my teeth so hard my jaw cracks, my eyes squeezing shut tight.

Why is everyone in this house so obsessed with her?

Including me.

I hate her.

There's something wrong *with her.*

There just might be something wrong with me.

"Excuse me, please," I think of what Thorne always tells me, speak my request loudly, hold my head high, River's hand tangled in my hair, his warm breaths comforting against my throat, giving me the strength to be assertive.

Rachel continues to stand there, half blocking my way, I could squeeze past if I turned my body to the side, but I don't. I stare at her, her arms still outstretched in River's direction, and I have this incessant need to *break her fucking hands*. She blinks, looking at me like I'm stupid. And I think that's it. The way she takes control of my children when *I'm* already dealing with them, snatching a stick of cheese out of my son's hand, scolding him with words really meant for me. The *looks* she throws my way when there's no one else around.

She thinks I'm dumb...

I don't think you're all that clever either, I think to myself, *because I'm the bigger monster.*

I don't realise I'm smiling at her until her arms drop back to her sides, the kitchen in silence, and she side steps out of my way, giving me *much* more room than is necessary. Pace slow, footsteps quiet, I wander down the hallway, taking a left and entering the boys' playroom.

Atlas is already perched on his haunches, front of his pink dollhouse folded open, his hands inside, wrapped around two small dolls. He looks up at me, chin pressed over his shoulder, big smile on his face for me, before he looks to his brother.

"Come play, River!" he beams brighter, River instantly wriggling in my hold to get down.

I bend forward, letting my toddler slide free, holding onto the waistband of his joggers until he gets his feet under him, before he's rushing Atlas, throwing himself at his brother with a high-pitched squeal. I cup the back of Roscoe's head, jigging him a little to keep him settled, until suddenly Hunter is snatching up my elbow, the one Roscoe is hooked in against my chest, dragging me out into the hallway.

Scowling, I look up at him, tugging to free my elbow, but his fingers hold firm, a pain needling in my chest when I look at his face. He passes a big hand through his dark hair, pushing it off of his face and drawing in a deep breath. We hover in silence, me staring up at him, him not looking at me *at all*, and I think of Dad marrying a woman he didn't even *like*, and my itchy skin gets so uncomfortable that I want to claw it all off.

"You look at her like you're going to tear her throat out," he hushes, and I don't respond because, well, *I do*.

But the way he says it… it doesn't exactly feel like a scolding.

Curious.

"Gracie."

"Hunter."

He blinks at me, "where the hell did this attitude come from?"

I blink back, Hunter steps into me, my bare toes brushing the tips of his boots. He feels impossibly taller when he dips down, his forehead pressing against mine, his dark eyes flicker between my own, and I wonder what he thinks he sees when he traces his lips across my mouth, his breathing picking up.

"I think I like it," he rasps, fingers squeezing my elbow, Roscoe caught in the tight space between us.

I lick my lips, tasting blood and the breath stills in my lungs as his dark eyes track the movement.

"Tell me why you don't like her, Gracie," he flicks his gaze back to mine, tongue rolling over my top lip, his front teeth tugging at my torn cupid's bow.

Hand slamming into his chest between us, I shove him as hard as I can, his teeth only sinking deeper into my sore lip, body crowding mine. A whimper whips its way up my throat, fingers fisting in his t-shirt. His tongue strokes mine as it invades my mouth, forcing its way between my lips. His big hands smother me, the one latched over my elbow still tight, but his fingers massage the tender spots his grip leaves behind, the other clutching at my back, white material of my dress fisted in his hand.

When he draws back, I gasp, the sound almost silent between us, his mouth works its way over my cheek, a trail of sloppy kisses against my skin. He tugs me in closer, Roscoe still between us, in the safest place he could ever be. Neither one of us would ever let anything happen to him, no matter what kind of games we find ourselves playing.

"Tell me."

Harsh tone rumbling up his throat like a low growl, I tilt my head back, fingers twisting in the soft cotton of his t-shirt, his scent fills my nostrils, mixing with our son's. Hunter smells like the forest, wet moss, daisies, the brook, our son swirling through, that delicate baby smell, fresh and clean. Every time I nuzzle my face against him, sucking down a lungful of that smell, I just feel better.

I am better.

I am not Mother.

But I don't wanna talk about this.

"She looks at me like…" nose twitching, I glance away, attention on our two eldest boys, playing nicely at their dollhouse.

Hunter carefully releases my elbow, his hand smoothing over Roscoe's head of fluffy black hair. He has my eyes, my hazel colouring, warm and striking. River has my light hair and pale skin, his dad's dark brown eyes, matching shards of gold speared through them just the same. Atlas is our split. Hunter's darker, olive skin tone, his black hair, and eye colour from us both, one a deep dark brown, the other is me. Bottom half a dark brown, top of it an icy blue. His mannerisms are all me too, but he has more life than the both of us combined.

So beautiful.

"She looks at you like what, beautiful girl?" Hunter

asks quietly, my eyes slowly rolling back onto his, face angled where his hand runs up and down Roscoe's back, eyes on mine.

Mouth dry, I look down, my bare feet, pale skin, toenails painted white, resting over the tip of Hunter's suede boots. I rock slightly, our sleeping son our aid, quieting our demons. I have the overwhelming urge to cry, and I lean just a little further into him, the very small space between us being eaten up as I do. Hunter watches my face, even though my eyes are dropped again, I know he's watching me. I can *feel* him. Always tracking me. Keeping me safe.

"Like I'm *strange.*"

Wings of a hummingbird, that's the way Hunter's body vibrates, the hand on my lower back stroking gently up my spine, a dangerous contrast to the clench of his strong jaw.

"And when-"

He snaps his attention to me, and the words dissolve on my tongue. Cocking his head, facial expression blank, his face and body the only thing that fills my vision. He slides a hand between me and Roscoe, hand beneath his round belly, knuckles grazing over my chest, hand curling around his boy. He turns him, tucking our sleeping son into his throat. Eyes on mine the entire time he resettles him, running his nose over the top of his head as he does so. It makes my insides hot and twisty, seeing him with our baby.

The air is heavy, a thick blanket that leaves me feeling cold. I lick my lips, swallow down the taste of blood, my breathing picking up the longer he stares at me in silence. And then his hand is snapping up, wrapping around my neck, and I instantly find myself feeling *better*.

"And when…?" he prompts, wanting me to finish.

All of the things I think I want to say about *her* sort of die, with the possessive way he surrounds me, his hands so, *so* gentle on our baby. His other still soothing, but in a different way, wrapped around my throat. Thumb and finger controlling where my gaze lies, pinching on my jaw, but it feels safe, to just, let him be in control. My brain relaxes, muscles melting, and I let him hold me up, eyes dropping closed, his breath fanning over my face.

He's hunching forward, pulling me in closer, my feet shuffling up onto his boots, thumb and forefinger directing, he tilts my head back. My eyes opening, his on mine, lips slanted over my own. Insides coiling tight, I shudder, letting out a breathy sigh.

Pupils blown wide, his eyes wander over my face, dropping to my lips before running back up my face. Shattered fragments of gold carving through the rich brown, his top lip pulling up and over his teeth in a wicked smirk. My heart sings, blood boiling, he flicks out his tongue, warm and wet, swiping over my parted lips.

A sharp breath of cold air slices through my lungs as I gasp, a soft whimper of need whispering through my teeth. My thighs clench beneath the floaty fabric of my white cotton dress. Heavy knit cardigan, a powder blue, draped over top, slips free of one shoulder, pooling in the crook of my elbow where I fist Hunter's t-shirt. I shiver, exposed skin prickling in the cool air of the large house.

The warmth of Hunter, Roscoe between us, seeps into my skin, Hunter's hand hot around my neck. Feet arching, pressing up onto tiptoes, balancing atop Hunter's boots, I pucker my lips, wanting, *needing*, to glide them over his.

Fingers tighten around my throat, cutting off my air, my eyes gathering tears at the corners, I stare at him through bleary eyes. My heart thumping so hard I wonder if it might burst into flames.

"Tell. Me."

The harsh growl rumbles through his teeth with a hiss, his sharp canines driving into the point of my cheekbone, making gathered tears spill over. They stream down my face, my lungs shrivelled and contracting on nothing, desperate for the permission of life.

I will die at your hand, beautiful boy, and I don't care.

I crave.

Us.

You.

It.

I want you to rip me to shreds, whisper that you love me and break me and hurt me and hunt me.

I am haunted.

I am hunted.

I am hurting.

I always want to hurt.

But not without *you.*

Never without you…

I always need you.

I need you, Hunter.

Save me from myself.

Hunter's fingers flex, readjusting just as the edges of my vision darken, allowing me to breathe for just a moment, tongue lapping over both cheeks, collecting my tears on his tongue. He draws back, mouth open, tongue out, as if for me to see, before he closes the distance, and his lips slam down over mine. Hungry and desperate, slow and gentle, love and tenderness. Something we're good and not so good at, but we do it, sometimes, with each other, be gentle.

My tongue licks into his mouth, long, languid strokes of my tongue over his. A growl rumbles in his chest, inner beast stirring, his hold on my neck light and controlling. Slowly, he draws back, looks at me, lips swollen and red.

"They like her more."

Confession a whisper, dark and empty and frightening, I slip down onto the heels of my feet, off of Hunter's boots, curl my toes into the carpet runner.

"Who, our babies?" he asks me quietly, not forcing me to look at him as I make my confessions.

Throat working, I swallow hard, nod my head, hung in shame, squeeze my eyes shut tight. I feel him shift, silence a low buzzing in my ears.

"What else, baby girl?" he asks quietly, because he knows, he always knows.

"Do you?" I whisper, it's so low it's almost silent, but as my eyes flick up to greet his, black swirling vortexes grip me in their vices and I still so completely, I feel as if I'm turned to stone.

He readjusts his grip on my neck, and I can feel him trying not to hurt, but I want him to. *Let go.*

Let go. Let go. Let go.

"*Do. I?*" he repeats, it's my question echoed but it sounds different coming from his tongue, disgusted, more venomous.

This is it. What I wanted. What I need.

Treat me badly, Hunter.

Make me hurt.

"Yes. Do. *You?*" It's a whisper, but there's so much of myself bleeding in the words, I don't know how I'm still breathing.

The look he gives me, the way he stares, his eyes feel like they're peeling my skin from my bones. Fingers twisting and plucking at my veins, picking through the mess of my insides, my brain, my heart, my soul.

Hunter licks his lips, like he's going to devour me. Stepping even closer, head dipping down to meet mine, our noses brush, his breath rushing through his teeth, fanning over my face. He nips my lips, squeezes my throat, lets his eyes fall closed even as he assaults my mouth in punishment.

And I want it this way.

I need it.

I'm lost without having any rules.

Make me follow you, make me serve.

My lip pops free, his tongue lapping over the split, a low moan ripping through his chest as he tastes my blood.

"You're going to stand right here and wait for me, whilst I go get *her* to watch our boys, *Mama*," it's almost a taunt, the way he avoids using her name, eyes on mine, intense.

And then he's tearing his hand free of my throat, my feet stumbling, trying to catch myself, his back already to me, Roscoe's sleeping face over his shoulder.

Lungs aching, breath being drawn in at a rapid pace, I look down at my feet, hands splayed over my stomach, white fabric cinched between my fingers. Ice runs through my veins and I close my eyes to catch my breath. I can hear Atlas and River playing together. The beat of my heart thumping in my ears, blood rushing, and I feel myself start to calm down, but then his boot-steps echo, cutting through it all, and my heart rate kicks up again. And he's right there, hands grabbing at me roughly, dragging me down the hall.

CHAPTER 16

GRACE

The snow is painful as my bare feet drag through it, sinking into the hard packed snow-fall, ankles already burning. Splinters of ice pierce my veins, a full body shiver wracking through me. Hunter half drags behind him, across the stepping-stone pathway that's currently hidden beneath half a foot of snow, his fingers pinching where they're gripped tight around my upper arm. He didn't seem to care that neither of us had outdoor clothes on, although he at least has boots on.

I want to ask what we're doing, where we're going, but my instincts compel me into silence, knowing he would never lead us to danger. My arm hurts and my feet are numb, but I can see the stables quickly coming into view, the outside burns a warm glow of orange beneath the heavy grey snow clouds. Hunter doesn't look back at me, doesn't speak, but I can hear him breathing, see his back heaving with breaths beneath his tight black t-shirt. The snow crunches beneath us, his heavy steps sinking him down, my feet raking across the top, barely having time to sink down.

Hunter unlatches the door when we finally reach the dark wood building, pulling me ahead of him and shoving me roughly inside. Warmth prickles at my skin, ice cold flesh pained with the sudden wash of heat. He bolts the door behind us, me a few feet away, spun around to face him, shivering beneath my thin dress, heavy knit cardigan not enough to make up for the freezing temperatures.

Silently, I wait, watching Hunter grip one of the empty stall gates, thick, strong fingers curl over the top, head dropped forward between his shoulders. A shudder rolling through him has his spine straightening just slightly and it's as though I watch the moment something shifts.

Hunter turns his head, still dropped forward, dark eyes rolling to the corner so he can see me. He licks his lips, gaze roving up my body, it makes me burn. Tiny little fires lighting up beneath my skin, singeing me from the inside out and I'm suddenly so hot that I can hardly stand still.

"Do you really think that I would *ever* even *look* at another person, *woman*, Gracie?" his words are so slow and so careful, and they give me the urge to run, but I stay where I am, nowhere to go.

"Archer said-"

"*Archer said…*" he chuckles, cutting me off, a dark, menacing low sound carrying from deep inside of him.

"Archer said that you don't have to like someone to stick your dick in them."

His eyes narrow even more, tendons in his forearms flexing beneath his warm olive skin.

"Yeah?" he asks after a too long pause.

"Yes," I answer quietly, wondering where this is going.

"You think I give a *fuck* what Archer says?" the question is lost on me, because the eerily gentle way he asks me has me backing up a step. "Where you gunna go, Gracie?" he taunts, dark narrowed eyes laser focused on my every twitch.

And I hate that it's with violence because that's all I ever crave.

Something is wrong with me.

"You think you can run from me, baby girl?" I shake my head, my feet still taking me back, bare and cold against the concrete, hay scattered beneath my toes. "You think I'd chase someone else?" I swallow down the doubt, don't answer. "Not going to answer me now? No head shake? Words, beautiful girl. Use. Your. *Fucking*. Words."

"I can run from you," I whisper hesitantly, nothing but empty stables surrounding me, echoing back my whisper.

"Yeah?"

"Yes."

"You know what I'll do about that, *little sister*?" the wood beneath his hands creaks before he releases the gate, slowly standing to his full height, he takes a singular step towards me and my shoulders bunch. "I'll fucking chase you. I'll fucking catch you. And then I'll fucking punish you for it. What d'you think about that, Gracie?"

"I think you *fucking* like it," I bite back instantly.

His lips kick up into a broad grin, at my swearing, the quick response, straight, pearly white teeth glinting ominously in the low light. He stalks closer, the air getting impossibly heavier and I'm well aware that my chest is already heaving, and my palms are stinging where my nails bite into them. And my knuckles pop beneath my pale skin as I watch him track closer. He stops, just a foot or so away and I stop breathing, watching his dark eyes stripping me bare, pulling off every layer I've built and turning it to ash.

He reaches to his right, hand going to the latch on an unused stall door. His veins are bright beneath his naturally tan skin, greens and blues raised across the backs of his hands, trailing up his flexing forearm. The door swings open, I see it from the corner of my eye, but I don't lose sight of my predator. You must never look away, the possibility of having your throat ripped out because you're distracted by something else is far too high.

"Get in the stall," the order is hissed, his throat working as he swallows, tension in his face, neck and shoulders.

Instead of answering, I slowly make my way inside the stall, being careful not to brush up against him where he stands half in the opening.

"On your knees."

I tremble, staring at him when he follows me inside, hands hidden behind his back, eyes trained on me, tracking my every breath. My skin so, so hot, the stables warm, sheltered from the wind and snow, the floors lined with straw that stabs into the soles of my feet. Hunter bangs the gate shut at his back, making me flinch, the breath rushing out of my lungs, feet tracking me back another step, back colliding with the wooden slatted wall, my heart squeezes in my chest.

Trembling on the spot, Hunter watches me, excitement and nerves a delicious mixture of adrenaline zinging through my veins. He strips me bare with his gaze, eye fucking me and furious from only four feet away.

Slowly, I glance at the floor, think about defying him, he's being patient with me right now, allowing me time to decide if I want to follow his orders or not.

On your knees.

I can feel the words sinking into me, something inside of me preening with this kind of attention, the darker parts of me demanding I fight back, stay on my feet, lift my chin, tell him no. With the talk inside my head being muted, I drop down onto my haunches, strips of hay rough beneath my bones, it hurts and I like it.

"Good girl," Hunter rasps, my lips parted on a silent breath as he uncrosses his hands from behind his back, a long, black riding crop in one hand.

My eyes follow it as he steps in closer, the tip of it

dragging through the hay before it's rising slowly, my eyes never leaving it. The leather tongue on its end pressing beneath my chin, tilting my head back. Up, up, and up, until my gaze is firmly fixed on Hunter.

"There she is," he coos almost silently, my skin prickles, a cold shiver running through me. His head tilts, "you're such a good girl for me, aren't you, Gracie?"

Nodding, the thick leather nudging the soft underside of my chin as I do, I tremble, anticipation for what's to come rushing through me like ice water quickly freezing in my veins.

"Always doing as I say. *Trusting in me.*"

I blink at the way he says the last part. The riding crop dropping from my chin, trailing down my chest, my belly, the skirt of my dress, to the space between my exposed knees. Hunter flicks the tip of the crop, the leather almost caressing the insides of my knees.

"Spread 'em."

I glance down, my pale skin milky, almost the same shade as my white dress, hay and straw scratches my shins as my knees slide apart. My cheeks heat, hearing a low growl rumbling in Hunter's chest, the riding crop still taps at my knees, stretching them so wide my muscles burn. Dress rucked up, thighs exposed, long jagged scar, crotch of my white lace knickers almost on full display. I keep looking down, even as Hunter traces the crop back up and over my body, the leather cool, my skin breaking out in goosebumps everywhere it touches.

"Look at me," the crop sails through the air with a

low whistle, heat suddenly blooming on the outside of my left thigh.

I look up, breathing harsh, Hunter looms over me like a dark god. My nipples pucker beneath my thin cotton dress, tight and aching as he swiftly hits my thigh again in the same spot.

"You know why we're doing this?" Hunter asks me, but I don't answer, waiting. "Gracie, when I ask you a question, I expect an answer, so pay attention." I watch him, riding crop twirling between his fingers. "Yes or no?"

I nod, quickly remembering myself, "yes, Hunter."

"Good," he nods his approval, my heart rate spiking. Pacing in the space before me, my thighs starting to tremble where they're spread so far apart. "I want to show you something, Gracie," words soft, his flicks his eyes to me, heavy and dark beneath his brow. "Will you let me, baby girl?"

"Yes."

His lips curl into a sinister smile at my lack of hesitation.

"I want you to listen to me, shut off your brain, all of those nasty thoughts swirling around in that pretty head of yours, I want you to banish them. Can you do that for me?"

A single brow raises on his forehead, my tongue wetting my lips, "yes."

"Good girl," he purrs, the praise rumbling from his chest, heat coiling in my belly. "You're only going to hear my voice now, no one else's, not *Archer's*, not even your own. Just mine."

"Okay."

"Take your dress off, show me everything that belongs to me."

I tremble, nervously, slipping my arms out of my cardigan, folding it in on itself and placing it beside me. Rising up on my knees, painful on the unforgiving ground. The smell of the horses, leather, hay, rich and heady, floods my senses. Eyes on Hunter's, I slip my fingers beneath my shoulder straps, let the light fabric fall down my body, pooling in the bend of my knees. His dark eyes survey me, dropping down my body, gaze caressing over my swollen breasts, down the dip of my stomach, exposed underwear and bare thighs.

"So beautiful," he husks, the sound rough and entranced, and it feels good, to have him look at me with hunger, his words low, like a nectar I desperately want to devour.

He steps in closer as I settle back down onto my haunches, weight balanced more evenly now on the length of my shins, dress caught around my knees. Hunter circles me, my body quivering as he traces the leather tongue of the crop over my exposed breasts, tapping both my nipples, the smooth leather making my nipples tighten further. A shudder rolls through me, the crop whispering up the length of my back, he flicks one of my twin plaits over my shoulder, the gentle thwack of it hitting my breast.

"Take your braids out," he instructs from behind me, his heavy breaths almost louder than my own.

Finger and thumb pinching the band around the braid's end, I tug it free, comb my fingers through the lengths. Once both are out, my hair down my back, Hunter shifts behind me, coming down onto his knees, thighs spread even wider than mine. Knees on either side of me, he brings his hand to my throat, moss, daisies, the brook, all of him overwhelming the stable smells.

One by one, his fingers are slow to curl around the front of my throat, his forearm slanted across my chest, he holds my jaw tight, tilting back my head, crown against his chest. Neck arched back as far as it can go, I look up, his head tilted down, eyes on mine.

"Open your mouth, stick out your tongue," the dark order is whispered, a sinister calm settled in the words.

Mouth opening, a sharp breath assaulting my lungs as I gasp, Hunter aggressively brushes his thumb over my bottom lip, pulling it down, and exposing my teeth. A strangled sort of growl threatens, but I keep it inside,

"You love me, beautiful girl?" he asks in a terse whisper, his face upside down in my vision, I nod, mouth open, tongue out, tears in my eyes at the bite of his grip on my jaw. "So perfect, Gracie," he hushes, lips against my temple, the tip of his tongue catching a tear as it spills over.

Humming, he draws back, my head still against his chest, breasts pushed out, spine curved. He looks down at me, a mess of emotion on his handsome face, dark eyes turned ebony, black as the night's sky, a mesmerising glitter of gold sparking through. He spits on my tongue. Thumb stroking along the lower half of my face, I feel his saliva slide back, my tongue still held out for him. He watches, adoration above all else cutting through the darkest parts of him.

"*Swallow*," he whispers, the word thick.

Violently, I shiver, goosebumps razing across my skin, my lips seal, swallowing him down and I'm instantly rewarded with a deep, rumbled groan of satisfaction. He grinds himself against me, shifting on his knees, my weight pulled into him, his cock already hard, digging into my lower spine.

"Don't move," he tells me lowly, lips brushing against the shell of my ear.

Standing, he steps around me, stopping a few feet away. Looking down, riding crop in hand, he uses it to sweep my hair back, brushing it delicately off of my shoulder. Reaching for his jeans, he unbuttons them, lowering the zip with deft movements. With the heel of his hand, slowly, he pushes at the gaping waistband, black boxers going down too, his cock springs free, thick and hard, glinting at the tip with pre-cum. He watches me intently, his hand stroking up his length, thumb rolling over his tip. I tilt my head, lick my lips, eyes focused in on his thick fingers squeezing tight around his cock.

"Crawl to me," his order whispered, the quiet space we've created here in the later hours of the morning, sun banished behind dark snow clouds, shutting out the light, feels safe.

Hands splaying over the concrete, thin dusting of hay beneath my palms, I shuffle forward. My loose hair making it difficult not to kneel or lean on it as I crawl, makes me slow. Dress disappearing down my legs as I move, I kick it free of my ankle. When I reach Hunter, still as a statue, silent as the dead in the basement, he places the crop beneath my chin once again, tilting my head back.

"Such a good girl," he breathes, his dark eyes wide, pupils blown. "Now, take me into your mouth, and choke on my cock, baby girl."

Opening my mouth, crop falling away from my face, I press up onto my knees, lash the flat of my tongue over his tip, making him jolt closer. Tongue twirling around his length, my eyes on his, where he peers down his perfect body at me, he lifts the hem of his t-shirt, tugging it over his head and dropping it to the floor beside me. My lips suck on the underside of his cock, veins throbbing beneath my tongue, I suck him into my mouth.

Hollowed cheeks, I swallow, his thick length tight in the back of my throat, salt and earth heavy on my tongue. Slowly, I reach up, hand gently massaging his balls, fingers of the other curling into his pushed down waistband, helping keep me as close as possible. My nose brushes the soft skin of his pelvis, fine trail of dark hair tickling my face, I nuzzle my face into him, his cock pushing down my throat.

He groans as I swallow, air cut off, one of his hands cups the back of my head, keeping me close, my eyes leaking tears at their corners where I stare up at him adoringly.

Hunger and devotion burn into me at the look in his eyes, swirling black pits of coal, caramel slicing through the darkness, love. My vision blurs, tears for an entirely new reason overwhelming me. His fingers crawl teasingly over my scalp, knotting into the roots, the leather of the riding crop resting against my back. A sharp bite of pain rips across my scalp as he yanks me off his cock. Strings of saliva connect us, my lips swollen and wet with it, the flavour of his pre-cum tart and clean on my tongue. I heave in breath, my lungs on fire with the assault of ice cold air.

"You going to make me come for you, beautiful girl?"

I stare up at him, my eyes wide, lips parted, and I nod my head so hard my neck cracks. Before I have time to register his movements, he's slamming me back down on his cock, my throat contracting as his length is forced deep, gagging around him as I try to swallow. Hunter takes control then, brutal, smacking thrusts of his hips, both hands fisted tightly in my hair.

"I'm going to fuck another baby into you, Gracie, you want that? To be swollen once again with my son, my daughter."

His words make my insides clench and pull, my pussy slick, wetness slides down my thighs, knowing what he wants from me.

My hands curl around his upper thighs, jeans still

around them, fabric rough beneath my hot palms. I hold on to him, letting him punish my throat and then he thrusts hard and deep, once, twice, pulling out so only his tip is suctioned between my swollen lips.

Hot cum pumps onto my tongue, my breath rushing through my nose as I try hard not to swallow. Gently, his thick fingers sweep over the back of my head, cradling my face in his hands, getting to his knees before me, adoration in his gaze.

His nose tenderly brushes over my own, mouth slanting over mine, I part my lips, his tongue licking deep into my mouth, his cum passing from my tongue to his. He kisses me savagely, wet, and sloppy and violent, our lips sealed tightly together. And then he's gripping the backs of my thighs, riding crop clattering to the floor, my spine colliding with the concrete. Knickers torn off, the lacy fabric pinching my skin, he throws my parted legs over his shoulders and then he's pushing his cum into my cunt with his mouth.

Fucking me with his tongue, my back arches up off the floor, his tongue exorcising our demons. The crown of my head presses into the ground so hard, stars shoot beneath my squeezed eyelids. Gasping for breath, hands slapping down at my sides, nails clawing into the ground, Hunter pins me down, big hand splaying over my lower belly, pressing me down, down, down. I push against him, my body bucking into his face, his mouth licking and sucking at my folds, over my clit, his tongue thrusting inside of me, I come. Shattering around him, muscles spasming, he holds me to him as I ride it out.

Bliss unfurls inside of me, blood hot, hearing sharp, eyes zeroed in on Hunter's mess of black hair. Just him. Just us. Everything around us dissolving like it's been doused in acid. Fading out until it's just him and I.

His large hands slide beneath my back, his knuckles scraping the rough ground, he pulls me up into his lap, kissing me tenderly, his lips move over my temple, my cheek.

"You're such a beautiful girl, such a good girl, so fucking perfect for me, Gracie, you are so perfect."

I bury my face in his chest, bare skin cool against my hot cheek, I let my eyes close as he strokes up my spine, nails gently clawing up and down my skin.

"Get on your hands and knees," he rasps against the top of my head, his heart thudding hard against my ear.

He shifts me out of his lap, turning me away from him, moulding me into shape with caressing hands. Spreading my knees, splaying my fingers, parting my hair so it hangs over both shoulders, head dropped forward. He moves up behind me, still standing, when leather kisses down my spine, making me shiver. All of me naked and exposed to him, he circles me like prey, his captive, something he both cherishes and wants to destroy all horrifically twisted into one. He moves in behind me, dropping into a crouch, the riding crop slowly moving down the length of my back, over the globe of my arse and back up. I can feel his cum, mixed with my arousal, trickling out of me, the cool air against my damp skin, making me tremble, I bite my lip, close my eyes, pray for death.

To have my life taken by him, oh, what a beautiful death it will be.

My head disconnects from my body as the first gentle lash of the crop lands on the base of my spine. His big hand smacking my arse cheek at the same time. My body rocks forward with the force, the softly stinging heat on my spine, harsh bloom of pain on one cheek. Thick fingers caress the burning flesh, pulling and spreading me apart, the riding crop whistles through the air, connecting with the same spot of the first hit and my back bows, spine arching and curving. I push back against Hunter, into his rough hand, the feel of his jeans a harsh texture against the heat of my flesh. His hand disconnects from my skin, only to connect with my other cheek in a hard smack.

A moan tempers its way up my throat, raw and strangled, my head dropping forward, hair trailing down around me, hiding me from view.

"I. *Own*. You." Voice deep and strained, every word punctuated with a harsh clap of his hand. "You. Are. *Mine*." The words are clipped, growled, the riding crop making a high-pitched sound as it cuts through the cold air.

I can feel myself getting wetter. Pussy dripping with him, my arousal slick, the combination coating my inner thighs. Every single place he hits on my body is crackling with fire. I'm needy and desperate, rocking back against him as much as he'll allow.

"So beautiful," he rasps against my stinging spine, bowing over me, lips mouthing the words over my lashings, his tongue swiping out, worshipping the marks he created.

He lifts off of me, back going cold with the loss of his warm skin on mine. I can see his hands splayed on the concrete either side of me where my head hangs forward, hair trailing around me like a golden curtain. He shifts between my thighs, his hands going to my hips, grasping at me with desperate fingers. I feel the head of his cock at my entrance, hot and wet and throbbing, before he's pushing himself inside, a grunt and groan of pleasure rattling his throat.

Using his grip on my hips he pulls me onto him, sheathing himself deep inside of me with one last rough thrust. The flesh of my arse burns where I slam into him, his huge handprints likely painted red upon my cheeks, a wailed cry drops from my lips as he starts to pound into me. Curling over my back, draping himself on top of me, his hands come beneath me, groping my breasts, thumb and fingers pinching and pulling on my nipples. My swollen flesh aching for release, heavy with milk, everything so overly sensitive and responsive to his touch.

One of his hands skates down my body, his thumb finding my swollen clit, I jolt at his touch, the coarse pad of his thumb circling it hard. My fingers claw into the concrete beneath us, straw and hay rough and scratchy against my skin. I'm the only thing holding us up, his weight on my back, my hands on the floor, I feel myself almost tilting, elbows wanting to buckle, but Hunter's strong hands keep me upright.

"I own you. Your heart, your blood, your soul, everything inside of you, eyeballs to fucking entrails, right down to your beautiful bones, baby girl. You are fucking mine."

His hips smash into me over and over, his hand groping and squeezing my breast, fingers and thumb rubbing everything above where he slams his cock in and out of me, and it's too much. My hands claw at the floor, nails bending, my brain short circuits, everything disappearing in darkness for a moment and I'm flying. Soaring my way through my orgasm so high I can touch the moon. I'm panting, slipping down to my elbows, but Hunter keeps me from falling, holding me to him, his dick still slowly moving inside of me.

His hand collars my throat, pulling me upright, on my knees, my back flush to his chest, a sheen of cold sweat between us. His free fingers push between my lips, sliding over my tongue, into the back of my throat. Saliva runs from the corners of my mouth, the urge to cough almost too much to contain when teeth sink into the side of my throat.

High on my neck, pain blooms, exploding through my veins, the pressure so intense, tears sluice down my flush cheeks, dripping off my chin, onto his forearm. Red ruptures behind my closed eyelids, spots of colour bursting open like rapidly unfurling roses, heat rushes down the column of my throat, my head relaxing back against him as the flat of his tongue catches my crimson essence.

The muscles in my neck ache, heat ricocheting down

my spine, warmth flooding my pussy as Hunter finishes inside of me. His cock hard and throbbing, forcing its way through my contracting muscles as they try to push him out. His mouth comes to my ear, head tilted back against his shoulder. Hunter holding me up against him, his fingers pulling free from my mouth, hand sweeping through the mess on my chest, blood, saliva, milk, tears. His fingers swirl through it, almost absentmindedly, as he nips my earlobe, sucking it into his mouth with reverence.

He makes his way down the side of my neck, over the broken skin, his tongue laving the sting as he continues his bruising assault of my throat. When he tilts my head, rotating it on my shoulders, he descends towards my collarbone, sucking his way along the sharply defined bone. It hurts and I sink into it, let the pain tear me from reality, plunge me into the darkness, the safety, the place Hunter and I ascend to in moments just like this.

My dark protective angel.

The biggest monster of them all.

"There's one thing you seem to keep forgetting, beautiful girl." He bites my neck, sucking on the fresh wound and my blood hums with approval as he drains just another little piece of me and consumes it. "It's that you own me, Gracie. You fucking own me too. You command me, I go where you go. We thrive together, we die together, no one else is ever going to be able to fill that for me. The space you fit inside of me, it was carved out by you, for you, nothing and no one could ever fucking change that. I love you, Gracie. You have, you own, you *are*, my whole black fucking heart."

Something inside of me is strung so tight I can hardly breathe. Can't open my eyes, can't swallow, can't think. My spine tingles, my blood burns hot, my soul fucking sings, and I feel like I'm dying.

But I'm alive.

Even when he makes me want to die.

For him.

With him.

For us.

"I love you, Hunter."

I can't help the tears that spill down my cheeks, the way my chest aches and caves and my heart beats in a way it wants to explode, wings ripping free to fly it into the heavens.

I slam my head back against his shoulder, over and over and over, and he lets me. Helping me exorcise my demons, purge my soul of doubt, of pain, of hate. And then he's grabbing my face, cradling the back of my skull, and smothering my lips with his.

He pushes and I pull, he gives and I take and then he's forcing his breath into my lungs to make sure I really know he owns every single incomplete piece of me. So, I do the same to him, he breaths, I breathe and it's *strange,* freeing, ownership and possession.

Our obsession is black and depraved. Carved with jagged, sharp edges and slick bloodied kisses. My heart beats for his, and his for mine.

And in the stable stall, closed off from the outside

world, we hurt, and we love, and we fuck, and he owns me and I own him and we punish each other for all of our sick, blood drenched sins.

"Tonight," he rasps, hours later, his deep voice burning a shiver down my spine. "I'll absolve your sins, you'll absolve mine," he whispers, repeating something he told me so long ago, the words feathering against the shell of my ear.

"I love you, Hunter."

"I love you, Gracie."

CHAPTER 17

GRACE

I push my shoulders back, something I watch Dad do when he means to talk business. It's Thorne's permanent posture, head held high, confident. He lifts my chin when we speak, he doesn't ever force eye contact, it's just to — help me remember I am allowed to speak with confidence, I don't have to mumble at my feet anymore.

It's okay to tell truths that are sometimes hard to find the words for, to say.

I've put the boys down, Hunter has an early start. I left him upstairs, didn't tell him exactly what it is I planned to do, but he looked at me knowingly all the same. He always knows everything. I wonder if I'm very easy to read or if he just simply knows me that well. Perhaps it's both. We're the same, him and I.

My bare feet are silent along the hall, my white silk pyjama pants loose and wide, swishing across the tops of my feet, strappy black vest top tucked into the waist-band, white oversized cardigan pulled over top.

The light of a television flickers out into the hall from one of the many sitting rooms we don't often use. Stopping just short of the open doorway, still hidden in the darkness, I blink, drop my gaze. I twiddle the end of a braid between my fingers, my hair parted in two, a French plait on either side of my head.

Is this what I really want to be doing?

Trying to make peace, start fresh? With *her?*

I don't want to feel uncomfortable in my own house. But the day I walked in on Hunter and her, he was too close. I missed their quietly hushed words, but she was flushed red, and that only happens to me when I feel a certain way, lust, anger. She certainly didn't look angry. Hunter did, but he always looks angry. It's one of the things I like most about him. That I can smooth out that expression just by being there.

I worry my lip, thinking about what's real and what's not. Mother is dead. I am not. Hunter loves me. The shadows are safe. Rachel is… *something else.* But I'm not sure I've been reading her right, perhaps it's just me. Maybe I unnerve her, the same way she rattles me. Perhaps it's just all her.

Head up, shoulders back, I push out a breath, take the final couple of steps forward, turn into the room and hover just inside the door for the single second it takes them to see me. Archer smiles wide, winking at me with mischief.

"'Sup, baby sis?" he calls quietly, just loud enough to be heard over the quietly playing TV.

Chest bare, arms spread wide over the back of the sofa, Rachel an entire couch cushion away, but still just within touching distance. I stare at her, her eyes on mine, and I cock my head to one side, Archer's fingers trailing just over the ball of her shoulder.

I glance at my brothers, the two youngest, on the opposite couch cloaked in darkness, bar the occasional flicker of blue light illuminating their faces. Arrow laid back, legs spread wide, head tilted, resting on the back of the couch, eyes on mine. Raine beside him, similar position, he flicks a brow at me, teasing smirk on his face.

I look back to Rachel, thinking I could just not say anything, or I could say it with the boys here.

"I would like to talk to Rachel," I announce quietly, my eyes remaining on hers, she glances at Archer, who doesn't look away from me.

It makes me feel better, more confident, holding their attention.

He's trying to work me out, but he's not as good at that as his eldest brother. Thorne, really, the only other person besides Dad that's almost always right.

Without another word, the three men stand, all of them well over six feet, they tower over me as the pass by, exiting the room.

"You haven't got a knife hidden away on your person, anywhere, have you?" Raine whispers, pausing beside me, breath feathering my hair.

I keep my eyes on hers, think of the pretty purple knife in my cardigan pocket, say nothing. Raine chuckles, following our brothers out into the hall. I wait until they're a little way away before stepping slightly farther into the room. My gaze flicks to the television, Rachel shifting in my periphery.

Scream plays on the TV, the character Billy smiling whilst nursing a stab wound to the gut. I watch it for a moment, standing in the centre of the room, my body angled towards Rachel, head turned, eyes on the television.

"You like horror films?" I ask her, still not looking at her.

"Not really," she says quietly, and I see her shrug out the corner of my eye. "You?"

I feel a small smile curve my lips, but I straighten it out, look at her properly this time.

"No," I tell her honestly, "I prefer books."

She nods her head, lips pressed together, the awkwardness too much, too hot, too cold, too tight, it makes me want to choke.

"We need to get along, I have some rules to help that happen," I tell her bluntly, my voice low, gentle, I don't really have a *tough* version of myself, but people tend to listen when I speak, if only out of curiosity.

Slowly, she leans forward, forearms resting on her knees, she eyes me, still in her jeans, tight top, I don't look like her, but that's okay, I think I like how I look, how I dress.

"Rules?" she questions, and there's humour in her voice that I choose to ignore.

I feel strongly about rules, and how they're supposed to be put in place to keep people safe.

These rules are to keep *her* safe.

From the monsters that lurk inside this house.

I'm the bigger monster.

"You are not the parent. *I* am. This is *my* house. You are here because I allow it. My sons are kind to you because I order it." My anger spikes with every word, although I don't show it, and she doesn't say anything to interrupt, but I can tell she finds this entire thing amusing. "If I say yes to something my children ask *me*, that is the answer. I don't like you talking down to my sons with words meant for their mother. If you have something to say, you address *me*."

My composure is calm and still on the outside, and I think of Thorne, wish he were here, to glance at, steal some courage from. I think of all the things my brothers and Dad have told me over the years, things Hunter has tried to reinforce inside my head, and I'm not sure I really believed any of it until now.

"I am not stupid, dim, dumb, if that is your assumption of me, you are very much mistaken. Do not underestimate me as a parent, as a woman. Do not treat me as though I am lesser. If you're not okay with that, you can go."

"Okay," she shrugs, a soft smile on her face that doesn't reach her eyes.

"I would like us to start fresh," I say next, ignoring

the way the light from the television dances through the shadows.

The shadows are safe.

"Fine," she says blankly, but I don't give her a reaction. "I can do that," she offers finally, but it feels strained, like the air inside this room.

I nod, turning to leave, unhappy with how this went, because I don't feel any better about her, but if she tries, then I will try.

"Grace?" she calls as I reach the threshold, seeing Arrow on my right, standing just a few feet away down the hall, listening.

I turn, head over my shoulder, eyes flicking back to hers.

"Thank you," she says, "for letting us start over," another forced smile on her face.

I nod, turning away, from her, from Arrow, my feet taking me back up to our bedroom. The whole way there making me wonder just what trouble she's going to cause inside this house. And how much of that trouble I'm going to be able to let go.

CHAPTER 18

GRACE

D ad said Michael called again. He didn't answer because I've asked him not to. And Dad always respects my wishes. He just wants us all to be happy and if I'm happy without hearing from my b____ ____ather ever again, then that's what he'll ens____ ____

Rachel ____ ____s a____eeping Ro____ie off to Rosie, her small smile is nervous as she glances at me just inside the foyer as she readies herself to leave for the day. And I wonder, not for the first time, that perhaps I *have* read her wrong. It makes my tummy twist with unease.

I'm trying not to let my mind play tricks on me when it comes to her.

I also made a pinky promise to A____ ____that I would try and be a little kinder to her after he listened in on our conver____ ____on the other night. I still don't understand how that action binds me to a promise, our little fingers curled around one another, but he says it does, so, I will try. And apparently, so we were clear, that involves not backing her up against a wall whilst holding a knife. Who knew.

Dad and the boys went into London early this morning, on task for the Swallows, one of them seems to have gone missing, and their leader is tearing apart the city to find her twin. Which requires an entire family of clean up experts on hand, so it meant Hunter had to leave the mill. He said he'll be back tonight, even if the others aren't, because it's Valentine's Day.

That leaves Rosie and I here for the day with the three boys, Rachel's day off, and it's only early, but so far, it's been *nice*. Calm and quiet. The absence of Rachel's loud voice makes for a nice change, I haven't once had to cover my ears with my hands or had any impulse to slash through someone's vocal cords with a butcher's knife.

River tugs on the hem of my white dress, thick woollen tights beneath, his little face peers up at me, dark brown eyes, gappy, toothy grin broad on his face. I look down at him, white puffer coat that matches mine, zipped up to his chin, black thermal trousers beneath, bright yellow welly boots, matching coloured beanie pulled down over his head of blonde hair.

"Mama, snow!" he squeals, fingers going to his mouth, other hand fisted in the skirt of my dress.

He turns towards the back door, pulling on the fabric, tugging me behind him, when he suddenly stops, fingers popping free of his mouth, he looks up at me, mouth opening.

"Attyyyyyyyyy!" he giggles, watching my face for the reaction he knows is coming, I wince on instinct, making him chuckle.

Shaking my head gently, I grab his mittens off of the kitchen side, dropping to my knee, I thread his wriggly, little wet fingers through them, fold the mitten piece over the top. I hear Atlas's pound of footsteps as he runs down the hall towards us. Rounding the corner, he skids into view just as I push to standing.

"Atlas," I say quietly, his mismatched eyes darting to mine, a slow smirk twisting his mouth, the corner of his lips tucked between his teeth.

"I'll get it!" he yells, twisting on the spot, running into the foyer.

I hear the coat cupboard latch click, his little grunt of effort as he unhooks his coat. Then the door slams shut, making me flinch again, and River giggles, his little head thrown back, mouth open, his naughty cackle strangely infectious. I bite my bottom lip, Atlas trampling back into the room, his energy levels so high he can hardly stop himself as he knocks into Dad's dining chair.

"*Atlas,*" it's a scold, to be careful, and he knows it.

He looks up at me, big eyes wide, gaze flicked up beneath his dropped brow, I close my eyes, shake my head. River's hands grabbing at my knee, he buries his face into the back of my leg, mouth open, dribble wetting my tights. Atlas is stepping into me when I open my eyes, blue coat on, pink hat, pink boots, hand outstretched to me in black mittens. I clasp his fingers in mine, River squealing as he bounces on the spot, I detach him from my leg, push out of the back door and down the steps, whistling over my shoulder for Tyson and Duke.

The boys and I wander, hand in hand, through the deep snow, tiny fluffy flakes drifting through the cold air, the sky is bright, the sun's rays finally managing to break through the dense snow clouds in places. The Dobermans bound out ahead of us, kicking up snow as they race through it, rolling around and then zipping back, nosing at the snow and tossing it over the boys.

When we reach the meadow, the house at our backs, forest to our right, I start rolling a snowball, letting Atlas push it around once it's big enough so we can get the base of our snowperson. The snow hits me just above my ankles, knee high leather boots protecting me from getting wet, which feels strange, not being able to wriggle my toes freely. I watch Atlas roll the growing ball of snow around and around with careful hands.

River runs and jumps, throwing himself onto the floor, snow poofing up and around him in a fluffy white cloud. Duke pounces, using his nose to roll him over and over like a snow sausage. River squeals with glee, calling out for his big brother through broken laughter. Atlas ignores him with a naughty chuckle as Tyson dives on my toddler too, nuzzling into River's face, his little hands grabbing at his short-hair coat, pushing him away before dragging him back to him.

"Uncle Archer said the next one has to be smaller, or it won't stack," Atlas informs me seriously as together we push and roll another large ball of snow.

"Okay," I nod, following his instructions, doing it the exact way he shows me.

Once we've arranged our three snowballs, one atop the other, I pull out some shiny stones I collected from the brook in the warmer months, from my pocket, fingers brushing over my little purple flip knife as I do. The one from inside my bedside table I've started carrying in a pocket ever since I took Atlas outside in the middle of the night. Hunter told me it could make me feel better, could protect our boys.

I hold out my palm, knife secured in my pocket, pebbles in hand. I bend down, free hand splaying over my thigh as I watch Atlas make his choice. The concentration in his decision brings a small smile to my face. He runs his little fingertips over every single one before he looks up at me, studying my face with rapt attention, it almost makes me squirm, but I hold still, keep his gaze, one dark brown eye, the other split, ice blue on top, dark brown the bottom.

He takes a tan coloured stone, a white one, studying me just once more before he turns away, toward his face-less snowperson.

River drapes himself over Tyson's back, like our dog is a horse and then closes his eyes. And I think about taking both boys back inside once our snowperson is finished, River is soaked right through already and it's supposed to snow again this afternoon.

Atlas reaches up, pressing his light stone into the place for the right eye, the tan stone going left. He steps back, un-popping the button on his coat pocket, taking out the short carrot Rosie handed to him at breakfast. His back still to me, he steps forward, and I expect him to push the carrot in the place of a nose. Instead, using the pointed end of the orange vegetable he stretches up on tiptoes, and scrapes a curve into the lower half of the snowball face.

He goes over it a few times, my eyes wandering to River every now and then, just a mere few feet away, his eyes closed, body limp, where he hangs over Tyson. Duke closed in on one side of them, their eyes, too, on my eldest son.

Atlas steps away, walking backwards until he bumps my legs, he looks up then, as I look down, a soft smile on his face, he lifts the carrot to his lips, and takes a big bite. I laugh, not expecting it, and he beams brighter.

"Your nose doesn't look anything like a carrot, Mama," Atlas whispers up at me, teeth crunching his mouthful of snack before he swallows. "She's you."

Blinking quickly, I look up, gaze on the snowperson, and it's like my eyes are staring back at me, as my *actual* eyes fill with moisture.

"Why?" I ask quietly, swallowing down the lump of emotion in my throat.

Unable to look back down at my son, I stare at the very small curve of a smile on the snowperson's face.

"Because you're my favourite person," he whispers back. "And you protect us."

Reaching up, a tear rolling down the side of my nose, I quickly wipe it away, blinking hard to clear my vision. I place my hands on my son's shoulders, squeezing gently. I look down at his soft face, his head tilted back, resting against my thighs, wonder how it is Hunter and I could make something so soft. So caring. So loving. So innocent. My heart thuds hard, breath held, I offer him a small nod, and he grins so wide, my insides churn.

Duke rumbles a low growl, my eyes snapping to his, his gaze focused on the tree line, Tyson's gaze focused there too, Duke steps forward, shielding my sleeping son. Their pointed ears pricked, tails straight, hackles raised on Duke's back. Atlas munches his carrot; completely unaware anything is happening when the hair at the nape of my neck stands to attention.

Slowly, I turn my head toward the snowperson, flick my gaze towards the treeline. Four large figures in black stand stock still between the trees, exposed by the bright white of the ground covering, the shadows beneath the dense trees highlighted by the reflection of the snow. I lick my lips, keep myself calm. I know they're real, the dogs don't usually sense when I see Mother. This is real. And my boys are in danger. These aren't visitors, or they'd have been using the large knocker on the front door of our house.

I turn Atlas with my soft grip on his shoulders, dropping into a slow crouch, carrot suspended halfway to his mouth he frowns at whatever he sees on my face.

"Atlas," I say quietly, gaze flicking to the stationary figures in the trees. Licking my lips, I swallow, "I need you to do something very important for Mummy."

His mismatched eyes flick between my own, before slowly, he nods, hand with the carrot dropping to his side.

"I need you to take your brother back to the house quickly, you're going to have to run with the dogs, okay?" Tyson growls and I swallow hard, razorblades jagged the whole way down. "Do you remember that special space Daddy showed you, where you and your brothers would always be safe?"

Atlas nods confidently, a look of determination on his face, I glance over his shoulder, seeing the blacked-out figures approaching unhurriedly.

"Where you and Daddy will always find us," he says, eyebrows drawn together.

"Yes, I need you to go there now and not look back, okay? You take River and Roscoe in there, and you don't come out of there until your Daddy, Grandad or one of your uncles comes to get you, okay? Not for anyone."

"What about you?" he asks with a wobble to his bottom lip that cracks my heart.

"Mummy's going to be gone for just a minute, baby," I tell him in a choked whisper, stroking my hand over his head, thumb sweeping across his cheek. "You're Mummy's brave boy, Atlas, you're going to look after your brothers. You know where Mummy keeps the nappy bag?" he nods in confirmation. "Good boy," the words rush out of me with a relieved breath.

My heart thuds harder and harder in my chest and I think it's about to explode when he leans into me, kisses my cheek, and walks directly to the dogs, gently waking his brother and taking his hand as he gets to his feet.

"Go home," I order them sternly, eyeing both dogs as I do, and at that, the four of them, both dogs, both sons, hand in hand, start to run, dogs on their heels.

Standing, I take in a steady breath, step forward, around the snowperson, keep my hands loose at my sides, and wait. I've been prepared for this, Thorne telling me that if something like this were to happen, outnumbered, outweaponed, nobody home, that I'm to let myself be taken. Hunter growling about it, before telling me he would always find me.

'I will always find you in the dark, Gracie.'

I let those words sink in.

Think about Wolf telling me I'm more capable than I think, Arrow telling me I have a kind heart. Thorne smiling in that Thorne way he only does for me and the boys, telling me I'm strong. Archer laughing at my unfunny jokes, his arm around me in comfort. Raine telling me not to reveal my advantage too early, save your weapon until you really need it, don't let on you have one.

I'm lethal.

I'm my own weapon.

Something strange and underestimated.

'You are the darkness, baby girl.'

Shoulders back, I stand tall, face clear, I swallow down my fear, anxiety at leaving the boys, but none of these people seem to be interested in them. I want to hold their attention, so when they're within calling distance, thirty-feet or so, I run.

I fly right, into the trees that I know and love so well. Booted feet hammering through the hard packed snow. My teeth chatter, arms pumping, fabric of my coat swishing as my arms pass over my sides. I fly through the trees, panic clawing at my insides, I duck beneath bare branches, decorated in the recent snowfall. The snow crunches and cracks beneath my feet, heavy footfalls not too far behind me. Breathing hard, puffing in a cloud before my face, I bear left, push off of a trunk, slip around behind it and stop. Breath burning a hole in my lungs, desperate to escape, I strain my ears, closing my eyes to focus on my hearing.

Twigs snap, snow crunching, waterproof fabric swishing, I count three, picking them out easily, I wait, ears searching for the fourth, chest threatening to cave in, rib bones feeling as though their bowing in towards my shrivelling lungs, I take in a breath, a gasp, my lungs too tired without oxygen, and I'm too loud.

My eyes spring open, and I see him instantly, I twist on my foot, ankle crunching, I push off the tree, a cry choked off in my throat as a large hand wraps around my neck. The air knocked out of my lungs, the figure in black slams me into his firm chest, lifting my feet clean off the ground.

"Sorry, gorgeous," he rasps on a chuckle as something solid collides with the back of my skull, vision turning black, my eyes fall shut, pain exploding in my head.

The last thing I think of is Hunter telling me he'll always find me.

CHAPTER 19

HUNTER

A rrow glances to his left, side eyeing me from the driver's seat as he takes us through the outer edges of the city, trees finally starting to come into view. My chest seems to expand with easier breaths the further from the city we get, deeper into the country, it's nothing but open spaces, fields and pastures of endless green.

It makes me think of Gracie now, her scent, sweet like honeysuckle, soft and fragrant, ferns, a woodsy undercurrent. How she smells after we've been out in the rain, fresh and clean. I want to consume her, every single piece of her, mind, body and soul.

Obsession.

That's what I have for her, a deep, dark, twisted obsession that has me wanting to devour her. Destroy her. Possess her. Protect her from everything that isn't me.

I think about tonight, Valentine's Day, something she

doesn't understand the concept of, but it gives me an excuse to dote on her, *obsessively* so, and she lets me because I've told her that's what's supposed to happen. It's also something I've now missed most of, but I know she'll be waiting up for me, a fire burning behind the grate, fur throws dressing the sofa in the den, her naked body needy for me beneath them.

Arrow's dark eyes flicker back to mine, and I still don't look at him. I feel uncomfortable, my black clothes are soaked in death, my skin, my hair, we wiped down all of our visible parts with wipes before getting into the car, but it's all still there, even though it's invisible to the eye. It's still fucking there.

Blackwells are death.

Bringers of it. Disposers of it.

It's been the Blackwell legacy for as far back as our name goes. The Blackwells have been everywhere, palaces, castles, underground criminal organisations, black markets, the dark web, our history even showing us as executioners for Kings and Queens of England. Executions may have been abolished now, the royals may no longer be putting on shows of blood and death for entertainment purposes, but it's still the Blackwell's sole purpose.

"You killed that guy," Arrow says with a quiet sort of disbelief.

An eyebrow tracks its way up my forehead, and I shift in my seat, turning to face him fully. Tilting my head, I stare at my younger brother, thick black hair a little longer than mine, but still shorn short around the sides, it flops forward over one of his black eyes in the same way that mine does.

"Congratulations, you can use your eyes for observations, Dad will be so proud when I turn in my report."

He snorts, a curve to his plush lips, a little swollen on the left side where he got headbutted, his top lip a little larger than his bottom one anyway, a little unusual, much like his personality, but it makes him prettier, softer.

"You tore out his spinal column," he says quietly.

"Yeah, my hands ache," I snort, turning back to face the front of the car. I see him smile, a small one reflecting my own on my lips, "Arrow…" I bite into my top lip, tongue worrying behind my bottom teeth. "Are you okay?" I ask, and it feels strange, to ask, want to hear the answer, because we don't really do this kinda shit.

I don't really do this kinda shit.

We drive in silence, the dark of the night pitch, white snow lashes the windscreen, window wipers working overtime to clear our view. Headlights on full beam, rear fog lights switched on, no street lamps lighting our journey home into the country.

"I'm okay," Arrow whispers in the quiet, but his words rake up my spine like demonic claws, our car finally climbing the winding roads that lead us to Heron Mill.

Swallowing, I keep my eyes on the road ahead, no cars passing us for the last ten miles, no one comes up here.

His answer unsettles me, it feels wrong, a dark secret weighs heavy on his shoulders, and I'm not going to pry, take it from him, share the load, because, I'm not sure I know how to do that for anyone other than my Gracie. And I should, because he's my brother and I love him, even though we don't share that shit, and I want him to be safe, to be happy, to feel as though he can tell me the shit that haunts him inside his head. But I don't do any of that as we finally start to climb our gravel driveway, snow heavy and thick as we park inside one of the garages.

"Okay," is what I say, but it's a far away sound as I look up at the mill.

The house looks like a corpse. Lights out in all the windows, ominous shadow of the building looming like a living, breathing thing that's just died. It unsettles something inside my gut, a swirl of unease licking at my insides. Hair prickles up on the back of my neck and I slip my hand into my jean pocket, finger the phone I haven't looked at since eight-am, and a sense of fore-boding falls over me, but I still don't take it out.

In silence, we exit the car. The garage door coming down behind us with a creak as we walk towards the house. Arrow slips his hands into his pockets, shoulders hunching up by his ears, both of us in nothing but blood dampened jeans and t-shirts, but I don't feel the cold as ice wind whips around us, snow hitting my exposed skin, eyes blinking hard as flurries of it assault us.

We take the stone steps up to the front door, two at a time, both of us increasing our pace. I push the door wide, Arrow calling out for Rosie, I can't speak, my mouth dry, unable to swallow as acid burns its way up the back of my throat. I can feel something wrong here, taste it.

I start to run down the hallway. Hands propelling me around the corner at the end, I sprint through the dark house, skidding to a stop in front of the library. I stop, squinting my eyes into the darkness, listening, I hear them, Tyson and Duke, a very, *very* low rumbling of a growl.

Rosie quickly gets to her feet, wobbly as she stands, wide eyes on mine from the couch, room in darkness.

"They're safe," she tells me, a tremble in her voice.

"Thank you," I breathe the words as Rosie steps up to me. "Are you okay?" I ask, knowing something is very wrong here.

Her hand squeezing mine, she nods firmly, passing me by, softly spoken words for the brother at my back as she does.

I step into the library, the growling heightening, Arrow and Rosie's footsteps echoing at my back.

"It's me," I tell the dogs loudly, and the noise stops instantly, a whimper from Tyson, sniff and snort from Duke as they get to their feet behind a leather couch, both of their heads peering around the side of it.

I walk over to them, rubbing their heads, "good boys," I say roughly, knowing something is very wrong, but I need to see my babies before I can think about the other thing that's wrong inside this house.

I step between them as they part for me, drop into a

crouch, finding the second from bottom shelf of books, large black leather spine eleven from the right. I hook my fingers over the top of it, press them to the screen that sits inside it, a single beep of recognition, and then the bolts start to grind and click, sliding free of the steel panel they lock into. The bookcase starts to sink into the wall, sliding back and to the right.

Automatic lights blink on, running the length of the short hallway and down the curved, narrow stone stairs. I take the six short steps down, following the tight curve, lights on each stair, lighting the way. I can hear Atlas shushing his brothers as they hear my bootsteps over their heads, and my heart twists, because I know they're by themselves. When I reach the bottom, I drop into a crouch, knock on the panel beneath the staircase, the small eight-foot squared cubby hole we carved out for the boys, their mama. I push those thoughts away, into a far corner of my mind to focus on the task at hand.

"Boys, it's Daddy, open the door, it's okay now," I say calmly, a very quiet shuffle, and then a smack on their door release button, another shuffle, the door sinking into the space and sliding left.

My three brave boys stare back at me, and my eyes fill with tears, heart singing with relief. Atlas on his knees before me, shielding his bothers behind him. He rushes into my open arms, throwing himself at me so hard he knocks the breath out of me. I hold him so tight I'm sure he can't breathe but I need to feel him. My chin over his shoulder, River leans against the far wall, a big blanket wrapped around him and baby Roscoe, a bottle in River's chubby hand, he holds it in his baby brother's mouth, Roscoe's fingers clasped around his brother's over the bottle.

"Daddy! You found us!" he beams at me, like we've been playing a big game of hide and seek.

"I'll always find you, Trouble," I half choke, thinking about what this means, what I'll have to do next.

My eyes stick to my two youngest like glue, Atlas firmly secured in my arms, the safest fucking place he could ever be. There's a box of open crackers, biscuit crumbs on the floor, fruit juice boxes pierced with straws, crushed water bottles, nappy bag open, milk, blankets, clothes. Much more than what we stocked this space with.

"You get all this for your brothers, Atty?" I ask him, my lip pressing kisses to the side of his head, he nods against me.

"Mummy told me to get the nappy bag," he mumbles against my throat, his face buried in my neck.

"You got the rest, and you got them down here safely," he nods, little fists screwed up in the back of my t-shirt. "You're my brave boy, so clever, such a good boy, Atty." I praise him, hot little tears soak into my skin and I don't let go of him, I stroke a hand up his back, the other pinning him to my chest.

"You're a good boy, River, for doing what your brother told you to do," I call over to him, tears threatening to spill over.

He beams at me, "Atlas looking after us!" he shouts

with excitement, and my chest caves, heart thudding so heavy and hard.

"Good, that's good," I force out, breath shuddering through me.

Atlas's little arms loosen, and I reluctantly give him the space to pull back from me, mismatched, watery eyes on mine, he licks his lips.

"Mummy told me not to look," he confesses, keeping his eyes on mine, I wait, let him huff out a breath. "I looked." He drops his gaze, sniffing hard.

"It's okay, baby," I coo, reassuring him, still holding onto his waist as he stands before me.

"Mama ran, but I think the bad men got her."

CHAPTER 20

GRACE

Cymbals crash inside my skull, stomach swirling with sickness, eyelids sticking together, I try to pry them apart without moving my aching body. The surface I'm laid on is cold, hard, smooth, I'm on my side, cheek flush with the ground, something stuck to the skin of my neck, hair stuck to it, my head spins again even though I don't move, my throat constricting as my belly revolts, it makes me curl into myself tighter, my coat's still on, but there's a chill down my spine.

I breathe through the shooting pain that explodes in the front of my head, eyes heavy and thick. I want the ground to suck me down, my body sink into it, disappear with the darkness, safety suffocating me. The back of my hand rests against the smooth surface beneath me, knuckles tight, fingers half curled into my palm, I flex them, the pain enough to make me stop but I do it anyway, my stomach lurching as I do so.

Head pounding, I pry my eyes open, desperately trying to keep the contents of my stomach exactly where it is. I try to swallow, throat dry, lips cracked, sticking together with the saliva that's escaped my lips, dried on the side of my face where I lie in a ball. Blinking, eyelids weighing a hundred pounds, I crack them open, slits of vision all I can manage.

Droopy eyes roll down to the surface beneath my face, darkness greets me, but I can make out the black and white chequered floor beneath my cheek. I take my time, not moving anything but my tired eyes, the space I'm in feels large, echoey, like the ceilings are really high. Taking it slow, I glance up above my head, nothing to see but dense darkness, I blink slowly, trying to clear the gritty feeling on my eyeballs.

A door slams, and I jolt awake, slight panic at having blacked out again, I force my eyes open, and it's still dark. I swallow, sickness threatening but I swallow it down, the feeling of needing to throw up over-whelming but I take in a slow breath through my nose, nostrils flaring. I curl my fingers, try to focus on staying awake.

Footsteps echo around me, could be one pair of feet, could be fifty, everything loud and echoed back to me, confusion making my head spin. I breathe, nice and slow, tempering the sick feeling in my belly. The foot-steps receding, silence blanketing me once again. Curling my fingers, blinking slowly, trying to keep my eyes open, bring myself into awareness, I roll onto my back. Brain sloshing around inside my skull, I lie still, stretch out my bent legs, my arms, starfishing myself to the floor.

I blink open my eyes, crust in my lashes, I reach up, wiping at each of them, picking at my eyelashes, rubbing my knuckles over my closed lids. The effort feels exhausting, and I lie still for another long moment, time seemingly ungraspable. I feel suspended, my head and body and the world all disconnected from one another. An internal struggle, sickness, rush of breath, I swallow it all back, force myself to keep my eyes open.

My mind wanders away from me as I lie still, my body slowly starting to switch back online. I think of Hunter, when I was giving birth to Atlas, how wild his eyes were, overwhelmed with love.

"Hunter," I call from the bathroom, underside of my bare feet sweaty on the floor tile, I curl my toes beneath my feet where I perch on the edge of the tub.

The bathroom door open, our observatory style window is all I see, fingers curling tightly over the rim of the bath, I squeeze the porcelain as pain slices through my lower back. Breathing evenly, deeply, in through my nose, out through my mouth. I focus on the trees beyond the window, the sun just setting, the sky a sea of pinks and lilacs, beautiful. It'll be dark soon, it's already late but it's July ninth, the start of the summer is here, and it's been hot, it is hot. And I'm carrying a lot of extra weight with our son snug inside of me.

I glance down myself, my swollen belly decorated with jagged thin lines, my pale skin stretched to what feels like breaking point.

It's itchy and tight and uncomfortable, it makes me want to claw it all off, but, instead, I press my hand to the top of my exposed belly, nothing but a bra and knickers on my body, run my palm over my bump. Muscles cramp in my lower belly, my bum, my back and I grit my teeth.

"Hunter?" I call again, knowing our bedroom door is open, he'll hear me.

I twist to the side, drop the stopper into the bath, and twist the taps for some water, cold on full, hot on half. I test it with my fingers beneath the steam, warm water pumping out quickly. I let it run, turn back to face the open bathroom door. Watch the pale pink sky change to deep orange-reds when he appears.

My chest heaves as he stops in the doorway, shadow falling across me, those dark, penetrating eyes on mine, rolling down my body.

"Gracie?" his brow drawing in, he steps into the bathroom, eyes studying my face.

"The baby's coming," I tell him softly, even as pain fires across my belly, my insides feeling like they're shifting and churning, I work hard to keep my cool.

"Yeah?" he asks me so softly, so awestruck, not a lick of fear on his beautifully handsome face.

"Yeah," I whisper.

He crosses the space between us, wide toothy smile on his face, I expect him to grab my belly, but he clasps my face in his large hands instead. Kissing my forehead, my nose, my cheeks, my lips, I smile beneath his kisses, his tongue slipping into my mouth, long, luscious licks of his tongue against mine. I grip a handful of his t-shirt, twist it between my fingers as pain pinches my lower back. I kiss him, pull him in, keep him close. He holds my face, cradling my cheeks, pulls back to look down at me, his nose brushing mine.

"You're so beautiful," he breathes, the words pressed into my lips where his mouth remains slanted over mine.

I look up at him, watching as he stands, his warm hands leaving my face. He tests the water, sweeping a hand through the filled tub, fingers curl into his palm before he flicks the droplets of water from his skin, shaking out his hand. He switches off the taps, offers me a hand. Heaves me up to my feet, pulling me into him, kissing my forehead, he unsnaps my bra, peels it down my arms. Hooks his thumbs beneath the sides of my knickers, pushing them down my legs. I lean on his shoulder as he bends down, crouching at my feet, eyes up on mine, he lifts my feet free, placing a kiss on my arches, one at a time. Kissing up my calves, the inside of my knees, his knuckles grazing my soft skin, leaning back, he holds my ankles in his fists, a little tight, but it's what we do.

"I love you, Gracie," he tells me with something thick in his throat, a sheen to his dark eyes.

"I love you, Hunter."

And in the early hours of July tenth, bathed in the heavy darkness of the night, Hunter delivers our son. A single candle flickering on the other end of the tub, my knees wide, bones pressing into the porcelain. Bathroom door shut, separating us from the bedroom full of health professionals for those 'just in case' moments. My arms hanging limp over the sides of the tub, head laid back, water cold, tired eyes on Hunter's, our tiny baby protected in his giant hands, nestled in the crook of his neck.

"Atlas," I breathe the word quietly, my eyes bouncing between the two of them.

Hunter looks down at the bundle in his arms, reddened skin, mess of thick black hair, Hunter looks up at me, his face in shadow.

Reaching out to cradle my face with his free hand, "Atlas," he whispers.

Staring up at the ceiling, the darkness clearing a little, my vision still cloudy, I stare through the shadows, the ceiling so high I can't see where it ends. Letting my head loll to the side, I see huge light-coloured columns, arched windows with clear glass, darkness beyond them. I turn my head to the other side, liquid sloshing around inside my brain, survey all parts of the room I can without overworking my aching head, and there's nothing. Pillars, arched windows, clear glass, black and white chequered floor for as far as I can see.

Lifting my arm that feels like a piece of lead, it trembles as I lift it into the air, let it flop down hard onto my tummy. My fingers crawl towards my coat pocket, tugging open the popper that requires a ridiculous amount of effort, I slide my hand inside, finger my switchblade. Grateful it's still there, amongst the little handful of leftover stones I offered up to Atlas. Tears sting my face as they seep free, but I don't cry, I slow my breathing, keep my eyes open, vision slowly clearing the longer I manage to keep them open.

Another door slams and I flinch, closing my pocket, and dropping my arm. The footsteps approach this time, closer and closer until they stop just behind my head, I don't try look back, my head pounding, shoots of pain fizzing around the inside of my skull.

"Grace," the voice scratches, and my mind tumbles, trying to seek out the familiarity. "No hello for your dear old dad?" he chuckles, an awful crackling sound that makes me wince. "Oh, maybe that knock to the head I gave you damaged your vocal cords as well as your brain, huh?" I lie still. "Fuck, you're strange, come on, darlin', up ya get," he crouches behind me, arms sliding beneath my upper back, hands hooking beneath my armpits, he drags me up to sitting, yanks me roughly to my feet.

Everything tilts, vision flickering with white spots, my feet not under me, he shakes me, hold on my upper arm not enough, I feel myself sliding until his other hand grabs me from behind. He drags me over to a dark corner, hefting me up into a chair. I collapse as he releases me, sloping down in the chair, my head dropping back, neck cracking, eyes fixed on the ceiling. My stomach churns, throat burning with acid, I swallow, trying to get my body to dissolve itself of pins and needles.

I try to curl my fingers, but I can't feel anything, a thread of panic tumbles through me, then Michael's face fills my line of vision and I feel sick all over again. He grabs my face roughly, finger and thumb pinching my chin, tearing my floppy head up. He's so close I can hardly focus, his nose way too close to mine.

"According to my girl," I blink at that. "You got a

thing for rules," he raises a brow at me, something knowing in his gaze, and I think of Mother.

Mother is dead…

"So, here's how this is going to go," he hisses, his breath like stale cigarettes, making my stomach roll. "You're going to sit quietly, do as you're told. I've already made a call to your new daddy for ransom. He'll pay my debts, line my pockets with a little extra, and you get to go home, but I'm making him sweat a little first for disrespecting me. And *you,* I haven't quite decided what I'm going to do to you yet," he pauses, eyes flicking between my blurry ones. "For disrespecting my girl, thinking you're better than her, just 'cause you got money now," he snarls, top lip pulled high on his face, muddy brown eyes narrowed. "You understand?"

I blink hard, trying to get my bearings, pick through everything he just said.

"Yes? No? Are you dumb? Damaged? Rachel said you were thick as shit, didn't realise just how bad." He shakes his head as though in disgust, like my intelligence has anything to do with him. "The fuck is *wrong* with you?" he spits the questions rapidly, shaking his head. "Do you fucking understand?" he snaps, using his grip on my face to nod and shake my head with his words.

"Yes," I choke out, my own voice rattling my brain, everything too loud, too fuzzy, too much.

He releases my face, stepping back, turning away from me, muttering under his breath, "dumb cunt," he disappears back into the darkness.

Rachel.

I knew she was wrong, something bad, but Thorne checked her. What is happening?

I can't do anything but try to get my head to stop spinning, stomach to stop churning. I manage to pull myself up straighter in the chair, my elbow bashing into what I feel out is a table. I run my hands over the wood surface, fingers seeking anything that might be sat upon it. I pull myself to my feet, head spinning, body tilting, but I cling onto the table, bow over it a little, helping me find my balance.

I think of how unlucky I was in the parent department, Mother who hated the very sight of me, locked me up in an evil school. Father who only sought me out for something sinister, wanting to use me for money.

And I've let a stranger into my house, care for my children, roam about my safety, presumably report back on it all. Maybe I am stupid.

He's wrong about Dad though, Dad won't pay, he'll come and get me instead, with my brothers, my Hunter.

Shuffling along the side of the table, feeling my way as I go, my fingers touch cold metal, I run my fingers over it, the smooth surface curved, a little nodule raised on one side, I push on it, clicking, and a sudden burst of light has my eyes squeezing shut. A lamp.

I keep my eyes closed, not really wanting the light, because with the light comes the shadows, but I need to be able to see what's around me, see if there's anything I can use. Something to get me away from here. But I don't know where I am, I don't know how to drive, despite Dad's best efforts to get me behind the wheel. I told him everything I need is already at the mill, what would I ever need to leave for. I think my question stumped him because his mouth opened and closed so many times with silence, he reminded me of a fish in the lake. I'm wondering now if I should learn to drive, after all.

There's nothing on the table, just the lamp with no wires, so it must have a battery or something to make it work. I peer through slits, my eyelids trying to protect my painful head from too much brightness. Some papers and a pen, a bottle of water that's already open. I contemplate the risk with drinking from an open bottle, but my dry mouth decides it's worth the gamble and I take a small sip of the cold liquid. It tastes like water, but I'm unsure if poison tastes of anything, so I only drink enough to wet my tongue.

I take the metal pen, placing it into my pocket, the one without the knife and then I make my way back to the chair. Slump down in it, feeling grateful I still have my coat, because it's in the minuses and this room is the largest space I think I've ever been inside of.

The glow from the lamp allows me enough light to take in the delicate wooden carvings on the wall behind me, chair and table I'm at, set up in a corner. I can't see any doors and the windows are huge but high up and they don't look like the type of window that opens, just ones that draw in the light.

I snuggle down in my coat, unsure what I should do. What I *could* do. The longer I sit, the easier my head feels, my stomach finally settling, a bubbling in it every now and then but nothing that gives me the urge to vomit. I only got morning sickness with River, it's why Hunter calls him Trouble, because he was always causing trouble even from inside my belly. My morning sickness came at all hours of the night, my head permanently down our toilet for the first five months, and then one day it just stopped.

My numb fingers start to fizz back to life, arms folded over my chest, hands tucked beneath my armpits for warmth. I breathe a little easier, thinking about how I'm not tied up, but I could be. Hands tied behind my back or wrists and ankles secured to this chair. I wonder if it's to make me feel more comfortable before they do something horrible to me. Or if it's just because they think I'm stupid. Not a risk.

Either way I'm grateful, everything hurts enough as it is.

I watch a little brown moth throw himself into the bulb, his shadow much bigger than he is, he bashes into the warmed glass, wings fluttering, vibrating with the effort of reaching the light. If only he knew he was far safer in the dark. *Like me.*

I let my chin drop forward, the tip of it resting in the puffy fabric of my coat, think of the Victoria sponge cake I made yesterday, filled with cream and strawberries, carved in the shape of a love heart. I told Rosie it was for Hunter's after sex snack, themed for Valentine's Day, she snorted so hard she choked on her tea. It brings a small smile to my face. I let my eyes fall closed, keep my arms tight around me.

"Grace!" Mother hisses, her fingers snapping in front of my face, her nails catching the tip of my nose.

My eyes fly open, hands gripping the seat of my chair, I lean far back, my head and neck protesting as I draw back as far as I can get.

"Stupid girl!" she shouts, her spittle hitting my face, I blink, eyelashes fluttering as she gets in my face. "You can't sleep, there are things you need to be doing, you *idiot!*" she screams, words snarled through her bared teeth.

Blonde hair perfectly coiffed, delicate curls around her shoulders. Hazel eyes burning into my skin, I instantly drop my gaze, instinct kicking in, never to look Mother in the eye. I push my hands into my pockets, feel the smooth pebbles inside, the cool metal of my blade, pen in the other. I keep my gaze down, feeling her hot breath down the side of my neck. My head swims, memories and thoughts trying to wade their way through thick sludge, but all I can focus on is the way she looms over me.

Pressed pencil skirt, tucked in cream blouse. I glance up at it, the part covering her chest, pearlescent buttons done up to the base of her throat. Red blooms there, slowly spreading like unfurling wings of a butterfly. Seeping and soaking into the silk fabric, I watch it spread out like an exploding firework, the dark crimson mesmerising my achy head. I focus on it in front of me, ignoring her taunts whispered in my ear.

She isn't stopping, even as blood has overtaken the cream of her blouse, soaking into her skirt. And I wonder if this is even really happening at all, but Hunter told me what to do, who I am, how I can beat her.

'If you see Mother again, you kill her dead, Gracie, you hear me? You close your eyes, you count to five, that's enough, that's all you have to do. Show her how little you care; how little she matters. You are the darkness, baby girl.'

I'm not afraid.

I close my eyes, breathing evenly, I count to five, taking my time, but even as I get to five, I can feel her there, her fingers on the outside of my knee. I jolt, eyes snapping open, murky blue ones stare back, it takes me a second to process, my head pounds, eyes blinking heavily as a man leans over me. It's *his* breath down the side of my neck, *his* face too close to my own, *his* hand on my knee where my skirt has been pushed higher over my thick tights. I don't even think about it. My fingers curl around the pen in my pocket, elbow tearing back, I slam the pen into his eye.

With a bellowed yell, he jerks back, grabbing his face, I keep hold of the pen, blood dripping from it onto the skirt of my dress. My chest heaves and my stomach churns again, but I blink my way back to consciousness. The guy I just stabbed on his knees, yelling at me, but I don't pay attention. I peer around in the darkness, the little lamp a dull orange glow. I don't need the light from the lamp to see, my eyes will adjust, despite how tired they are, I'll be able to see. It's where I spend most of my time after all, in the darkness.

'We're safe in the darkness, aren't we, baby?'

I force myself out of the chair. Hands propping me

up on the table, wobbly legs beneath me, shaking as I reach across the wooden surface, I click the lamp off, plunging the small area into darkness.

The space I'm in is huge, everything echoing, the one-eyed man's cries wail now with whimpers over anger, the sounds bouncing. I slip away, my head still spinning but a new sense of determination strengthens me, darkness injected into my veins, penetrating my bones, I find the wall, wooden carvings beneath my palm. I follow it along, my footsteps silent, the crying man far away from me now. I hear a door open on the other side of the room, and I focus in on the sounds.

Another man barking something, obviously finding his bleeding friend, I rest against the wall, my back flush with it, bloodied pen in one hand, switchblade in the other. I finger the button on the little knife, but I don't press it, I just hold it, not too tight, but firmly in my grip. I calm my breathing, adrenaline rushing through me like a living thing, feeding my monster, stroking the fire in my belly.

Another door slams shut somewhere, another set of footsteps, a voice I recognise, *gorgeous*. I shudder, thinking of the pain in my head, but I push it back, stay still and silent. I can hear them rushing around the room to find me, which means there can't be any working lights, or they'd have turned them on to seek me out, which works to my advantage.

The table lamp goes on again, I can see it's dim glow, it's easily a hundred-feet away. Someone drags the wounded man across the floor, telling him to *shut the fuck up*, they shove him into the chair I vacated, his hands over his face.

Another man steps into the small circle of light, and I know this one too, Michael.

"What the fuck were you even doing out here?" Michael bellows, bending forward, getting in the bleeding man's face, even though the man sobs now. "Fucking idiot!" he smacks his hand into the side of his head, making the man in the chair cry out, hands still over his eye. "You can't fuck the merchandise before we get the money, you dickhead, I told you *after*," he snarls and my insides knot.

I don't want any of these men touching me.

I don't want to have to hurt anyone.

Kill them.

But I'm not prey.

My heart thuds hard in my chest, short, shallow breaths of panic hissing through my teeth. With my hand, I cover my nose and mouth, letting my eyes squeeze closed. In my other hand, I fist the pen hard, feel the warm metal of my little knife against my lips. Take comfort in the fact I decided to start keeping it on me whenever I head outside.

The men start to scramble, knowing I can't escape, I stay stock still, mouth covered, but eyes adjusted to the dark, open. Four men took me, which means there could still be one man left in this building that isn't in this room right now.

Alert, ears pricked, I listen, peer through the darkness, no one finding me yet as they pace the room with torches, and I start to wonder how much of what is happening is real.

I think of Hunter, how very, very real he is, how he protects me, will always find me. My fingers uncover my mouth, stroking across my jaw, down the column of my throat, dipping into the fresh tooth marks he chewed into the side of my neck. I think of the scar on my left thigh, something *I* chewed there, the last time we were separated. Taste the blood, feel the scar burning.

I'm real.

This is real.

Mother is dead.

"*Graaaaccce,*" someone calls in the darkness, and I realise he's much too close to me, but I don't run, I don't play games with strange men who want to hurt me.

I bide my time, half hoping he finds me, the other half of me hoping he doesn't. I flex my curled fingers, pen in one hand, knife in the other, I take a few steps to my left further away from where they started their search and I bump into someone.

"Boo!" he hisses in my ear, grabbing for me.

I lurch to the side, slipping past him, but his fingers knot in my hair, wrenching me back, my head screaming with pain, I can't stop the strangled sob from leaving my mouth. I lash out, arm arcing out, but he grabs my wrist, twisting my arm up and back, and the pen goes clattering onto the tile floor.

"Little bitch," he hisses in my ear, venom spat with each word.

He shoves me forward, my head tilts, stomach

rolling, my foot rolls, crunches and a sharp pain pulses in my ankle as my knees hit the floor. I brace on my hands, a single torch light getting closer now, footsteps approaching, I fist my knife tighter in my curled fingers. I heave, acid burning its way up my throat, but I keep it down, pant hard through my nose.

Torchlight flickers across the floor, and I tuck my knife tighter into my palm, the blade still closed. The guy behind me shifts, his hand coming down hard on my back, splaying over my spine, my hips pressing into the floor. Puffer coat the only thing separating me from his touch, his weight comes down on his hand, squeezing the breath out of my lungs, my stomach tightening.

Michael shines the torch over my face, my eyes squeezing shut, I try to peer up at him through slits, his shadowed face twisted in a disgusted snarl.

"Let me teach her a lesson, Mike, for Letty," the guy pressing me down says, a heightened bite of excitement in his tone.

I stare up at the man with whom I share blood, his eyes narrowing slightly, and I think that maybe he'll say no, get this man off of me. Instead, he grunts, shaking his head and turns away, fast, clipped footsteps echoing in his wake.

The man at my back chuckles, dipping his head down so his words are spoken directly into my ear, the darkness engulfing us once more.

"This'll hurt," is all he says on a sinister breath, he

holds me down, hand flat on my spine, and I hear his belt buckle clink.

My head thuds, heartbeat roaring in my ears, but I stay still, I keep calm, even as he flips up my skirt, rough knuckles grazing the soft skin of my lower spine where he tugs on my woollen tights. I wait until he leans back, his weight on my spine shifting, and I kick out. My heel connects with his chin, his teeth clacking together, he tears his hand off of me, and I use the freedom to flip over onto my back.

My brain feels like it's sloshing around inside my skull, eyes bursting with spots of white, dizziness making me want to vomit. I kick at him again, flat heel of my boot catching him in the centre of his chest, and he shouts a howl, my cold, clammy hands hurrying me backwards. All too quickly he's on me again, trying to pin my legs, his hand pressing down on my lower belly, I grit my teeth even as my head swims and black edges my vision.

"Now I'm really going to make it hurt, you little cunt," he snarls at me, shoving his trousers down, his belt buckle clinking as it hits the floor, and I'm grateful I can't see.

I breathe out, my lungs burning, a sheen of cold sweat dampening my face, long hair tangled and caught beneath my back. He tries to hold my ankles, unable to grip both as I kick my legs, flailing now, because if he pins me I'll never be able to get him off. He smacks at my inner thighs, my skin on fire with the force, but I don't stop kicking out my legs. Sometimes connecting, sometimes not.

But when he drops his body down onto mine, weight crushing my chest, hand locked around my ankle, knee bent and flush with the floor. His arm shoved between us, chubby fingers tearing into the crotch of my tights, I press the button on my knife and slam it into his cheek.

He rears back screaming so loud I want to cover my ears, instead, my fingers stay firmly secured around the hilt of my knife, I don't let go, don't pull it free. Holding on tight, the force of his movement dragging me up from the floor with him, double edged blade slicing through the flesh of his cheek, right to the corner of his lips, where it pops free of his mouth, carving through his cheek.

Warmth splatters my face and I stumble back, trying to find my feet, eyes adjusted to the dark, I see the skin of his face flapping, his hands hovering over his face, his tongue clucking in the gaping hole. I slip, landing hard on my arse, a shock of pain bolting up my spine, fizzing in the back of my skull like an electrocution and I blink hard to clear my vision.

A door opens and closes again, the slam of it echoing across the vast, empty space and I look to the far corner, lamp on the table showing the guy, Letty, still slumped down in the chair, arms flopped at his sides now.

The huge man in front of me wails, flailing around where he writhes on the floor, and I panic, because I'm not a killer. I don't want to put corpses on the cold slab in my basement, I just want to play with them once they get there. Sometimes I make them better, sometimes I take their insides apart, but I'm not hurting anyone when I do. Tears spring to my eyes then because I feel all out of sorts, and I don't want to be here, doing this, I just want to go home to my boys.

Footsteps are rushing in my direction, two pairs this time, the man by the table still slumped in his chair. Torchlight bounces around the floor, two sources of light aimed at the man I just made bleed. This second pair of footsteps has to be the fourth man that took me, and I can only hope that there aren't any more hiding away behind the walls.

I walk on my hands back across the floor, using the cover of darkness, and the sounds of his sobbing to hide the sounds of my hands, wet and slippery on the tiles. Their torches honed in on their bleeding companion, I get to my feet, walk backwards until my back is flush with the opposite wall. My hands are slick with blood, sliding over wooden carvings, smooth painted surfaces.

I'm moving in the opposite direction to them, when my fingers find what feels like a doorframe. I slide my palm over it, my hand disappearing inside a gap, knocking into more wall etchings about a foot deep, it's an alcove.

I run my fingers over the carved frame, my booted foot knocking a low platform, I lift my leg, the cold air prickling my exposed skin, on show through my torn tights. Finding the small step up, I tuck myself inside the space, my back to the side of the arch, and torchlight flares over my hiding space, continuing on along the wall.

I listen to the men talking, low murmurs, angry tones, Michael's voice booming over the rest.

"I want her found!" he bellows, his accomplice hissing something I can't catch in return, "we need her alive until the money's deposited, then you can get your revenge. And not a single second before our debt's paid, Tony. The Ashes don't fuck around; we need to sort this shit today or we're all fucked."

There're grunts of agreement, a lower groaning now from the bleeding man and no one seems to see me yet. I watch their lights dance frantically across the huge space, and I can see it a little better now, the black and white chequered floor looks like marble, the walls at least thirty-feet high, domed ceiling even higher. Perhaps some sort of showroom.

I watch as Michael crosses the room, his torchlight flicking side to side as he goes, he leans over the guy by the lamp, Letty, shaking his shoulder, making him grunt, but he doesn't seem to rouse. Not that it looks as though Michael cares anyway, his posture is tense, and he seems more aggravated than upset by the state of his friend. I follow him with my gaze, tracking him across the room, his light not even attempting to locate me, he disappears inside a door, no light from inside spilling out. It makes me think there either isn't any electricity, or they shouldn't be inside this building and are trying not to draw attention with lights on.

I contemplate my options, wonder if I should

attempt to make my way there. Maybe find a door out of here I could escape through, find a place outside to hide in until my family comes for me. My head thumps, legs trembling, and I feel like I might be sick. Needing to be quieter, no matter my decision, I peel off my knee-high boots without further thought. I swallow down the bitter taste in the back of my throat, acid burning in my chest, and I feel my eyelids droop, a shiver wracking through me.

It's only when I start to slide down the wall, the swishing sound of my coat rubbing against it alerting me, that I suck in a sharp breath, just as a gun goes off. I jump, instantly forcing myself to freeze, the room in silence, my heart in my throat, ears ringing like a high-pitched siren, and it's the first time today that I think I might die.

"Get out here, right now, or when I find you, I will fucking shoot you, girl," my father barks and my blood runs cold as his tone reminds me of Mother.

The way she would get in my face, force my gaze to the floor, her spit against my cheek as she screamed at me. When she would tie my hand to the metal pole of our kitchen island, leaving me alone beneath it for what felt like days until she returned, only for the abuse to continue in a different way. How I've spent my whole life trying to get the courage to pluck out my own eyeballs, avoiding my own gaze, reflection, making sure to never look anyone directly in the eye.

And I'm not sure how I make my way so silently across the floor. Woollen tights whispering across the marble, but I'm only a foot or so away, his back to me, and rage boils through my veins like a volcano readying to erupt. The feral roar that rips its way up my throat has Michael spinning around, a look of complete horror on his shadowed face as my blade connects with his neck.

It sinks into the hollow of his throat, blood spurting from the wound as I pull the knife out, gun clattering to the floor, I stab him in the neck again. His eyes wide, mouth open, I tear my knife back out. Hands grabbing his throat, he squeezes, and even in the darkness I can see the dark blood oozing out quickly between his clasped fingers.

Coughing, blood and spittle splashing my face, I blink, eyelashes heavy with crimson. Stepping back, I watch as he drops to his knees. Hands quickly going slack, they start to drop from his neck, body falling to one side, he slumps unforgivingly to the floor. I keep my eyes trained on him, even as my feet move me away, and despite the throbbing of my head, thudding of my heart, I feel suddenly lighter inside.

I wonder for just a moment, why I couldn't have had a father like Stryder for all of my life, why I got so unlucky with Mother. Cursed, tainted from birth, something dark always looming inside of me. Maybe my darkness came later, did I find it, or did it find me?

I think of Hunter as I make my way across the room in darkness, hearing the other two men across the room, one heaving, probably the injured one, the other man shouting, but I can't hear him clearly. Can't pick through his words, can't focus on anything but the man slumped in the chair, illuminated by the orange glow of the lamp.

Unconscious when I approach, I don't hesitate, don't look at the grisly wound in place of an eye. I simply line up the edge of my blade at his throat, dig deep, carving a curved line straight across his throat. He doesn't wake, gurgling as his lungs start to fill with blood, it sputters out of his mouth, running like a river down the front of him from the slice in his throat.

Everything feels numb, teeth chattering, I feel as if I'm hardly here. Floating across the room, I find the man, Tony, crouched over his friend with the mangled face, and plunge my knife between his shoulder blades. Full force of my body weight behind it, since he's crouched, I have the advantage.

He goes crashing down to the floor, and I go with him. Landing hard on his back, knife handle stabbing at my chest, he topples on his friend, the guy sobbing beneath us both. He tries to throw me off, my knife still in his back, I huff as I free my blade. He elbows me hard in the chest, and I fly backwards, the wind knocked out of me, he looms over me as he stalks closer.

"God, I'm going to enjoy carving you up," he says sinisterly, my chest cramping, he reaches down, big hand grabbing my throat.

I arc my knife up, an ominous grin on his face, I stab him in the shoulder. He shakes me off, my blade stuck in his flesh. He drops me to the floor, *hard,* breathing like a raging bull, he peers down at me, goes to grab me again. I scrabble backwards, my hands and arse and feet all shuffling me away as fast as possible. Slick hands slipping with the blood on them, elbows hitting the unforgiving marble, I land flat on my back.

Taking the open opportunity, he drops down on top of me, straddling my stomach, his hand splaying over my chest, I arch up from the floor, one of his hands squeezing my throat, the one from my chest gripping both my hands high above my head, bashing my knuckles into the ground. He laughs, fingers tightening, breath cut off, heart thudding harder and harder, I spit in his face. He roars, wiping his cheek on his good shoulder.

"Fucking cunt!" he screams at me.

Dips his face down into mine, tip of his nose brushes my own, panting breath on my lips, my knife still protruding out of his shoulder. He seems unaffected, like he can't feel the stab wound in his back, the blade in his arm.

"I'm going to take my time killing you," he whispers over my mouth, and I snap my teeth down over his top lip.

Sucking his lip into my mouth, I bite down as hard as I can, lungs burning without air, he keeps squeezing my throat, my eyes forced shut with the pain, but I don't let go. Even as he slams my already painful head down into the marble floor, teeth aching, I bite harder, tearing at his mouth, I shake my head side to side. The inside of my skull sloshing around like the spin cycle of a washing machine without the laundry.

Head shaking side to side, he releases my hands,

smacking the heel of his hand into my temple. Stars bloom beneath my closed eyelids, blood flooding my mouth, running down my closed throat, urge to gag strong, I clench my jaw, and I feel when it tears. He wrenches his head back, his lip in my mouth, throat released, I slam up to sitting, twist the knife free from his shoulder and plunge it into his chest, twisting and shoving it deeper and deeper.

I spit his shredded lip out, blood and saliva dribbling freely from the corners of my mouth. I spit again, tear my knife out of him, shove him backwards with my shoulder to his chest, and he's dropping to the floor with a thud. I gasp for breath. Throat burning, pulse hammering in my neck, head dizzy, I brace my hands on the floor, get to my knees. Sit that way for what feels like seconds and days all twisted and warping into one when I hear a whimper.

Breathing hard through my nose, I blink, try to clear my cloudy vision. I find my knife, dropped beside my splayed hand, clumsily curl my numb fingers around it and crawl my way to the last man alive. The one who tore up my tights, so I tore up his face. It's slow going, dragging my beaten body to the worse off one in the centre of the room.

I hear him before I see him, peering through the darkness, his large form appears before me. A collapsed heap on the floor, his hands are up by his face and I shudder thinking of them all over me.

I'm not quiet in my approach, wet hands slapping over the marble, but he doesn't move, I can hear him muttering to himself, wet flapping of his baggy cheek, tongue clucking against his exposed teeth. I crawl right over him, and he doesn't try to fight me.

The darkness my friend, my safety, I let it fuel me, peer down into his droopy eyes, "*fuck you*," I whisper and slide my knife into his neck.

CHAPTER 21

HUNTER

The sky is pressing in, dense clouds bursting above us, heavy flurries of snow smattering my windscreen. I think of Atlas as I tucked him up in his bed before I left, telling me that it feels like his sky is falling down without his mummy.

His sky is falling down.

Bones in my fingers popping and cracking, knuckles blanched white, hands fisting the steering wheel, I careen around the tight corner, Arrow in the passenger seat this time as the city skyline comes into view. My heart is hammering beneath my rib bones, call with Thorne connected through the speakers.

"It's a gallery, Fernsby Hall. That's where Raine's traced the call back to," Thorne informs, deep voice rumbling through the car.

I think of the ransom call made to my father, from *hers*. Think of wrapping my fingers around his scrawny little neck and squeezing until his fucking face pops like a balloon.

Foot flat to the floor on the accelerator, tires screeching, I whip us around another corner, mounting the curb, dropping us back down onto the road with a thunk. Arrow's arm up in the air, hand curled through the handle above his door, he keeps his gaze focused on the road, even as I drive us like we're on a rally track and not dark, neglected, snow covered streets. Window wipers squeaking, they rocket back and forth, clearing the thick flakes of snow as they hit the windscreen like ice bullets.

"I'm going to fucking kill him," is what I say in response, Arrow doesn't look at me, but I see his nod of agreement from the corner of my eye.

"Not if you kill yourselves first," Thorne tuts, and I imagine him shaking his head, just the once, his expression not changing from his usual stoicism even once.

I laugh at that, a demonic chuckle, because I'd get to her dead if I had to.

"We're good," Arrow replies, even as he holds on tighter, free hand bracing against the dashboard as I swing us around another corner.

Back-end fishtailing before I right us, accelerating faster down the straight road.

"You're pushing one-ten," Thorne says, again, with indifference, everything synced up to Raine's monitors at a back-alley office in Bethnal Green.

I don't answer, I just rock back and forth in my seat, willing the car to go fucking faster.

Thorne stays connected, but the three of us share silence, nothing to be said, not until we get there. I think of her tied up, frightened, hurt, and my nostrils flare. If there is one single mark on her perfect fucking skin, I'm going to skin her fucking father alive and make him eat it.

"She'll be okay," Arrow says quietly, he's softly spoken, the *feeler*, the only one of us, other than Dad, that really knows how to be soft, or, well, show it.

"Shut up," I tell him through barred teeth, my tongue pushing up against the back of my teeth.

I grit them so hard my jaw cracks, and then I force out a breath, shake my head, suck in another.

"Sorry," I utter.

"Don't be," Arrow shrugs, and I hear Thorne shift, imagining him pushing a hand through his perfectly styled hair, black, wavy length always kept short and swept to one side.

"What don't we know?" Arrow asks after an extended silence. I glance at him from the corner of my eye. "I mean, how has this happened, how would anyone know we're not at the mill today? That we'd be out the way. How would anyone even *find* Heron Mill?"

We haven't invited anyone home since the boys were born, the last time anyone was over, other than the Swallows, was my twenty-sixth birthday party, and even that was extremely low-key.

"Raine's looking into camera feeds, see if we can track anything to or from the house, we only have the cameras we set up on our own land, the best we'll find is a vehicle to trace back to the city."

I don't say anything, Arrow silent too, and I decide I'm never leaving my family home alone ever a-fucking-gain.

A headache hits me again, and I grit my teeth at the shooting pain in the back of my skull, wipe my tired eyes with my knuckles.

"You're fifteen-minutes out," Thorne rumbles, Arrow answering him, we lapse into silence again.

There's no traffic, the outer edges of the city all sleeping peacefully in their beds as I whip past houses, flats, schools, closed up community buildings. Everything is bright, even in the dark, with the fresh snowfall. This is the most snow I've ever seen, and it's still falling.

"Black van, Mercedes," Thorne rattles off the number plate, Arrow responding.

There's a pause, a shuffle and Thorne clears his throat, his line buzzing as he switches to loudspeaker, all of our brothers there.

"It's- oh, woahhh," Archer's voice coming through, a low whistle on his last word.

"Who ran checks on the nanny?" Raine asks quietly, and I feel my veins freeze.

"I swear to fuck, if you didn't check her out properly!" I bark, my stomach fucking knotting, because Gracie said, she fucking told me something was wrong.

"What are you looking at, Raine?" Arrow asks calmly, softly.

I breathe hard through my nose, keep my eyes on

the road, squeeze the steering wheel as Raine's voice comes through.

"Michael and Rachel, I think-"

"*Think?*" I growl, interrupting him.

"I'm pulling up images, anything caught on a street cam with the van, over the last week…"

"They're kissing," Archer says, and it sounds as though he wants to vomit, but it's just his dick he's been sticking in her, I left my fucking kids with her.

"FUCK!" I roar, smashing my fist into the dashboard until my knuckles split, the entire car bouncing as I rock angrily in my seat.

"How did this happen?" Arrow asks quietly, but fuck that.

"Thorne!" I bark viciously, "how have you fucking missed this shit?!" I bellow down the phone.

"I…" he starts, sounding unsure, and my blood heats as quickly as my boiling temper.

"THEY'RE MY FUCKING KIDS!" I scream so loudly I can't even hear myself.

"I've fucked up," our eldest brother says quietly, a confession, and I can't even form words. "I don't- I'm sorry."

My lips pop open, but my mouth goes dry, I can't even respond. Thorne does not *fuck up*. It isn't in his fucking nature.

"Thorne," it's a hiss, his name feeling like acid on my tongue.

"Lay off him, it was a mistake, we all make mistakes," Wolf pipes up for the first time and I scoff.

"Where is she now? The fucking nanny?" I bark the question, not worrying about the boys, knowing Dad's at home with them, with Rosie, having arrived just as we were rushing back out of the door.

"I'll call Dad, update him," Archer says, "I'll find her," something dark twisting his tone.

"I want to deal with her," I growl lowly, "don't let on we know anything," I instruct, and no one argues with me.

"Two minutes," Arrow says, breaking the growing silence.

"Keep me on the call," Thorne instructs, and I want to smack him upside his fucking head, but I bite my tongue, don't say anything, focus on getting my girl back first.

Fernsby Hall comes into view, a tall, looming, white building, windows dark. I straighten, hitting the break hard as we approach the building, wheels skidding in the snow. Tires slipping, I pump the breaks, but the car starts to spin, I'm going too fucking fast, the back bumper slams into a lamppost, stopping the car with a loud bang, but I'm already throwing the door open, running up the front steps of the huge dark building.

There's no life around, all of the surrounding buildings closed up and in darkness too and it all feels too quiet. Snow crunches beneath my boots, brick steps taking me up to the huge arched doors. White marble columns on either side of the porch style front.

Arrow is close behind me, Bluetooth earpiece

connected to our oldest brother, being pushed into his ear.

"You 'ear me?" he asks Thorne, who must reply with confirmation because Arrow replies, "sweet."

And I'm grateful for my brothers, unable to be by my side physically, but still making the effort to be with me all the same. And although I'll never admit it, especially with what's just been uncovered, but it's Thorne I need in situations like these.

I twist the huge handles, expectantly finding them locked, but it still frustrates me all the same. Arrow pushes in front of me, shoulder shoving me back a step, moving me out of the way. Dropping to one knee, lock pick kit in his hands, he starts to fiddle with the handle. I'm too brash, impatient, tapping my foot and grunting with irritation.

Bitter wind rips around us, snow melting into my clothes, soaking my skin beneath, my cheeks ice, prickling with cold, I try to keep my breathing easy. Force myself not to knock Arrow out of my way, start throwing myself against the doors like a battering ram until their hinges crack, wood splits and I can get to my girl.

It doesn't bear thinking about, the possibility that she's not still here.

If she ever even was at all. Just because Michael called from here, doesn't mean he brought her here.

She has to be here…

Because if she isn't, I'm going to burn the whole fucking world.

I'm fucking coming for you, baby girl.

I let her down once.

Swore to never do it again.

And I'm not breaking my promise to her for anything.

Especially not her low-level, gang lackey bio-dad. Not fucking happening.

I roll my shoulders, crack my neck, shake out my fists, feel better with the weight of the gun resting against my lower spine, shoved down the back of my jeans. The one in a holster beneath my arm, knives in every pocket. It's overkill, this fucker and whoever he's got helping him with his suicide mission are no challenge for me and my brother. Arrow appears as the gentlest of us all, but behind those soft, reassuring smiles, kind, black eyes and poetic words of wisdom, is a blood thirsty fucking killing machine.

So when the locks click open, handle releasing and I'm barrelling past my younger brother to get to my fucking girl, I don't worry about him at my back, because I know he's got it, just as I have his.

I only have to rush through two short hallways, the building in ominous silence, my footsteps, although hurried, are long and quiet, boots whispering over the marble flooring. Darkness surrounds us, my brother close at my back, his almost soundless words to Thorne, we are silence, prepared, ready, vipers waiting to strike, bears waiting to maul. I am a fucking predator, *the* predator, and every fucker in this place is my prey.

The doors leading to the main gallery are locked,

Arrow once again down on one knee, he works quickly to get us entry, these doors opening far quicker than the first.

Further darkness greets us, I blink, heart thudding so slowly in my chest I wonder how I'm still functioning. I slip my way inside, door opening just enough for my brother and I to get our wide bodies through, Arrow closing it at our back. We're flush with the wall, his shoulder brushing mine, as we let our eyes adjust.

Blood, its rich, metallic smell, for most, is something you either gag on or are seemingly unaffected by, it's unpleasant but you're not particularly triggered by it.

But for me, usually, it gives me a dizzying sense of power, a high. Be it a life taken, body disposed of, death caked up my elbows, soaked into the fabric of a t-shirt, a hoodie. Sometimes it's the taste of it, on my tongue as it laps over my Gracie's plush pout, defined cupid's bow split by my teeth.

And other times, it doesn't feel as though it gives me any sort of power at all, quite the opposite in fact, draining me empty, filling Gracie with its power instead.

The room is silent, the air is thick, almost hard to breathe, as though, if you inhale just a little too quickly, too sharply, you'll choke on it. Straining my ears, the only thing I can hear is my own heartbeat, Arrow's slow breaths. There's nobody alive in this room.

I step forward, pushing off the wall, panic swirling around in my gut, but she can't be hurt, I would know, *feel* it.

I would have fucking felt it.

There's no way anything has happened to her. My breaths are faster, heart hammering, my ears buzz and I think of her not being here. Struggling against grown men, people much larger than her, stronger, and the panic is making it hard for me to feel anything when I hear it.

I still. Arrow stops moving, still flush with my back, when the almost silent 'wet snick' sounds again. Head tilting, eyes wide, I glance to the other end of the large space, the whole room echoes, the ceilings so high. Heart banging against my chest, threatening to crack my sternum, blood rushing in my ears, I think the familiar sound is just a wishful memory inside my head. But then I hear it a third time, and I *know*, but I still don't move.

Instead, I turn to my brother, wishing I could see his face properly in the dark, and I don't have to say anything, because he's already dropping his hand onto my shoulder, I'm handing him the gun holster, the one shoved down the back of my jeans, and he's turning back to the door we entered through.

Gracie doesn't like to be watched when she works.

CHAPTER 22
HUNTER

I follow the sounds on quiet feet, everything inside of me feeling uneasy, because despite what happened with her mother, my Gracie isn't a killer. She's nothing like me in that sense, she doesn't want to murder anyone. She still has an innocence about her that I want to help her keep forever.

A gentleness that she's instilling in our sons. How she never swats flies or crushes insects, the way she has one of our brothers hike her up onto their shoulders so she can catch and release spiders from ceiling corners. Switches off lamps to save moths, lets them settle, scoops them into her hands and takes them out into the darkness.

Darkness is our safety.

And I think I got it wrong. How I compared her once to a butterfly, poison-winged. That's not my Gracie, she's delicate, needs to be handled with care, is safer in the darkness, enjoys drifting through the shadows, but can still survive the light. She's a moth. Beautiful and fragile, strong and resilient. And there's nowhere I'd rather be, than fluttering through the darkness, with her.

Once upon a time, I wanted to destroy it, that seed of innocence, *her*, the whole fucking world could have been destroyed with her and I thought I wouldn't care. I lied to myself, then, now. Gracie isn't innocent, but she holds onto it like a candle in the dark for those of us without it. She's mine, my whole black fucking heart, and I will always protect what's mine.

"Gracie?" I call quietly, deep voice soft, breathing evening out.

The quiet noises stop, and my heart threatens to beat out of my chest.

"Hunter," it's not a question, there's relief in her voice but a knowing too, and then she says, "you always find me in the dark."

And I think of when I told her that, tears streaking her beautiful face, our bathroom flooded with water, grief, fear.

I smile.

"I will always find you in the dark, you beautiful girl."

"Hunter," she whispers, my footsteps carrying me closer, I can't see her yet, but I follow her voice like she's pulling my strings.

"Are you okay?"

"Yes," she answers. A small pause, and then, "I did a bad thing," she whispers so, so quietly, anyone else would miss it, but we don't speak loudly in our house, everyone using quiet voices.

She gets too overwhelmed with lots of noise, and being a family of seven men with a choir of deep voices, it certainly took some adapting, there's been more than one occasion where family dinners have ended with Gracie covering her ears. But we're better now, all of us.

"It's okay," I whisper back, "you're not in trouble," I coo softly, pausing in my approach. "Baby girl, I need you to tell me if I'm going to trip over anything."

"Oh," a short sound of surprise, and I picture her face, lips popped open, small crease between her brows. "Um, yes," she decides, my arms loose at my sides, I flex my fingers, knuckles cracking. "I'm going to come and get you."

"Okay, I'll stay right here," I tell her quietly, my voice just above a whisper.

I hear her shift, the swish of her coat, the water-proof fabric rustling, and I feel relief that she still has it on. Her silent steps don't give away her location, and it takes everything inside of me to wait, to be patient, when all I want to do is tear through the shadows, throw back the veil of darkness and sink into everything that's her.

I smell her, my nostrils flaring, thick, heavy, cloying blood hits me first, sharp, metallic, and so strong I can taste it on my tongue. Then her sweetness hits me like a shot of adrenaline to the heart, honeysuckles, ferns, that woodsy undercurrent. She's like our favourite places all rolled into one, the basement, the darkness, the forest.

I'm greedy, I inhale her deeply as her small body stops just before me, her silhouette revealing her in the obscurity.

"Hunter," she whispers, her wet, sticky fingers stroking along the sharp angle of my jaw.

My blood hammers through my veins, kickstarting every single inch of me, and my hands are fisting in her hair, my mouth is over hers, tongue sliding between her teeth. Her hands fist my t-shirt, one of my arms banding around her, forcing her up onto tiptoes, she arches into me as I devour her. She tastes of blood, strong, and rich and my dick kicks at the closed fly of my jeans.

Untangling my hand from her hair, I reach between us, tear the zipper of her coat down, soaked through with what I can only assume is blood. The thought makes me pull back, try to get a grip, control myself for just a second to check, to make sure, I need to know. Mouth slanted over hers, I break our kiss, hear her whimper, my breath pants across her lips.

"Did they hurt you, Gracie? Is any of this blood yours?" I ask her quietly, running my hand down the front of her body.

I know she has a white dress on, the neckline is square, exposing the upper portion of her chest, collarbones, her delicate shoulders with the palest smattering of light freckles from her time outside. Index finger tracing down her chest, between the valley of her breasts, I flick the tip of it over her hardened nipple.

"One of them hit my head," she whispers over my lips, and despite my insides fucking burning with the power of a hell demon wanting to raze the entire fucking world, I stay calm, let her finish.

But she doesn't, and I know there's more to the story.

"What else happened to you, baby girl?"

She pushes further into me, like she thinks I'll let go.

I'll never fucking let you go.

"This one…" and I feel her turn away from me, chin over her shoulder, eyes peering through the darkness at something I can't see.

Gently, I take her chin between my thumb and finger, turn her back to me.

"This one?" I repeat as a question, a calm whisper, I bite my tongue, to stop myself from rushing her, she won't tell me if I'm not patient.

Gracie came from a world of living in fear, following rules. There's no fear now, but we still have a few rules, just for her benefit.

"Blackwells don't tell lies," I remind her gently as I feel her swallow, my flared fingers grazing her throat, chin still in my grip.

"He ripped my tights," she says almost silently, but I stiffen, pinching her face, hand dropping to her throat, my fingers tighten around her like a collar, making her yelp.

My hand instantly drops from her neck, panic making my heart gallop beneath my rib bones.

"Gracie?"

"One of them hurt my throat," she says quietly again, but there's a thread of a sob in her words.

"Okay," I soothe, hand stroking her sticky hair back, thumb sweeping beneath her eye, fingers smothering one half of her face, thumb resting on her bottom lip. "The one who ripped your tights, Gracie. Did… did anyone touch you?"

My worst fucking fear is this, her getting hurt because I wasn't there. And I know I'm holding my breath, and I want to shut my eyes, but I keep them open, to face whatever it is she's going to tell me, because whatever happens, we'll always face everything together.

"No," she tells me, her breathing laboured. Then she whispers, "I cut off his hands, after I…" stopping herself from confessing her sins.

"After you?"

"Killed him," and the breath I held rushes out of my lungs and into hers as I cover her mouth with my own.

Tongue licking over hers, her teeth nicking the tip of it as I push my way inside her mouth, I groan into our kiss, her throat echoing something similar back. I kiss her hungrily, slowly, taking my time, I make fucking love to her mouth, before drawing back, pecking kisses all over her beautiful face.

"Rachel is-"

"I know, I'm sorry, I'm sorry I didn't listen to you," I rush out, interrupting her, "I'm so sorry I didn't listen to you."

She nods against me, swallowing, and I wish I could see her.

"The boys are safe," I tell her.

"I know," she replies instantaneously, knowingly, "that's why I didn't need to ask. You wouldn't be here yet if they weren't," tears spring to my eyes, and my heart explodes inside my fucking chest, and I wonder how the fuck I ever got this lucky.

Her breathy whimper draws me in closer, lips mauling across her cheek, tongue circling inside her ear, down the side of her neck, teeth scraping the column of her throat. She shudders, pressing herself into me, my cock throbbing against her lower belly, I shove at the shoulders of her coat, her arms shimmying the puffy fabric free.

Her coat hits the floor, her fingers on the button of my jeans, mine sliding beneath the shoulder straps of her dress, shoving that down her body too. She pulls my jeans open, fly zipper torn down, her small hand shoves beneath my boxers, fingers closing firmly around my dick, making me rock into her wet hand. Her breath hot and heavy on the hollow of my throat where she peers up at me, despite the room being bitterly cold.

I hook my thumbs beneath the sides of her tights, push them down her legs. She holds onto my shoulder with one hand as together, we thread her legs out of her knickers and tights. With that same hand she tugs at the shoulder of my t-shirt, I dip forward, skimming my lips over hers as I let her pull it over my head. Her hand squeezes tight around my cock, slowly rolling her fist up and down, I push my pants and jeans down with the heel of my hand, cup the back of her head with the other.

"Lay down for me, baby girl," she takes my hand in hers, letting go of my cock, she gets down onto the floor with me, both of us on our knees.

I smooth her hair back, clasp her face in my hands, kiss her lips. She shifts to sitting, parting her legs for me, I dip down with her, our lips sealed. My hand cradles the crown of her head as she lies back, shivering as her spine makes contact with the cold marble.

She smiles against my mouth as I cover her chest with my own, my lips plucking at hers tenderly. I run a hand down the length of her body, fingers and thumb bumping over rib bones, the dip of her belly, over the curve of her hip. Hand skating down her left thigh, feeling the jagged, raised scar, evidence from the last time she was separated from me. I squeeze her flesh, her body trembling beneath me, she nips my lip, her hands curled over my shoulders, fingers of one hand tangling in the hair at the nape of my neck.

Cock heavy and swollen, weeping against the silky skin of her belly, I lift up, her fingers, once again, closing around my length. This time, guiding me towards her tight entrance, pressing me against her slick flesh, the head of my cock leaking pre-cum. One hand planted beside her head, the other cradling her skull, I dip down, press my forehead to hers, our breath mingling.

"I love you, Gracie," I breathe into her, making sure she can taste the truth in my words.

She presses her lips to my mouth, tongue flicking over my bottom lip, before she draws back, lips still brushing over mine.

"I love you, Hunter."

She kisses me at that, tongue sinking into my mouth with ease and grace, gentle and loving, and then I'm snapping my hips back, surging forward, cock sinking into her in one harsh thrust. Spine lifting from the floor, nails clawing into my shoulders, gouging my flesh, she cries out in my ear, her pussy clamping down around me. I hiss through my teeth, our foreheads pressing tight together.

She clings onto me, nails carving in deeper, I feel it when she finally breaks skin, the little dribble of blood the slithers down my shoulder blade.

"Hunter," she breathes, my cock slamming into her harder and harder, shunting us across the floor.

"Gracie," I reply on a grunt, my teeth clenched, jaw popping.

"Please," she pants against my lips, "make it hurt."

My thrusts into her tight cunt slow, fingers flexing where I hold her skull in my hand, knotted in her hair. My eyes flick between hers, darkness not allowing me to see her fully. I swallow, her fingers untangling from my hair, she sweeps her fingers over my face, still sticky with another man's blood. But I think it's how I like her best, bloodied and innocent and in love with me.

I'm just about to give in, let her have any fucking thing she wants from my right now, and say *okay*, when her hand cracks across my face so hard it makes my ears ring, my lip splitting on impact, teeth aching. I blink away the flare of white in my vision, slowly turn back to face her.

"Gracie," I growl, catching her wrist just before her hand connects with my face a second time.

She wriggles beneath me, my dick getting even fucking harder, my blood dripping down onto her face and I know there's something wrong with me. With her. With the fucking both of us. But I don't fucking care.

I don't fucking care.

Because no one else has to understand our love.

It's toxic and fucked up and dangerous.

But we like playing these games.

Give in.

Let go.

Play with me.

Make me hurt.

All things her psyche whispers to me in the dark, phantom claws curling beneath my flesh, secreting their poison, infecting me with a sickness I already fucking possess.

I give in.

Squeezing the fragile bones in her little wrist, I slam her hand down onto the marble, dip down to her face, snarling over her mouth and she fucking giggles.

"*Yes*," she whispers, coaxing and taunting me from the safety of shadows, waiting for them to swallow me up too, have me join her, and I shatter.

The last piece of man inside of me dies, the monster taking over, feral and hungry. My teeth sink into her bottom lip, tearing through the delicate flesh, tasting iron, I suck blood from her lip, pull my cock out of her, tear my lips from hers. I cover her bleeding mouth with my hand, roughly drag it across her face, make sure I cover my palm and fingers with her blood.

Then, cock in bloodied hand, I smear it over my length, her blood, her arousal, I swipe blood from my chin, my lip dripping a steady stream where she slapped me. I smother my throbbing dick in it all, and then mercilessly, I slam my way back inside her.

Hips colliding with hers with a nasty crack. She groans beneath me, her teeth battling with mine as she tries and fails to get her teeth into the split of my lip. I work my way down her throat, sucking and biting bruises over the ones that someone else fucking put on her, replacing them with my own.

I cover every inch of her neck, right around to behind her ears, every millimetre of exposed flesh has my teeth marks in now. I bite her all over, like a fucking possessive claiming. I fuck into her with my bloodied dick, she cries out beneath me, my hand still crushing her wrist, holding it hostage high above her head, her fingers clawing at the back of my hand. I snap my gaze up to hers and she stops clawing at me, stops moving, her mismatched eyes wide, staring into my own, savage, wild.

"Put your fucking hands above your head," I hiss at her, banging her hand to the floor with the order before releasing it. "Both hands," I bark, hushed, "keep them there."

Her hand slips free from over my shoulder, slick with my blood, and I can just make out the move-ments in the dark. She crosses her wrists above her head, fingers knotting together, eyes on mine all the while.

"Good girl," I whisper, nipping at her lips, the top then the bottom, my tongue laving over the wounds, blood congealing, I lap over it, swallow it down.

Then I rake my teeth down her throat again, cock slipping free of her hot, tight cunt, I bite her skin, down her chest, tongue swirling over her bloodied skin, I take a puckered nipple into my mouth, massaging the other with harsh fingers. She whimpers, back arching, tits pushing up and into my touch, I suck hard, pulling as much of her flesh into my mouth as possible. She whimpers as I loosen my hold on her other breast, milk sliding over my knuckles, down my throat as I suck her nipple between my teeth, creamy and sweet just like her.

I pop off of her breast, grope both in rough hands, run my tongue up the valley of her breasts, lapping at her milk, our blood. My tongue runs down her belly, dipping into her navel, swirling around, teeth marking her hips, before gliding further down, over her mound. Arms curling beneath her thighs, I tug her down sharply, pulling her hips up to meet my mouth, her weight resting on her shoulders, I suction my mouth over her clit.

She thrashes beneath me, unable to escape my hold, I squeeze her legs in the crook of my elbows as the heels of her feet pummel my ribcage, sucking harder on her clit. The flat of my tongue gliding up her, from clenching entrance to swollen clit, sucking and biting the lips of her cunt, I bury my face in her pussy, fingers digging into her thighs. She screams as my teeth sink into her clit, *hard,* her body trembling harder than an earthquake beneath me.

Lazily, I lap at her as she comes down, sucking up everything she rewards me with, before gently placing her legs back down. Crawling back up between her open thighs, legs flush to the floor, my cock leaking, and twitching to sink back into her. She lifts her shaking arms, body trembling beneath me. She runs her fingers up the back of my neck, pushing them into my hair. Breathing hard, she stares up at me, and then she yanks on her hold in my hair, my head smacking hard into hers as she welcomes my cock back inside her.

I fuck her then like a punishment. For her. For me. For us. A show for the Devil, a fuck you to the gods. Like filthy little heathens, beautiful creatures of the night, we fuck beneath the cover of darkness. I spit in her open mouth, her tongue sticking out to show me, even though I can't really see, before she makes a show of swallowing me down, moaning as she does.

My lips reconnect with hers, and we kiss as I hold myself deep, hips joined, let it all fucking go. Shiver racing up my spine, I paint the entrance of her cervix, cock pumping her full of my cum. She holds me to her, her hands curled in my hair, my arms curling beneath her back as I come down on top of her, let her feel the weight of me, chest to chest, cock twitching inside of her.

She sighs against the top of my head where I lie snuggled into her chest. Heaving bosom beneath me, heart hammering in my ear, she smooths her fingers through my hair, over the side of my face, holding me to her.

"Marry me, Gracie," I whisper seriously, her hands pausing in their soothing strokes.

She holds her breath, but I don't hold mine, listening to the elevated beating of her heart, after a long quiet moment, her fingers continue their soothing combing through my hair, nails scratching gently at my scalp.

"Okay," she whispers, making me smile, craning her neck, she presses a kiss to the top of my head, my arms tightening around her.

"The darkness is beautiful, isn't it, baby?"

"I think *our* darkness is beautiful, Hunter."

EPILOGUE

GRACE

Atlas holding my hand gently inside his, I sit on the floor at the foot in our bedroom, Rosie seated behind me, fingers in my hair, finishing the tiny braids weaving through my long curls. Atlas's soft lips press kisses to my knuckles, River slobbering all over the other hand as he holds too tight, and tries to copy his older brother, making me laugh. He looks up at me, big goofy grin on his chubby face, proud of what he's doing to make me laugh.

"Thank you, boys," I say quietly, River licking my thumb, giggling with glee. Rosie clucks her tongue at him.

He throws his head of dark blonde hair back, cackling with his mouth open wide. Atlas laughs, little shoulders shaking as he smiles wide at his brother. I glance at Rosie in the mirror, her eyes wet, smile on her face, she drops the end of my plait, sniffling with a laugh, she drags a handkerchief up to her face, patting her eyes dry.

"Allergies," she sniffles, her warm green eyes shining.

"It is April," I say, offering her an excuse and she smiles, throwing me a quick wink.

"Okay, boys!" Raine says excitedly from the door, clapping and rubbing his hands together and making me flinch. *'Sorry'*, he mouths from the open doorway. "Let's get you two ready, so you can go help Daddy, yeah?" he says with a wide smile, he dips down, hands braced on his knees.

Both boys hurrying towards him, Atlas glancing back, my small nod of encouragement widening his smile. His beautiful, mismatched eyes check over his shoulder once more, as River squeals, Raine heaving him up into the air. I open up my arms, Atlas running back, he throws himself into them, squeezing me tight.

"You're coming down soon, aren't you?" he whispers into my hair, breath warm, tickling down the skin of my throat.

I think of the way he hugged me so tight just a few short weeks ago, the night Hunter brought me home, the way he sobbed in my arms, made me promise to never leave again. I swallow down the emotion, the fear, give him one last squeeze, and we both pull back, so his eyes are focused on mine.

"I'm going to be there, just a few minutes after

everyone's ready," I whisper back. "Daddy will need your help to get ready. Will you make sure he's there for me on time?"

Atlas nods vigorously, having something to focus on, helping him clear the little cloud of anxiety. He runs back over to Raine, waiting in the open doorway, he cups the back of his head, ushering him out of the door, winking at me as he pulls it closed behind them.

I stare at the closed door for a moment, think of my first night inside this room, the fear and excitement upon discovering I wasn't locked in. How I was too afraid to explore, worried what Mother would do if she caught me not following the rules.

Memories of the last five and a half years flash through my mind, all of the things that have happened in this room. Giving birth to all three of our sons right here in our en suite bathroom, Hunter spending five months attending birthing courses because I didn't trust anyone else to deliver our son. The countless hours he spent reading me baby books, rubbing my feet, brushing my hair, kissing my belly.

I think of the feeling inside of me, warm, fluttering, full, a swirling eclipse of moths, wings spreading happiness through my veins. I drop my gaze, tears beading in my lower lashes, soft smile on my face as I stare at the gold ring on my finger, a twisted antler, for our love of the forest. Yellow canary diamond in its centre because my hair reminds Hunter of sunflower fields.

I think of all the years before I found my home here, my family, my heart, and I breathe it all away with a breath I didn't quite realise I've been holding onto for so long. Looking up, eyes flicking to the observatory style window, I stand, crossing the room, feet treading between the laid-out carpets, cool wood on my bare feet. I peer out, across the trees, the sun shining, the first warm day of the year, April fourteenth, and I get to bind myself to the other half of my soul forever today.

I feel his eyes on me before I spot him. Strong hands on our youngest son, Roscoe cradled to his chest, black shirt tight across his broad shoulders. Hunter stares up at me, I down at him, black flop of hair hiding one of his dark brown eyes, a smile curls his lips, and I feel my own mirror his. My heart clenching in my chest, my soul reaching for him, I bite my lip, drop my gaze and turn away from the window.

Rosie smiles wide when I look up, white clothing bag crushed excitedly in her hands.

"Now, how's about we get this bride ready for her groom," she asks, eyebrow tracking up her forehead on one side, I nod, giving her permission to continue her fussing.

I glance over my shoulder, peer out at the bright sky, and finally feel peace.

EPILOGUE

HUNTER

My palms aren't sweat, there's no sickness swirling around in my gut, I didn't go out last night and get fucked up on my last 'night of freedom'. I'm not nervous. I've never felt more sure of anything in my entire fucking existence. The air is crisp, but the sun's rays beam down, warming my skin, even with the chill from the cool breeze.

Archer straightens the cuffs of his black shirt, tugging them down, twisting one of his gold cufflinks. He pushes his hand through his black hair, wavy like Dad's, Raine's and Thorne's. His gaze flicking up, squinting as he looks towards the sun, making the green shards piercing the dark brown of his eyes spark to life.

"You're going to do this shit properly, aren't you?" I

raise an eyebrow; it tracks slowly up my forehead with my question.

Smirking, he drops his gaze, looks to the floor, attempting to suppress his smirk. My fist collides with his shoulder, making his laughter belt out of him.

"For her," I growl at him, wondering why the fuck I thought having Archer marry us was ever a good fucking idea.

But then I think of Rachel, finding out my headaches and deep sleeps were from the fucking drugs she kept slipping in my food, so I'd be tired constantly, slip up and miss things I'd usually notice. The way Archer and I tore her apart, mind and body, his chest heaving, face splattered in blood as I locked the chains on her prison. She can stay there and rot until I decide it's time to put an end to her suffering. She deserves to have it drawn out. No one's going to look for her and no one fucks with my fucking kids.

We're the closest in age, Archer and I, him only ten months older, but we're the most different, we love each other but he drives me in-fucking-sane. *All* of the time.

"Yeah, yeah, yeah, I know the drill, dude. Chill out. I'll behave," he rolls his eyes, broad grin on his face, taunting, my eyes narrow, muscles flexing, readying to pounce.

"Enough," Thorne's strong rumble interjects, appearing silently behind me, hand firm on my shoulder, stopping me before I strangle our brother. "Ready?" Thorne asks.

Archer backing away, hands sliding into his pockets,

Thorne blocks my view of him, stepping in front of me, hand dropping from my shoulder.

I stare at my eldest brother, his dark eyes on mine, posture so proper and formal, but his eyes look tired, his skin a little ashen. He looks very un-Thorne-like. I think about asking him what's going on, he hasn't been here much the last few weeks, since everything happened with Michael, maybe longer. I make a quick calculation in my head, try to work out when he started staying away for longer periods at a time. Wonder where he goes. I know he feels guilty, but none of my boys got hurt, Gracie is fine. Everything worked out in the end.

"Let's not do this now, Hunter," he says quietly, my silence enough, he knows I know something. "I will tell you after, let's enjoy your day."

He doesn't wait for a response, doesn't offer me anything else, I don't try to speak, I just exhale, watch him walk towards Wolf, whose eyes were already burning a hole into the back of our brother's head. Now he stares him down, waiting for something, which he gets almost immediately, because Thorne nods without a spoken question, and then Wolf turns with him. Both heading towards the small cluster of chairs set out, facing the forest tree line.

An arch crafted by Wolf, twisted wood, branches, ferns and flowers woven through it, whites and lilacs and green. The forest beyond is full of life, everything sprouting and thriving, roots finally pushing up what they protected all winter. Wild garlic, lavender, magnolias, rhododendron. The air smells sweet, birds tweet, and butterflies are just starting to reappear.

I watch my family, all of the men dressed in black, slacks and shirts, shined shoes. Smiles on all of their faces. Raine bounces River in his lap, his infectious giggle making me smile. Atlas sits in the first chair, all of the seats in an arc around the floral arbour. Little legs swinging, hands clamped over the edge of it. Arrow cradles a sleeping Roscoe beside him, his little mouth popped open, head thrown back over my younger brother's arm.

Thorne and Wolf take a seat on the other side of the aisle, heads bent together in secrecy, I watch them for a moment, brow creasing. When a sharp whistle from Archer gets my attention.

Rosie bustles towards me as I turn to look over my shoulder, following his head jerk. Her hurried steps, bright smile and warm eyes, she glances at my outfit on her way over, no doubt checking I'm dressed correctly. She stops before me, green eyes shining, greying hair twisted into a fancy plait, pulled forward over one shoulder, light blue, floral dress on her short frame. She cups my cheeks, kisses my forehead as I bend to meet her halfway.

"I'm very proud of you," she whispers, and I swallow hard.

"Thank you, Rosie," I say quietly in return, and then she's hooking her arm through mine, turning me towards my brother where he waits beneath the arch.

She drags me down the aisle, her pace all business. I

stand in place before my brothers, my sons, the woman who helped raise me.

Soft music starts to play, small wireless speaker beneath the seat empty for Dad. Everyone quiets, stands, and I feel her.

Our tether.

She tugs gently on her end, making sure I'm exactly where I'm supposed to be. *Meant* to be. I tug back, a smile to my lips, skin prickling with warmth.

I hear a small gasp from Atlas, and my eyes are still fixed to the floor, my toes inside my shoe tapping at the sole. The nerves I didn't have seem to slam into me all at once. Adrenaline shooting through me like a bolt of lightning. And I suddenly wish it were dark, because I would feel better, a little more secure. In myself. But it isn't and I'm not, but she is mine and I am hers, and all of this is just to prove it to the world, because we don't need to prove it, *anything*, to each other. We already know.

And then I look up.

Dad walks Gracie across the meadow, grass thick with wildflowers, buttercups, daisies. Her hair shines like a halo, hanging down her back in loose, gold curls, tiny braids pulled through. Small body in white, tight lace bodice, strapless, a V shape to the bottom of the corset style top, carved high above her hip bones. And from there there's silk, lengths and lengths of shiny white silk, layered and trailing. My breath stills in my chest, her beautiful, mismatched eyes wide on mine, she doesn't look away from me.

Even when they stop before me, Dad pressing a kiss to her knuckles before placing her curled fingers into mine, she's still looking just at me, and I her. Like we're the only people here, just the two of us. Archer begins, but I don't hear a single word he says, eyes locked on her face.

Tiny dark freckle beneath her left eye, a warm hazel, gifted by the Devil, the other an ice blue, instilled to her by a god. Small nose, slightly upturned at the tip, her pout plump, glistening as she licks her lips, further drawing my attention. Cupid's bow sharp and pronounced; a tiny white scar slashed through its centre.

I think of that first night I saw her, high up in the window, no idea who she was, why she was in my house. How I snuck into her bedroom, watched her sleep, touched her face, an angel in the dark. I knew then what I know now; this girl is my undoing. And I am nothing but insanely in love with her.

She squeezes my fingers, a soft giggle carrying to me on the breeze, I snap my gaze to Archer, a knowing smirk on his lips. He instructs me to repeat after him, which I do, Gracie taking the words a little slower, a gentle curve to her mouth as she tries not to laugh. And when Archer pronounces us husband and wife, her bare feet climbing atop my shoes, pressing up on tiptoes as they do. Arms wrapped around her back, her hands curled securely over my shoulders, I kiss her with my entire soul.

Later that night, both of us breathless after a chase through the trees, her naked body entangled with mine.

The sky full of stars, her gaze unwavering, eyes lost on the view, just as mine are irrevocably lost in her, I tell her that I love her.

And in the darkness, coveted in the safety of the shadows we know so well, I make love to my wife.

THE END

AFTERWORD

Hey you!

I hope you enjoyed the ending for Hunter and Gracie. I intended to leave them in Heron Mill. But I couldn't do it, Hunter demanded further attention, and Gracie wanted to play... How can I say no to that?

So I hope you enjoyed them coming full circle. You'll still get little glimpses of them in the Blackwell Brothers' upcoming books, so it's not *really* goodbye. Just a ta-ta for now.

I hope you enjoyed the little cross overs and the little teasers... did anyone catch the little nod to Wolf's book title? The little one liner about the Chaos Twins from Swallows and Psychos? The Ashes tie in? And Thorne... 'nuff said.

I'm excited to bring you more of this series, for Rook Point, for Thorne and Haisley. Anyone wondering more about that? Who the Kelly's are? What Thorne's been up to? You know what would be good right now? One last little surprise.

Why don't you turn the page for Rook Point's blurb?

ROOK POINT

It started when I was just a boy.

My obsession.

An inheritance the men in my family seem to be gifted, one that feels a lot like a disease.

It was love at first sight.

Hair the colour of fire, eyes crafted of the deepest jade.

I was captivated by her instantly, enthralled, but it was not meant to be, our worlds were already vastly different. Destinies not meant to intertwine. My family *worked* for people like her, they didn't marry them. The Princess of the Irish Mob. The eldest son of The Firm's disposal crew.

So, I grew up, I moved on, and I spent long nights in bars drowning dangerous thoughts of her.

But, it seems, with time, things can change. One night, one debt, one single game of cards.

And in a sick twist of fate, a treasure that should never be mine was suddenly within my grasp.

COMING SOON

ACKNOWLEDGMENTS

Markie, for always finding me in the dark. I love you more than words can ever express. It's you and I.

Kendal, you are my whole world. I love you more than anything.

Mum, for listening and talking through every idea I have ever had for a book, and encouraging even the most violent, disturbing scenes. Thank you for keeping Nan far, far away from these pages…

Addie, I love you, I love you, *I love you*. For coaxing me through the writing of this book, encouraging me, spurring me on and staying up all night working through the mess inside my brain. Thank you, you're my best friend and I am so grateful for you.

Leah, *ohhh, Leah*. Fuck, I love you! Thank you for loving Hunter and Gracie just as much as I do… if not *more*. For sending me songs at 1am that make you think of them, for reading this before anyone else. This one was for us. You're a goddess and a creative genius. I can't wait for more. This series is your baby, and I couldn't be more grateful for your passion.

Inga, you're responsible for the death of Rachel. There, happy?! Thank you for encouraging my original idea, spurring me on, and giving me the positivity I need to keep going. I love you so much.

Kristen, wifey, for video calling me when you're doing chores and making me laugh so hard I cry. I love you so much, so grateful for you.

Raeleen, for attempting to organise my messy life, and letting me whine AND for being an incredible friend, I am so very lucky to have you in my life.

To my Street Team, you girls are wonderful, Sam, Arielle, Alannah, Emily, Erin, Steph, Becky, Rebecca, Jess, Shawna, Elizabeth, Sue, Jennifer, Layla, Vic, Kiyahnah. So grateful for all of your hard work, and encouragement. Thank you.

Thank you to my ARC Team, you're all wonderful and I'm so grateful to you all.

And finally, to you, the reader, I thank you for giving my work a go, and if you enjoyed it, even better! But regardless, I appreciate you for reading, thank you.

ALSO BY K.I. TAYLOR-LANE

.

SWALLOWS AND PSYCHOS

KYLA-ROSE SWALLOW

A Dark Mafia Why Choose Romance

PURGATORY

PENANCE

PERSECUTION

CHARLIE SWALLOW

A Dark Mafia MMF Romance

RUIN

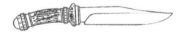

.

THE BLACKWELL BROTHERS

HUNTER BLACKWELL

A Dark Gothic Horror Stepsibling MF Romance

HERON MILL

HERON MILL TENEBRIS

THORNE BLACKWELL

A Dark Gothic Mafia MF Romance

ROOK POINT

WOLF BLACKWELL

A Dark Gothic MF Romance

CARDINAL HOUSE

(COMING SOON)

THE ASHES BOYS

A Dark Bully Gang Why Choose Romance

TORMENT ME

BURY ME

(COMING 2023)

FIND K.L. TAYLOR-LANE

BOOKBUB

AMAZON

INSTAGRAM

TIKTOK

PINTEREST

FACEBOOK

GOODREADS

FACEBOOK READER GROUP

Printed in Great Britain
by Amazon

35468037R00195